Praise for the novels of
USA TODAY bestselling author Jennifer Snow

"*All Signs Point to Malibu* is a sweet, sexy romp with lots of heart and a psychic twist."   —Nan Fischer, author of *Some of It Was Real*

"A spicy enemies-to-lovers dream so full of delicious tension and chemistry that I couldn't turn the pages fast enough!"
—Holly James, author of *The Déjà Glitch*, on *All Signs Point to Malibu*

"Funny, heartfelt and at times bittersweet, *All Signs Point to Malibu* is a joyful read."   —Melissa Baron, author of *Twice in a Lifetime*

"Never too late to join the growing ranks of Jennifer Snow fans."
—*Fresh Fiction*

"Prepare to have your heartstrings tugged! Pure Christmas delight."
—*New York Times* bestselling author Lori Wilde
on *An Alaskan Christmas*

"Jennifer Snow is one clever writer."   —*RT Book Reviews*

"Heartwarming, romantic, and utterly enjoyable."
—*New York Times* bestselling author Melissa Foster
on *An Alaskan Christmas*

"Readers will enjoy the mix of sexy love scenes, tense missions, and amiable banter. This entertaining introduction to Wild River will encourage fans of small-town contemporaries to follow the series."
—*Publishers Weekly* on *An Alaskan Christmas*

"This first title in the Wild River series is passionate, sensual, and very sexy. The freezing, winter-cold portrayal of the Alaskan ski slopes is not the only thing sending chills through one's body."
—*New York Journal of Books* on *An Alaskan Christmas*

Also by Jennifer Snow

Wild Coast

Sweet Home Alaska
Alaska for Christmas
Second Chance Alaska

Wild Coast Novellas

Love on the Coast
Love in the Forecast
Love in the Alaskan Wilds

Wild River

An Alaskan Christmas
Under an Alaskan Sky
A Sweet Alaskan Fall
Stars Over Alaska
Alaska Reunion
Alaska Dreams

Wild River Novellas

An Alaskan Wedding
A Wild River Retreat
A Wild River Match
Wild Alaskan Hearts
An Alaskan Christmas Homecoming

For additional books by Jennifer Snow,
visit her website, JenniferSnowAuthor.com.

ALL SIGNS POINT TO MALIBU

JENNIFER SNOW

CANARY STREET PRESS

**CANARY
STREET
PRESS**™

Recycling programs
for this product may
not exist in your area.

ISBN-13: 978-1-335-99395-3

All Signs Point to Malibu

Canary Street Press
22 Adelaide St. West, 41st Floor
Toronto, Ontario M5H 4E3, Canada
CanaryStPress.com

Printed in U.S.A.

To Dan, thank you for believing in this story enough
to want to bring it to life on-screen!

PROLOGUE

SUN BLAZES DOWN OVER THE MALIBU COASTLINE
as I dodge wedding guests in the posh, luxurious courtyard of
the Banks Resort Hotel. People wearing designer clothes and
flabbergasted expressions are in my periphery as I desperately
try to avoid eye contact. The music has stopped, but photog-
raphers are delighted to continue capturing the "festivities."
Bridezilla's approach sets off my fight-or-flight instincts and
I'm not sure I could take her, so I quicken my pace as I make
my way through the over-the-top flower arches lining the
wedding aisle. An overpowering stench of lilies makes my
eyes water, blurring my path, and I narrowly escape a tumble
on bunched-up pink velvet carpeting.

That could have been disastrous for the bride.

Instead, I bang my shin against a chair as I flee for my life—
away from eight angry bridesmaids in hot pursuit. Moving fast
in heels is a skill that should definitely be taught in finishing
schools. I collide with a server carrying a tray of champagne

flutes and grab one before they fall to the Astroturf. I down it quickly for liquid courage then toss the glass aside.

With the furious entourage closing in and dozens of cell phone cameras pointed my way, I jump over the short wall that separates the resort property from the beach, snagging the hem of my maid of honor dress. I hear a rip and pray my Wonder Woman underwear aren't on display. Though, once the guest videos go viral, my choice of undergarments will be the least of my worries.

Stumbling over my strappy stilettos, I run down the boardwalk, tripping over uneven planks of decaying wood, all the way to the beach. I kick off my heels and my feet sink deep into the scorching sand as I continue my escape.

I can hear the wedding guests in the courtyard behind me. A mix of shock, anger, and gossipy amusement drifts on the ocean-scented breeze. This day has turned from matrimonial bliss to a complete shitstorm.

Arguably, I'm to blame.

Desperate for air, I pause, bending at the waist. Deep breaths in and out as I glance over my shoulder. No one's following me. Absolutely no one. My gut tightens as *that* realization is heart-wrenchingly worse.

I straighten slowly and—gripping the fabric of my dress in one hand, my shoes in the other—I walk along the beach, getting lost in a sea of brightly colored umbrellas. Crashing waves along the shore mask the sound of my heart pounding, but nothing can drown the dread building in my chest.

How did I let this happen?

Life wasn't always so full of drama. Up until a few weeks ago, I had just the expected levels of stress, self-doubt, and anxiety. Then things started to spiral out of control. One mishap after the other culminating to this epic fuckup…

I knew that goddamn tremor was a bad omen.

ONE

HAILEY'S DAILY RULE FOR SUCCESS:
Start your day on purpose and with purpose.

Four weeks earlier...

IF YOU READ ENOUGH DAILY HOROSCOPES,
you'll eventually find one you like.

Sixteen astrology sites, three online tarot card readings and a Magic 8 Ball TikTok filter later, I find the prediction I'm sticking with for today.

With the lunar eclipse in your sign, shake up the day by embracing your bold and passionate side, but be prepared for some introspection late this evening when planetary shifts create opportunities for future growth.

Seems generic enough to relate to anything that happens today, and I like the reassurance that gives me—manifestations of success *are* predestined by fate.

I position my ring light and tripod next to my desk in front of the window of my home office. Dressed in casual chic, I'm polished to near perfection, but not too perfect—no filters here. My followers respond to "real" and I do my best to convey the fakest version of real I can muster this early in the morning.

Behind me on the walls are framed magazine covers featuring my smiling, confident face. The taglines boast "Top 30 Under Thirty," "Best Influencer of the Year," "Motivator to the Stars."

It's all true.

At twenty-nine, I have become a successful life coach with over ten million followers on my daily app, which doles out words of wisdom to get one's day underway.

I check the time on my computer and wait...4:59...5:00 a.m. Forcing a wide-eyed smile, I go live.

"Hey, Hustlers! It's Monday! New week, new goals. Get up. Get moving. Remember, if you're not up early, someone else is. Monday is the perfect day to try something new—so get out there and be adventurous. Set your intentions for the week and remember setbacks are just another test of your dedication and commitment. Keep hustling! Love to all!"

I post the inspirational Monday morning message to my devotees and views immediately come in, positive comments and heart emojis light up the screen. I genuinely enjoy all the love and the feedback. Over the years I've built a solid, authentic reputation by caring about my followers—from the early days when I was working to build my platform and I'd call out each viewer individually. Something I obviously can't do anymore as my business has blown up, but I still take the time to hear about Marsha from Utah, whose kids have gone off to college and she's trying to find herself again, and Kimberly from Texas, who just started a new health regime and is struggling with the early morning workouts.

Human connections are what this industry—this *life*—is all about. Unfortunately, my circumstances make getting too connected a little complicated.

Approachable but distant. Friendly but cautious. Open but not vulnerable.

The three guiding principles that have helped me reach this level of undreamable success without landing me in some research facility for the "gifted."

I log off and make sure the camera isn't still recording so no one sees my vintage She-Ra pajama pants and fluffy slippers as I shuffle my way out of the office.

In my bedroom, I remove the wrinkle-free button-down I'm wearing over my matching Masters of the Universe tank top, hang it in the closet, then climb back into bed. I set my cell phone alarm for 9:00 a.m., a reasonable hour to be awake, then hit a button on the wall. Blackout blinds close automatically and once again I realize how grateful I am to be living this life.

And that I'm just one slip away from losing it all.

My eyes fly open as the room shakes around me and I'm tossed brutally from bed, as though that solitary thought has shaken my entire foundation. As if I've opened Pandora's box and allowed chaos to finally track me down.

Face down on the floor, I hear crumbling above me and roll underneath the four poster, covering the back of my head with my hands. It feels as though my house has been swept out to sea as I ride out the nausea-inducing trembling and swaying of an earthquake that has to be a magnitude of six or higher. Cracking echoes all around me and I envision the whole house collapsing, the entire Malibu coast getting swallowed in a crevasse.

California is on a fault line and it's only a matter of time.

Luckily, today isn't that day. As fast as it came on, what will likely be deemed a "tremor" to prevent doomsday fanatics from freaking out, stops.

Today's horoscope was a tad too on the nose—won't be visiting that site again.

I roll out from under the bed, shakily get to my feet, and wait to see if there are any aftershocks. With one arm braced against the wall, I breathe deeply to steady my thundering heart rate. The health tracker on my wrist has gone offline—vitals unavailable. That can't be good.

Once everything seems settled, I survey the room. A few items on the dresser have fallen and the drawers are open, but otherwise no real damage.

I leave the room and move slowly through the rest of the house. Thankfully the previous owners had been paranoid enough to have the house earthquake proofed. Larger appliances are attached to the walls with safety cables, the ceiling lights and fans are secured. Safety film covers the windows and glass doors.

There's very little damage throughout.

Until I enter my office and see all the framed magazine covers have crashed to the floor.

With a shaking hand, I carefully sort through shards of broken glass to pick one up. The tagline boasting my success blurs as I once again feel faint—the lingering emotional aftermath of a natural disaster.

It was just a tremor…but all it takes is one small crack.

Hours later, I shake off that morning's excitement as I sit at my desk, wearing a Golden Bears jersey sporting number 18—"Laywood"—on the back. Matching baseball hat over a cute, sporty ponytail, foam finger and I'm ready to go. I take a deep breath and wait for the online chat to connect.

And wait…

I confirm the date on my calendar. This is decision day.

Maybe they forgot or lost track of time. Maybe I was sup-posed to call them. If so, I'd hate to keep them waiting. I hit the call button on the screen and resume my excited, confi-dent pose as it rings.

And rings… No answer.

I slump back in the chair as an email notification pops up—an announcement about a life coaching event next month at the West Beverly Hotel, where I'll be one of the guest speak-ers.

Only the biggest life coaching event of the year. No pressure.

I click on the notification and see that Spencer Stanley, a charming, slick new coach dominating in the sports division, has been added to the list of panelists. His smug smile grates on my last nerve. The guy has only been in the business six months and already he's got over a million followers and was deemed influential enough to be featured at the event. I'm not jealous of his success; I'm annoyed by it. Building a brand takes time and I'm not sure what horseshoe this guy has lodged up his ass to have reached the top so quickly.

Don't look. You don't want to know.

Opening his social media page, I immediately regret it as I see his latest post from…*4:30 a.m.!?* There's no way he ac-tually gets up that early.

Nothing better than waking up on a gorgeous Monday to a new client deal! That's right, I can now officially confirm the rumors that I am partnering with Kirk Laywood—pro basket-ball's hottest new rookie.

Damn it. I thought I had that guy.

The least Coach Riley could have done was give me a heads-up. I represent clients from all walks of life—actors, politicians, professionals, but I've yet to break into the pro-athlete market. Psychological research shows that motivators are a valuable part of an athlete's team and yet so many of them are reluctant to accept that type of assistance with their careers.

At least from me.

Four meetings with Kirk and his coach. Four expensive steak dinners. Four long, polished presentations on the benefits of life coaching…and I teed it up for Spencer Stanley to swoop in and seal the deal. I should have insisted on a signed contract at our last meeting when it seemed as though I had him on the hook.

Didn't I learn anything from watching *Jerry Maguire* a dozen times as sports research?

A minute of wallowing then onward and upward.

I pull the foam finger off, close my eyes, take a deep breath, and namaste Spencer right out of my mind.

"Checking out the competitor, smart."

My eyes spring open and my health tracker warns of a pending heart attack. At least it's registering this time.

"Alice? What the hell?" More professionally, "I mean, how did you get in here?"

Alice Kline, a former client and adorably neurotic bestselling author, simply shrugs as she stands in front of me. "Climbed in through the window." She gestures at the one open behind me.

I'll be repositioning my desk to face the window ASAP, feng shui be damned.

"I rang the front gate, but power's still out along your street. Manuel let me in," she says.

So much for my gardener's Christmas bonus this year.

I shouldn't be surprised by this unexpected, outside-the-box entrance. Alice is a low-grade stalker who solicited my services by following me to Whole Foods for my daily grocery pickup for a solid three months before finally approaching me about coaching at my semiannual gyno appointment. Sounds creepy, but anyone who subjects themselves to a Pap smear to get my attention is worthy of fifteen minutes of my time. That kind of dedication is admirable—the single-minded determination I look for in potential clients.

Still. "Alice, we've talked about boundaries."

"I know, but I need more time," she says with a hint of desperation, rearranging the objects that the tremor knocked from my desk.

Now that my pulse has returned to a less worrisome rate, I notice she's wearing old sweats with what I assume are coffee stains on the front. Her hair is piled high in a messy bun and the undeniable scent of a cheap dry shampoo auras around her. The vein in her forehead is pronounced and dark circles under her eyes suggest she hasn't been sleeping.

She's spiraling and I'd like to help, but... "I've explained how my services work. Six-month contract. No extensions."

Messing with fate is a delicate balancing act. I can set my clients on the right path or help them avoid the wrong one, but then it's up to them. Thinking about the ripple effects just one small suggestion has on the universe is anxiety attack inducing.

Alice sits across from me, undeterred. She takes out a copy of *Murder by the Dozen* from a deep sweatpants pocket and places it on the desk. I pick it up and reluctantly give in to the temptation to smile. This book and the previous bestsellers almost didn't happen, but they are truly addictive and imaginative.

"Thanks for bringing me an advanced copy. Signed?"

Alice nods, but her knees bounce as she scans the office.

"Are you all prepped for the launch?" I ask as I get up and place the book next to the others on my "client pride" shelf. This collection is my joy—I cherish it more than the one showcasing my own awards and achievements. The client shelf actually exemplifies hard work, grit, determination, and perseverance.

"Yeah, I guess..." Alice mumbles, biting her nails.

Against my better judgment I ask, "What's going on?" I sit down and give her my full attention, though waiving my own rules makes me more than a little uneasy.

Never let anyone get too close or stay too long.

"I want to write something different. Something a little out there..." she says.

"Out there?"

"A sci-fi Western romance."

I nod slowly, try to wrap my mind around it. "In addition to the bestselling mystery series? Under a pen name?"

Alice shakes her head. "I don't want to write the Cook-book Murder series anymore. After ten books, I'm tapped out. There's only so many ways to murder a person with a spatula."

I'm failing to come up with even one.

Alice deserves all the credit her books have garnered from readers and critics alike. Her creativity in coming up with new, fresh ways to kill people in the kitchen is actually terrifying. Alice doesn't host many dinner parties.

"But the books are fan favorites and your publisher is supporting them. You've reached every goal we—*you*—set for yourself since we launched the career plan." Not an easy feat. When I first started working with Alice, her originality needed to be reined in a little to secure that first six-figure deal.

"But I wasn't sold on the idea back then either. It was your suggestion to try the mystery genre."

I remember that glimpse well. Alice had pitched her sci-fi Western romance at our first meeting in the gyno office waiting room. Taking her hand in mine that day, I really wanted to see that the outside-the-box series would be wildly popular, but my glimpse into her future wasn't so promising...

Inside a busy, popular bookstore, a banner announced Author Meet & Greets. A nervous-looking Alice sat at a table, a stack of sci-fi Western romance books in front of her. No one approached.

A few feet away, a mystery author sat with a long line of customers eager to get their signed copy of the latest Murder by Recipe book.

I smile gently at Alice now. "And it worked."

Though maybe not so well for the other author I borrowed the idea from.

Ripple effects = anxiety attacks.

I pause for a breath before delivering advice I know she's not going to like. "Alice, I know you want to write the book of your heart, but the Cookbook Murder series are the books people want to read...and—" perhaps more importantly "—your editor wants to contract."

Alice sighs, her shoulders slump, deflated.

Offering advice contrary to what people want to hear has a soul-sucking effect that I try to avoid at all costs. That, along with the nagging voice in my mind that says, *What if I'm wrong? Will I have dashed their dreams for no reason?*

"I don't think I have passion for it anymore," Alice says, standing. Approaching my bookshelf, she rearranges the books by alphabetical order. She would make a fantastic organizer if she ever considers a career change.

"Passion is a big part in creating, but to be successful long-term…"

"I need to treat it as a business. I know." She stops organizing and sighs. "I should be grateful to be doing what I love."

Nope. We are not going to slip into that territory. Alice is an incredible writer, subject to imposter syndrome. If she gets sucked into this self-confidence quicksand, it could be weeks before she resurfaces, and her publicist has a full launch schedule planned.

"No. You should be proud. You did the work and now you're reaping the rewards. And I'm not saying don't write the sci-fi, I'm just saying do it for yourself. Maybe self-pub it under a pen name and see if it sells…" Safe enough not to destroy the career she's worked so hard to build.

Alice looks disheartened. "Good idea. That's what I'll do."

Soul. Sucking.

I stand and move around the desk toward her. I hesitate, but she needs this. More so, *I* need this reassurance that I'm still sending her down the right path. Under the pretense of a friendly gesture, I extend my hands and Alice reaches out to take them. I rotate our palms so that our lifelines touch and connect. Energy flows between us and, breaking my own rules, I sneak another glimpse into Alice's future.

A book publishing event is in full swing in a beautifully decorated hotel ballroom. Elegantly dressed guests are in attendance. Champagne flows freely and a dessert bar features offerings too pretty to eat.

Alice, dressed in a beautiful black gown, stands on the stage and accepts a Golden Novel Award for Best Mystery Series. The award is dated 2025.

I snap back to the present and gently release Alice's hands, confident again. "Just trust me, okay. It will all work out."

"You've never steered me wrong," Alice says as she moves away and starts to climb back out the window.

"You can use the front door," I say with a laugh. Alice is great at cheering me up…when she's not giving me an existential crisis. Under different circumstances we might even be friends. But I've yet to figure out how to have female friendships without complications. My psychic glimpses give insight into whatever a person is emotionally invested in in the moment, but I'm not sure how that would look on a personal level. Heart-to-heart conversations could be far too revealing.

"All good," she says as she slings her legs over the window ledge and hops down.

I stand at the open window and watch her go.

Success sometimes looks different than what we've envisioned.

Sometimes the opportunities we think we want are just distractions to the ones fate is trying to provide for us.

Today, the soothing words of affirmation don't hit the same way.

Once I see Alice wave to Manuel and exit through the gate I sigh, then get to work. This weekend I'm hosting another epic VIP influencer party in the hope of connecting with more professional athletes. In my brief experience with that clientele, they prefer more casual settings to formal meetings and I'm hoping mob mentality could help give some of them a push to commit.

The to-do list is long, but there's no party without guests, so I yank off the sports jersey and baseball cap, fix my blouse and hair, then open my social media app. Sitting straighter, excited expression in place, I go live to my VIP Only group.

"Hey, Exclusive Hustlers! I want to personally invite you all to an event this weekend at my place in Malibu. Open bar, food, live DJ, networking opportunities. And of course, a five-minute one-on-one with me! I'll even give your business a boost with a personalized social media shout-out at the event. Details below. Remember, this is an exclusive VIP event so bring your member code for access at the gate."

I log off and my cell phone chimes with a calendar reminder for the following day that reads: "Maple High Career Week."

And then there's that.

I've been turning down the invite to speak for years, but they keep asking because I'm a bit of an urban legend at my old high school since a pep rally junior year...

Jocks and cheerleaders were strutting around the hallways wearing the school's colors, while in a bathroom stall I fought with the mascot costume. Finally free of the stuffed Teen Shark outfit, I discovered I'd finally started my period. At sixteen, I was a bit of a late bloomer. A mix of anxiety and excitement washed over me as I'd finally reached this milestone.

Entering the gym, where the cheerleaders were practicing for the pep rally, I approached Angela—a perky, popular senior who had been complaining about cramps earlier that day—and whispered in her ear. She looked annoyed but handed me a tampon from her shorts pocket. When our hands touched, our lifelines connected and that's when I had my first glimpse...

...of a stunt gone wrong during the rally and Angela crashing hard onto the gymnasium floor.

I was freaked-out, unsure what had just happened or what to do about it. Obviously warning Angela would have committed me to social outcast status for the rest of my high school career and well, I was a mascot, so my popularity wasn't exactly stellar already. But as the pep rally played out in real time, the glimpse replayed in my mind inside the overstuffed Teen Shark head, the nagging twisting in my gut gripping tighter and tighter.

Angela performed the stunt for real, and I ran onto the floor as she was tossed into the air and dived...

The mascot costume providing a soft crash mat for her fall.

The crowd cheered and Angela was grateful—though not as grateful as one would have suspected—for me saving her life.

After that, everything changed. I don't know why or how I have this power, and I can't see my own future, but I learned to use it to increase my own popularity by helping others achieve their goals. Now it's turned into a lucrative career... as long as no one discovers my secret.

On a billboard promoting some life coaching conference at the ritziest hotel this side of California, Hailey Harris's face is as big as her ego. Gridlocked traffic means I've been staring at it for a full four minutes. My hands grip the steering wheel and I rotate my neck, trying to ease the tension from seeing her too-bright smile. Those perfectly straight, white teeth have to be photoshopped.

"You know, if you took the last exit instead you would've shaved five minutes off the drive and wouldn't have to see that billboard you love so much." My football team's star quarterback, Marcus Kent, is sitting in the passenger seat of my Jeep as we drive to practice, and he's full of helpful advice.

"This way avoids the bottleneck on Main, where that tremor caused a crater in the middle of the street." The morning's earthquake had registered a six point seven on the Richter scale and wreaked havoc all over the coast. Local news has been about nothing else and scientists are saying it came out of nowhere. No warning. Which in my opinion should warrant some defunding to their research, but whatever.

"If you avoid Main altogether and take 3rd, that's not a problem," Marcus says.

"Didn't you fail your road test last month?" The kid's right, but he's already too much of a smartass for me to admit it. "Let me do the driving, please."

A loud crunch sounds and our bodies are jerked forward.

"What the...?" I glare into the rearview mirror to see some Beemer on my bumper. "You good?" I ask Marcus.

"Yeah." He's giving the guy the finger and I slap it down, then climb out of the Jeep. Heat waves drift up from the pavement as I walk to the back of the vehicle to inspect the damage.

The other driver, wearing an expensive suit, Rolex on one wrist climbs out. Great—a douchebag who'll try to blame this collision on me.

Instead, he holds his hands up in defeat. "My bad. Sorry. That billboard." He nods toward it. "Talk about distracted driving, amirite?"

Hailey Harris strikes again.

I notice that his car has taken the brunt of the damage

with a dented bumper and army-green paint scratched into the sleek white finish. "We're good," I say.

"Holy shit, you're Warren Mitchell," the guy says, reaching into his pocket for his cell phone. "You used to be a big deal."

Used to be. I can feel Hailey smirking down at me from the billboard. "Nah, man, you got me confused with someone else," I say then walk away and climb back into the Jeep. "That fucking billboard," I mutter as I slam the door shut.

Marcus grins, lowering himself back through the sunroof. "You know, me and my boys could climb up the tower some night and give her a mustache or something," he says, sliding lower in the seat.

Tempting.

I turn to him. "After that last stunt you and your boys pulled at that corner store, what did I say?"

"Head down. Nose clean." He sighs. I hate that Marcus is hanging with the older boys in his neighborhood. All dropouts with zero ambition. All trouble. He has a bright future ahead of him if he can focus on football and not get distracted.

"Look those guys don't have going for them what you do and they don't want to see you succeed either."

"They're my bros. They're cool."

They are the complete opposite of cool, but the last thing I need is Marcus feeling like I'm against the friends he thinks have his back. I don't want him to stop confiding in me. As much as I hate being interrupted on a date to go prevent my player from getting charged with a misdemeanor, he needs to trust he can call me.

"All I'm saying is it's easy to be found guilty by association."

Marcus nods and his light blue eyes cloud over as he stares out the window at the billboard as traffic moves an inch. "I don't even know why they waste these advertisements out here anyway. Not like anyone from this neighborhood can afford to go to some bougie conference."

It's called aspirational marketing. With their heads so far up their asses, the event organizers can't fathom that some people would rather have groceries than pay a hundred dollars a ticket to attend a seminar that encourages them to work harder, dream bigger, invest in themselves—not acknowledging that not everyone has that luxury. "Not exactly great marketing," I say.

Marcus studies me. "Who is this Hailey chick, anyway?"

"Just someone I went to high school with."

"Ex-girlfriend?"

I shudder. "Come on, you think my standards are that low?"

"Dude, you'd be punching up."

I reach across and punch his shoulder.

Marcus laughs, then I hear his stomach growl. Loud.

"When was the last time you ate?"

"Breakfast." He avoids my gaze.

Most likely not today's. Marcus's dad is serving time for armed robbery and his mother works three jobs to try to support the two of them, but the family's struggling. Hand-me-down football gear and the love of the game is the only reason Marcus keeps coming to practice. For now. "Top of my bag, there's a sandwich."

Marcus shakes his head, but his stomach rumbles louder. "Nah, Coach, I'm already getting a ride from you. I'm not taking your food too."

"The lady at the deli made it wrong. She put olives on it. Top of the bag."

Marcus sighs as he reaches into the back for my duffle bag. "You gotta start telling her when she messes up your order. You eat there like every day."

"She's eighty years old," I say as I shoulder check and switch lanes. It isn't the best deli around and about half the time my sandwich order is wrong, but the woman lost her husband the year before and I think she likes having someone to talk to. "And besides, I have a dinner date tonight—gotta save my carbs."

"That chick from the game last week?" he asks.

The multilevel marketing guru who tried to recruit me to sell energy drinks? "No."

Marcus sits back in the seat and unzips the bag. "The red-head at practice the other day?"

Miss forty-dollar steak and didn't eat it? Definitely not. "No."

Marcus eyes me. "Shit, Coach, you get around."

"Shut up and eat the sandwich." It's not that I get around. It's that I can't stick. Casual dating is more than enough of a commitment. Besides, the women I tend to attract are lured by the championship rings and my faltering six-pack, not my dazzling personality.

Marcus takes the sandwich from the bag, then a course book. "What's this?"

I glance over. "Put that back."

He doesn't. Instead, he flips through the pages. "You study-ing to be a shrink?"

"No. It's just a course I'm taking. Put it back." I started the online sports psychology program on a late-night whim after too much whiskey and a trip down memory lane on the an-niversary of my brother's death. I have no plans of actually becoming a certified sports psychologist—I just want to be the best possible coach to these kids.

"You know, I was thinking maybe I should be looking into some sort of online course after graduation—school guidance counselor says a backup plan for athletes is smart."

I nod carefully. "It is smart…but for now, let's focus on plan A—football, okay?" He's talented enough not to need a plan B, he just needs to believe it and keep pushing hard.

I take the exit off the freeway and drive toward the football field. Cars up on blocks in driveways and run-down homes line the streets where kids play ball and neighbors try to cool off in small inflatable pools on overgrown lawns. I didn't grow up in a neighborhood like this one. Money-wise, I had everything handed to me. Giving back by choosing to coach a local team instead of accepting offers from elite high schools obviously reveals something about my psyche, but I haven't gotten that far into the course yet.

A block later, I pull to the side of the road. "Out you go."

Marcus belches and sends me an annoyed look. "Seriously, man? You're really gonna make me walk from here?"

"Don't want the others to think I'm playing favorites," I say, picking up his bag and giving it to him.

"Even though you are?"

"Even though I absolutely fucking am," I say. "Out."

Marcus grins as he opens the Jeep door and climbs out with his gear into the sweltering heat.

"See ya at the field." He closes the door and I drive away. My gaze drifts into the rearview mirror. Marcus, bag slung over his shoulder, scuffs his feet as he walks down the street. His broad shoulders are slumped forward and his head is down.

He's my star player, and he has every reason to think he can make it to the big leagues as long as he stays focused on what matters. But his lack of confidence is his biggest enemy. My help can only go so far, but I'm determined to do everything I can to make sure that kid survives the season, gets scouted, and gets the future he more than deserves.

TWO

LATE, I PULL MY CONVERTIBLE INTO THE PARK-
ing lot of the posh private high school in a rich area of town
where I absolutely did not live ten years ago. My mother
stretched the truth on the school application—specifically our
zip code—to ensure I could attend. Then she held three minimum wage jobs to pay the lofty tuition fees. She firmly believed that a good education would break our family's "curse"
of bad financial luck, even though she never fully explained
what that meant and made sure I stayed away from anyone
who could. Growing up I never knew any other family besides
her and I respected her enough not to go seeking. I knew she
had her reasons and I trusted them. She was the only person I
needed in my life anyway. Strong, independent, and fearless,
she taught me to trust my own instincts, follow my goals, and
never let anyone tell me I don't belong.

My job was to keep my nose down and grades up.

I delivered.

And now my zip code reflects the status of this high school. Unfortunately, after a valiant battle with breast cancer, my mother hadn't lived long enough to see it.

I take a deep breath as I stare at the "Career Week" banner draped across the front door of the school. A bell sounds and teens wearing school uniforms—altered to reflect their individuality—swarm inside the building. Ten years ago, the wrong shade of tights would have sent a student home with a detention warning. Now the skirts are shorter, worn with fishnet stockings or knee-high socks. Blazers are adorned with patches and the expensive, flashy runners are definitely a newly permitted accessory.

I lower the visor and stare at my reflection in the tiny mirror.

Deep breath in, deep breath out...

You belong here.

Inside the high school, nothing has changed. It even smells the same—a slightly nauseating combination of gym socks, pencil shavings, and disinfectant. Hallways are lined with lockers thick with generations of painted-over graffiti and stickers. An impressive trophy case displays the school's athletic achievements. On the walls are posters about next year's student council elections and the upcoming prom.

I round the corner toward the gymnasium and nearly collide with...

Warren Mitchell.

He swiftly dodges me as though I might set him on fire if our skin touches.

If only.

"Hailstorm." It's a mix of heavy disdain and physical pain.

I fold my arms across my chest and narrow my eyes at the old nickname. "I'm pretty sure I've asked you to stop calling me that."

"I'm pretty sure I don't give a shit."

Still the most immature person on the planet. "What are you doing here?" Please let him be coaching the high school football team or something. Unfortunately, he's not wearing athletic gear, but a pair of dress pants and pale blue dress shirt open at the collar and rolled at the sleeves. In my gut I know what's coming.

"I was invited to give a career week speech," he says as though it's the greatest honor of his life.

I knew it, but still, no fucking way. "Today?"

His smug expression is wiped from his face as his gaze flickers over my own professional-looking attire. "That's why you're here too?"

"They usually only ask one speaker a day. You must have gotten your date wrong."

Warren folds his arms across his chest and yeah okay, the muscular forearms are definitely his best feature. His *only* redeeming feature. Would I like to touch one? Absolutely. Will I? Never. I learned my lesson about touching Warren Mitchell the hard way. I mean if I was dangling from a cliff and he was the only person around to save me, would I consider letting him wrap those arms around my body? Perhaps…

"Maybe you got *your* date wrong," he says, bending slightly at the knees to jerk my attention to his face and away from the muscles that were holding me hostage.

"No, see, I put my appointments on a calendar, not on the back of my hand."

Warren opens his mouth to argue then notices ink smeared on his hand. I take a step closer and squint to read what's written on his tanned skin. The last two digits of a phone number are smudged and unreadable.

"I guess Sasha won't be getting a second date."

Warren shrugs. "One date was probably enough."

"For her, absolutely."

Warren starts to retort but Mrs. Miller, a twelfth grade teacher, approaches us. She looks overworked, exhausted, surviving on caffeine and teen angst. I have no idea how teachers do it. They are real-life heroes. I like kids well enough—from a distance. Zero desire to have any of my own. Risk passing along this...condition? No thanks.

Somehow, Mrs. Miller still has enough energy to greet us with a warm smile and genuine excitement. "Wonderful. You both made it!"

"Hello, Mrs. Miller. Great to see you," I say politely. "Um, question—isn't there usually only one guest speaker?" I cast a side-eye at Warren.

Mrs. Miller nods and looks apologetic as she glances back and forth between us. "There was a scheduling conflict, but we know how hard it was to get you..."

She's referring to me.

I catch Warren's look from the corner of my eye and I know what's going through that judgy mind of his. I think I'm too busy and important to give back to the next generation. He doesn't know me, so I don't know why I let his opinion—his *very wrong* opinion—affect me.

"My schedule's a little tight," I say to Mrs. Miller.

She nods. "We didn't want to reschedule either of you when we realized the mix-up, so we thought a joint presentation would be perfect."

In an alternate universe, maybe.

"Perfect," I say with a tight smile. I won't let this unexpected run-in with my arch nemesis derail me. I am a confident, successful business owner. I belong here. My daily affirmation seems to lack conviction the more I repeat it.

Another bell signaling the start of first period and Mrs. Miller checks her watch. "We're just bringing the students into the gymnasium now. Give us a minute to get them all settled. This close to summer break, they turn into assholes."

Ah, right there. Pure, unfiltered truth.

As she heads into the gymnasium, Warren turns to me. "Seems as though we'll be sharing the stage."

"Or you could offer to come back another day."

"Afraid a professional athlete will be more popular with the kids?"

"*Former* professional athlete."

The minute the words are out of my mouth, I regret them. One run-in without dredging up the past would have been too much to ask.

"And whose fault is that?" Warren asks wryly.

Shit went down two years earlier...

I was walking through LAX, dressed in travel chic, pulling an expensive carry-on behind me as I weaved through the travelers in the departures lounge on my way to a life coaching conference in New York.

Warren was walking in the opposite direction, a football logo'd duffel bag on his shoulder. Head down, looking at his cell phone, he bumped into me as we both entered the security line.

"Hailstorm! Haven't seen you since high school," he'd said.

"I dropped that nickname back then. And for the record, you were the only one to use it," I'd reminded him. I'd never figured out why he called me that. It's not exactly flattering and up until that day, I'd never done him any harm.

Warren gestured for me to enter the line in front of him. "Tough break about you and Liam."

I cringed internally at the mention of my ex. The breakup a few years before had made sense, but it still hit me hard and Warren being Liam's best friend, I suspected he'd heard the dude's version of the story, which most likely included phrases like: "She's too obsessed with her career." "She's guarded and closed off." "She's too stressed and busy for sex." That last one in particular wasn't a rumor I loved circulating.

"High school relationships rarely last," I said, giving the same excuse I'd repeated to myself while I recovered from the toughest disappointment I'd had to face since my mother's death.

Desperate to change the subject, I nodded toward his duffel bag. "Headed to preseason?"

Warren shook his head. "Try-outs for the Rangers. I went free agent this year."

"You gave up the security of a contract? That's brave," I said with genuine admiration. I wasn't too knowledgeable about the world of pro sports, but going out on his own—backing himself—was actually a sexy trait. Not that I'd ever looked at my boyfriend's best friend in that way, but anyone with eyes could appreciate Warren's six-foot-three muscular frame and dimples for days. His easygoing, carefree demeanor combined with his stardom was a lethal combination for those women inclined toward athletes...which I absolutely was not.

"Isn't your company motto all about taking risks, backing yourself?" he asked as we moved along the security line.

"You follow me on social media?" He didn't strike me as the scroller type.

"I've caught a post or two," he said flirtingly.

I didn't take the flirting personally. Warren was charming, charismatic, and as emotionally unavailable as he was gorgeous. I couldn't remember him ever having a serious girlfriend. Even "casual dating" was too permanent a description of his relationships. Football was his only obsession.

The line moved again and we shuffled forward. A kid, playing with a stuffed animal bumped me and I fell forward. Warren caught my hands against his and our lifelines connected.

Let the record show that I was not at fault for glimpsing into his future or the disastrous aftermath, but what I saw in that brief clip rocked me to my core.

Warren, dressed in his football gear, training with the Rangers. A few great plays...then a linebacker collided with him, leaving him seriously injured. Medics rushed out to the field and everyone looked devastated.

Then, he was lying in a hospital bed, hooked to monitors, fighting for his life.

I gasped as I stepped back from him. We'd reached the front of the security line. I had mere seconds to talk him out of these tryouts. "Are you sure this is the team you really want to play for?"

"It's my dream team, so yeah, pretty sure."

"Right, but what about home team loyalty and all that?"

"I go where the rings are," he said.

A guard motioned us to keep moving and I took my time putting my stuff into the bins on the conveyor belt. He motioned for me to hurry up, but I ignored him. Time was ticking.

Warren filled his bin and waited behind me with blissful ignorance. I tried to appear calm, but inside I was losing my shit. I couldn't let him get on that plane.

"I just think you should think about what you really want," I said. "Maybe when I get back from my conference in New York, we could meet…"

The flirty smile was back. "For drinks? Sure. For life coaching—pass. I'm good."

I needed to level with him. "Look, if you keep playing football you're going to get hurt."

"Part of the job." He said it like several concussions in a career were expected and some sort of rite of passage. He wasn't getting it.

"No, I mean, really hurt."

Something in my voice gave him pause. His grin faded and worry crossed his seafoam-colored eyes. "How do you know?"

The absolute toughest part of having this ability is knowing no one would take me seriously if I answered that question truthfully. "Just a feeling…"

"Like some *Final Destination* shit?"

If that's what it took to convince him. "Something like that."

He looked concerned for a brief second and my hopes rose, but then, "You've always been a bit of a weirdo, Hailstorm," he said teasingly.

The guard flagged me toward the metal detector.

I reluctantly passed through, but as Warren followed behind me and started to gather his things from the conveyor belt on the other side, I panicked.

All out of options…

"That guy is trafficking drugs!" I yelled, pointing a finger at him.

Warren scoffed, then his eyes widened as two overzealous guards grabbed him. Chaos followed until the next thing I knew he was pinned to the floor. He looked up at me. "Hailstorm—what the hell? She's kidding guys," he told the guards sitting on his back.

Apparently not something to kid about as one guard radioed for airport police.

From the floor, Warren shot me a desperate look for help, but there was nothing I could do. I'd just saved his life even though he didn't know it and I refused to overthink or regret my actions. This was for his own good.

I mouthed "sorry" with a sincere look, then grabbed my things and started to head to my gate but…

"That woman has a bomb!" Warren yelled after me.

Another set of guards chased after me with a large, menacing looking canine. I have an irrational fear of dogs, but this time it seemed warranted. The thing was snarling and foaming at the mouth as it approached.

So, naturally, I ran.

I didn't get far before the dog gripped my bag between its sharp fangs and the guards tackled me to the airport floor. Arguing was futile as the dog started sniffing me—my belongings, my ass...

"Hey! Cut that out," I told it. Who'd hide a bomb up their ass? I glanced across the room and saw another dog sniffing Warren's butt. That made more sense.

Moments later, after excruciating embarrassment, where I kept my head low and prayed no one recognized me, Warren and I were both escorted into a search room, where things happened that I will never forget or reveal. I watched the time tick away as we missed our respective flights and received a six-month travel ban for the "prank." I wouldn't be making it to my conference, but Warren wasn't in danger anymore.

But did he thank me?

Now, as we stand in the school hallway and glare at one another, it's clear I'm still not going to get any appreciation.

Mrs. Miller pops her head out through the gymnasium door, interrupting the silent stare-off. "We're ready for you both."

Showing up Hailey Harris wasn't on my agenda for today, but I'm more than happy to rise to the occasion.

As soon as this wave of nostalgia passes.

Maple High's mascot—a Teen Shark—and team colors have been freshly repainted on the gymnasium walls, but other than that, it still feels the same. The same excited energy of the Friday night crowd at the basketball game hits me. The thrill of the competition and the cheers from the home team fans. I spent so many high school nights in this gymnasium.

Now I'm back in a different way. Hundreds of students sit in their cliques on the bleachers. Faculty sits on the gymnasium floor behind the podiums and mics set up for the speeches.

And every last person in attendance is waiting for me to impart some words of wisdom.

I'd have said no if it wouldn't have made me feel like an asshole. Truth is, I'm much better on the field offering support and guidance than wearing dress clothes and needing to stay on script—minding my p's and q's. Getting through this without dropping an f-bomb will be a miracle.

And now there's the added pressure of sharing the spotlight.

Hailey isn't struggling at all with a lack of confidence. Dressed in fitted, fashionable dress pants, a loose-fitting blouse, and wedge heels, she's casual yet professional and looking cool as a cucumber. This is her thing. She lives for the sound of her own voice.

She does look good though. I can begrudgingly give her that. Not the same adorable team mascot desperate to fit in that she was ten years ago. Success agrees with her, I guess. I'd be happy for her if she hadn't stolen mine.

Mrs. Miller stands and addresses the loud, rowdy crowd. "Settle down…okay everyone…"

The students continue to ignore her. She wasn't kidding about teenagers being assholes. But who could blame them? This time of year, I'd been itching to be outside too, not stuck in a classroom. I'd never been studious…unlike Cliff. Valedictorian, top of his class, ambitious and driven, my brother was going places. He should be standing here delivering an inspirational speech.

Coach Green, dressed in a team logo'd tracksuit, stands and lets out a long, loud whistle. Everyone settles.

Mrs. Miller sends the man a smile that looks like a little more than just gratitude. Something definitely going on under the bleachers there. "Thank you, Coach Green," she says.

He winks at her and she blushes.

"Continuing our career week festivities, we are lucky to have two of Maple High's very own alumni here today for a special double presentation," Mrs. Miller says, gesturing for us to take a podium and mic. "We have Warren Mitchell, professional football player and winner of two championship rings…"

Jocks in the crowd cheer and I can't resist sending Hailey a look. That's right. They love me.

"And we have Hailey Harris, influencer and life coach to the stars, to provide some inspiration."

Of course, the social media–obsessed cheer for her. Which is arguably double the crowd. She shoots me her own smug look and I can admit it's warranted. The applause is definitely louder and goes on seemingly forever.

Kids these days are brainwashed.

"Who'd like to start?" Mrs. Miller asks, looking back and forth between us.

I gesture Hailey forward. "Ladies first."

"In other words, you have nothing prepared," Hailey mumbles under her breath as she reaches into the pocket of the curve-hugging pants and takes out what looks like a dozen pages.

Most likely a snore-fest. I'm not stressing.

"Or just saving the best for last."

Hailey shoots me an icy glare, then smiles confidently as she turns to address the crowd. "Hello, students and faculty of Maple High. It's an honor to be back in these old familiar halls. I think we all know the impact social media has on our lives…"

"Stress, anxiety, self-confidence issues," I mumble behind her back.

Hailey ignores me but her spine stiffens as she continues. "With so many people vying for attention and recognition these days, any successful business or professional requires that their brand be distinguishable from the competition."

"At the cost of putting their entire personal life on display."

I tried to shut up. I did. But I have this inability to not call out bullshit when I hear it.

Hailey swings toward me, a fiery look in her light blue eyes.

Uh-oh. I've angered the beast.

"Online personas are usually avatars of ourselves," she counters.

Okay, for the record she started it.

I approach the mic but keep my gaze locked on her. "So, it's all fake?"

I hear her teeth clench so hard, I'm expecting a tooth to fall out when she speaks. "No," she says slowly, as though I've had too many concussions to comprehend the single-syllable word. "It's deciding how much of ourselves we want to reveal, how vulnerable we choose to be. It's up to us to decide what aspects of our lives the public has access to."

"I'm just saying people—especially young adults—need to be more active, interact with others in real life, not through altered personas."

"Real life requires an edge. It's not all fun and games. Even athletes need the exposure that social media provides."

"Then why are you having such a hard time adding sports clients to your roster?"

One point Mitchell. Zero Harris.

The crowd acknowledges the sick burn and as much as I'd like to revel in the win, something in her expression makes me feel a tad guilty for calling her out like that. Just a tad. Or maybe it was the burrito I ate late last night after dropping Sasha at home, making my insides churn. Either way, my sympathy capacity for Hailey Harris is not enough to give it another thought.

Hailey checks her bajillion pages, skips a dozen or so, composes herself and continues. "Excellence is something we can all achieve. It just takes hard work, commitment, dedication, and perseverance."

I should let it go. I've got one win. Still, my mouth is on autopilot. "Today's society is putting so much pressure on people. This hustle culture isn't healthy or sustainable."

Hailey turns to face me again, her cool dissipating quickly. The front of my dress pants pulsates when her laser beam gaze tries to pin me in place. Riled-up Hailey is kinda a turn-on.

"Says the man who doesn't get out of bed until noon."

Oh, now it's getting personal.

"I'm just saying failure is not a fatal flaw. If it takes a little longer to achieve one's goals, that's okay. Life is not a race."

"You also can't stand still. There is nothing worse than having a great idea or product and failing to bring it to market before someone else," she says pointedly—to the crowd this time.

Damn, I cued her up for that one.

"We all know posting online is solely for praise and recognition," I say, running out of fuel.

"Successful people post to inspire and encourage others," she says turning to look at me again. "There's no shame in bragging about personal achievements and I think we need to normalize being proud of ourselves and what *I've* achieved."

And there it is.

Hailey realizes what she's said and coughs. "What *a person* achieves..."

Every argumentative fiber in my being wants to keep this debate going. I'm getting more turned on as we go. By the fight, not Hailey Harris—just to be clear, but I notice that the teachers and students are staring at us and I don't need a boner to fuel Hailey's ego.

I clear my throat and address the students. "I'll just say that sports are hugely important and not just for those of you hoping to go into professional athletic careers. Sports teach life skills and discipline. But it's also meant to be fun. If you're not enjoying it, what's the point?"

"What's the point?" Hailey scoffs. "Success, financial security... Some of us weren't born into luxury."

"Says the woman who lives in a multimillion-dollar mansion."

Somehow, we've moved closer to one another as we've been speaking and Mrs. Miller quickly stands and moves us back toward our respective podiums before things turn physical.

Kinda a shame. I'd like to see what she's got.

"Well, that was great," the teacher says. "Really...insightful and informative. Right, students?"

Pretty sure this speech was scheduled for an hour. I check my watch. Hailey and I have failed at the task epically enough to be cut short by forty-six minutes. I lower my head and stare at the gymnasium floor.

A low rumble through the crowd and half-hearted applause confirm the kids thought the whole thing was complete bullshit. Not a token of wisdom to be had between us.

Hailey and I have the decency to at least look suitably embarrassed.

I can't let things end this way. I lean toward the mic. "I'd like to conclude by offering a donation of five thousand dollars to the sports program."

Now the crowd cheers for real.

Hailey rises to the challenge. "I'll match that donation for the social and technology clubs."

More applause.

"Did I say five? I meant ten."

Hailey stammers slightly but, chin raised, she nods. "I'll match that amount."

Behind us, the teachers look flabbergasted by our generosity. Mrs. Miller steps forward, but Coach Green stops her.

"Wait, let's see how high they'll go," he whispers.

Mrs. Miller shoots him a look and goes to the microphone. "On that note, let's conclude today's career week presentation."

Smart. Cut us off on a high, before it goes sideways again.

"A special thanks to Hailey Harris and Warren Mitchell for their generous contributions," she says, applauding us. "Early lunch everyone."

I wave to the crowd as they quickly disperse from the bleachers. "If anyone wants an autograph…" No one's listening.

Hailey stifles a laugh, but I don't see anyone clamoring to meet her either. Kids are tougher to impress these days.

In the hallway a moment later, Hailey and I race toward the exit and try to leave at the same time through the same door, our bodies colliding again. She's actually stronger than she looks. Her five-foot-three frame should have been sailing across the hallway with the body check I just delivered, yet she holds her own as we lodge ourselves in the door frame in our struggle to get through.

This is ridiculous. I know it. Yet something about her turns me into an immature dick. I begrudgingly, generously, stand back and motion for her to go first. I can be the bigger person.

Nose in the air, she pushes through the door.

I slide my sunglasses on, then quickly catch the swinging door she's released before it hits me in the face. "Always a pleasure," I say through gritted teeth as we step out into the sunshine.

Hailey simply flips me off as she heads toward her convertible.

THREE

HAILEY'S DAILY RULE FOR SUCCESS:
Even bad press can promote your brand,
if you're creative enough to spin it.

NOT THE BEST WAY TO WAKE UP IN THE MORNING.
Normally, being tagged in a viral video would have my follower count rising, but the post from Sharksfan2008 of the career week presentations—or lack thereof—has me cringing as I peer at it through sleepy eyes at 4:25 a.m. Not just because Warren and I look unprofessional—debating one another instead of keeping our personal feud to ourselves—but because the comments are heavily in favor of Warren's point of view.

When did work/life balance become the current social narrative?

And there's no way this teenager has enough of a following to make this post trend. A quick search confirms my suspicion that it was "shared" by Spencer Stanley on his socials.

If I'm keeping tabs on my competition, the competition is definitely keeping tabs on me.

Time to do damage control.

Which means rolling over and going back to sleep, intentionally skipping my morning motivational post.

A few hours later, a refreshing fruity virgin cocktail in hand, Gucci sunglasses on, I float in my pool on my gold floatie shaped like a dollar sign—a gift from an investor client I saved from jail by advising him against a fraudulent get rich quick scheme. Cell phone in hand, I smile and go live to my followers.

"Hey, Hustlers! This is your midweek reminder to breathe."

A deep inhale and slow exhale as the floatie continues to drift toward the edge of the pool.

"Even hustlers need downtime. Make sure to take a few moments today and enjoy the rewards of your effort. Why else are you working so hard if you can't—"

My words are cut off as the floatie hits the edge of the pool. A loud hissing is all I hear before I'm swallowed by the toxic-smelling PVC.

None of today's nineteen horoscopes predicted this was how I was going to die.

Flailing my legs and arms, I hold my breath and struggle to free myself as the middle of the floatie sinks. Vinyl tries to swallow me whole. I continue to fight it off and finally tip free into the water. I shriek and hold the phone above the surface as my body is submerged. Cold water steals my breath (okay, let's be real—the pool's heated, but damn, it's still a shock). Seconds before my lungs are depleted of air, I resurface and reach for the edge of the pool. I quickly stop the live stream, but not before eight hundred followers have viewed the post. Hearts and laughy face emojis pop up on the feed.

At least they were laughing. Mission accomplished, I guess.

I climb out of the water and grab a towel from the lounge chair, then examine the pool. A large crack is visible in the concrete.

Shit. Now I have *actual* damage to fix.

Miraculously, my cell phone has escaped unharmed, so I pace the pool deck as I make a call. Two rings, then:

"Jensen Pools and Lawns."

"Mr. Jensen! Hailey Harris."

"Hailey! How are you?"

"I have a bit of a problem…" I barely have to say more before the most amazing man on the planet sets me up for a service call later that day. My ex's father is the only male role model I've ever had. He's a funny, thoughtful, wise man and the breakup with Liam was that much tougher because I was also losing him and his guidance. Luckily, through his business, we've found a way to stay in touch. But it's not the same. I'm no longer family.

I disconnect the call as my neighbor, Amelia Cranshaw, approaches. We installed a gate in our shared fence for easier access between the yards. She has to be in her late seventies but doesn't look older than sixty—the perks of being a former Hollywood starlet who always took self-care to the next level. She wears a beautiful kimono and carries a movie script and I know why she's here.

"I overheard you on the phone just now, dear. How bad is it?" she asks as she looks at the pool.

"Hopefully an easily repairable crack."

"Must have been that tremor earlier this week."

That hadn't even dawned on me as the cause, but it makes sense.

One small crack…

I nod toward the script. Best to get right to it. Amelia is lovely and her stories about Hollywood in the "good old days" are truly captivating, but if I'm not careful, my day will be gone before I realize it. We've been neighbors for six years and in a weird twist of fate, I'd say she's my only real friend.

"New audition coming up?"

Amelia nods. "My agent sent me this adorable family drama, and I was thrilled…until she told me which role they wanted me to read for. Take a guess."

"The mother?"

"The *grandmother*," she says as though she'd prefer to play Jabba the Hutt in a new Star Wars spin-off. She catches sight of her reflection in my window. "Guess time really does sneak up, doesn't it?" she says pensively, almost as though she's forgotten I'm even here. "Anyway, dear, can you read my fortune?"

"I told you, Ms. Cranshaw, that's not what I…" I stop. We've had this discussion a million times. Amelia believes I'm a palm reader after she caught me in action with a previous client at one of my VIP events and well, it's better than trying to explain the truth. "Sure. Give me your hand."

Amelia extends a thin, elegant hand, adorned in expensive jewelry. I take it and study her palm for effect. Then I press my lifeline to hers and the same inexplicable energy runs through me as I'm transported to some indeterminate time in the future…to Amelia's house next door.

A beautiful but lonely home. Movie posters featuring a young Amelia are on the walls and Oscars line the shelves. Amelia stands in her living room, delivering a monologue from one of her black-and-white films.

On her old-fashioned writing desk is a stack of unsent Christmas and birthday cards addressed to "Aaron Cranshaw." Her gaze lands on a picture of herself—middle-aged—with Aaron as a boy. She looks sad, regretful as the monologue comes to an end.

"Still haven't reached out to your son?" I ask gently as I release her hand.

"I'm busy. He's busy," she says dismissively. She hates when I get personal, but it's the only thing I see whenever I "tell her fortune." I hate to think it's because Amelia's days in the spotlight are over. I'd write her a starring role and produce the movie myself before I'd ever disappoint her with news like that.

"What about the role, darlin'?" she asks, almost diva-like. To Amelia, I'm a personal spiritual advisor, neighbor, then friend-adjacent. She has no idea how much I typically charge for this service or how much I value knowing her. While the support and advice giving doesn't flow both ways, I like to think she'd be there for me if I ever truly needed her.

"Definitely go for it," I say.

"Won't I be typecast as a grandma?" She looks worried that this role could prevent her from once again playing the leading love interest, and I genuinely hope she does get those parts again. But until then, "Two words—Betty. White."

Amelia's eyes widen with renewed hope. "You think so?"

"Absolutely. Now, go rehearse."

Amelia hugs me gratefully—the only payment I need—and I cling on a second longer, needing this contact way more than she does.

"Hug's over," she says.

"Yep," I say awkwardly as I release her.

She heads back toward her house. "Good luck with the pool, dear!" she calls over her shoulder.

Alone, I look at the crack in the concrete and my gut tightens with an eerie, sinking sensation. It's not my psychic abilities at work. This is more of an ominous vibe, as though the crack in the pool could be a sign of things to come...

Hours later, I hang freshly laundered sweaters on the treadmill in my state-of-the-art home gym, which is full of equipment I have no idea how to use. The sales rep at Fitness City must have made his monthly commission off me. But if I want sports clients, I need to get sporty. Or at least give the impression that I know what I'm talking about. Probably should scuff up some of the weights before the VIP party, when I'll be touring potential athletic clients through the facility.

I mean I *could* actually use the equipment. Right now, my health maintenance strategy is to avoid fried foods and hope for the best. But I hate working out and despite countless efforts, I'm not a huge sports fan.

Before the incident with Warren, I had zero interest in pro-athlete clients. I can bullshit my way through most industries, with some minor research, but sports seemed to have too many variables, too many unknowns, so it seemed too risky to fully trust my glimpses.

But after that day in the airport, something switched in my thinking. I tried to resist it, but I couldn't quiet the nagging voice that said maybe I could use my gift for more than success in business—my clients' and my own. Maybe there was a better purpose. Maybe I could—and should—use my gift in a more altruistic way.

After all, I'd saved Warren's life. Maybe preventing other injuries would balance out my karma a little. Make me feel less like a fraud for never having to implement the success strategies I advise my clients.

The front gate intercom sounds and I glance at my watch. Jensen Pools and Lawns—right on time.

I hit the intercom button on the wall and static sounds before a muffled voice announces their presence. Great, something else broken.

Upstairs, I open the front door and step outside as I hear the maintenance van drive up to the house. I wait and smile at the sound of Mr. Jensen's toolbox coming around the corner.

Only it's not Mr. Jensen.

My mouth gapes and I blink several times, but he's still there.

Liam Jensen.

My ex, dressed in a polo shirt with a company logo on it,

approaches and scans the property. He stops in front of me and I almost reach out to touch him to make sure he's real. With my "condition," hallucinations seem like just one step away.

"Hails, long time," he says with a familiar slow smile that used to make my heart thunder. Apparently still does. My health tracker can shut up anytime now.

"I was just in my gym," I say lamely to explain the loud, rapid beeping coming from my wrist. Technically, it's not a lie.

"Good to see you," he says, his gaze drifting over me. I glance at my athleisure wear—I may not work out, but I can appreciate the comfort of yoga clothes—and quickly try to tame my unruly hair.

"Is it?" Jesus, Hailey—sound more desperate. "I mean, good to see you too... What are you doing here?"

"Dad's crews were out on other jobs, so he sent me to check out your pool."

Right. He works for his father. Or at least he used to in high school. Now he's a big shot architect in New York.

"Oh right... I'll show you out back."

I lead the way toward the backyard pool and Liam follows, an impressed look on his handsome face as he takes in my view.

"Ocean view, like you always wanted. I remember driving to the beach every weekend and you'd always talk about owning one of these homes one day."

"Set goals and..." I stop and laugh, embarrassed. "Sorry, occupational hazard." Try to be normal, Hailey. "When did you get back in town?"

"A few days ago," he says and I can't decipher how he feels about it. But I know how I feel. Sucker punched that this is the first time I've seen him. Not that I expect to be his first stop when he's in town, but a quick text would have been nice.

"I was on the plane when the tremor hit. Had to circle the airport for over an hour."

An uneasiness settles in the pit of my stomach at the mention of the earthquake. "How long are you staying?"

"Not sure…at least a year."

My head whips toward him and I get a neck cramp. "What happened in New York? I thought you were designing the new skyscrapers along Seventh Avenue?"

Okay, so I stalk my ex-boyfriend online. Who doesn't?

"Your dad keeps me posted when he comes to maintain the pool," I say, slightly flustered. He peers at me with those dark brown eyes I thought I'd stare into forever—back when I was young and naive and thought someone like me could actually have a real, long-term relationship.

Back when I had no idea that fate had other plans. Because Liam's life was entwined with mine, I could never see *his* future either.

As far as "gifts" go, this one is severely lacking.

Liam stares at the pool and clears his throat. "Yeah, I, uh… had another opportunity here."

And maybe now I do too?

Nope. Not going full speed ahead with wedding plans just yet. We broke up for a reason. Though looking at him now, that reason—which I assume was a very good one—is eluding me. He's only gotten better looking in the last few years— definitely more muscular and his hair is slightly longer, curling around the collar of the shirt. Just the right amount of stubble covers his square jawline. He looks healthy and happy, but there's something about his demeanor that hints at unease.

"Let's take a look at this crack," Liam says, bending next to the pool and examining the concrete.

I stare at him, enamored, as not-so-repressed feelings start to resurface.

Liam was the first guy I ever dated. He was my first kiss. My first sexual experience. My first and last heartache. Opening up to people is not something that comes naturally to me given my predicament. Relationships are based on trust and honesty. Which basically rules me out of ever having one.

So many times over the years, I wanted to tell Liam my secret. Almost did a thousand times, but no one has ever known—not even my mother. And parting with it would mean making myself more vulnerable than I've ever found worth it.

Even for Liam.

Breaking up and going our separate ways once things reached that critical point of shit or put a ring on it was probably for the best. Although I can't help wanting to know his opinion on that.

"Doesn't look too bad yet," he says. "Good thing you caught it now, before it completely collapsed and you'd have an indoor pool in your basement."

Water damage is definitely not something I want to deal with. "Think you can fix it before this weekend?"

Liam stands and grins at me. "Another epic influencer party?"

My eyes narrow. How does he know about that?

"What? I follow you on social media."

He what? "The Liam I remember acted like he didn't even know what social media was." Anti-attention despite being one of the most charismatic, smart, athletic guys in school, Liam was modest and not a fan of what he always referred to as "Look at Me" culture.

Ah, right—the main catalyst in our breakup. Different worlds, different passions, different values.

"Someone once told me I needed to use the power of the socials to advance my career," he says with a shrug. "But before you get too impressed, I'm following like four people and I have exactly half that many followers."

I laugh. "Then I'm honored to be one of the chosen few."

Our gazes meet and hold in what Amelia would refer to as

a "beat of romantic connection," and my lack of recent sexual pleasure decides to fuck with me. Is there a statute of limitations on breakup sex?

Fortunately, before I can embarrass myself in the most epic way by suggesting it, he clears his throat and looks away.

"I can get a crew here tomorrow morning. If they only partially drain the pool, fix the damage and then give it a few days to set, we should have it up and functional for your party."

"Thank you so much," I say then hesitate before asking, "Would you like to stay...for a drink? I could make lunch." We could have that breakup sex we never took advantage of.

Liam checks his watch, shakes his head regrettably. "I have someone waiting in the van. Rain check?"

I hide my disappointment. "Of course. Yeah. Anytime."

We start to head around front and I turn to him. "If you're not doing anything Saturday night, you should stop by." I'm afraid if I don't set up an exact time to see him again this will turn into that thing where friends say "we should do this again sometime" and it never happens. A future relationship or second chance may not be in the cards, but Liam was my best friend for a significant portion of my life. He was there for me when my mother died, when I launched my business. We have history and if he was back home for a while...

"Thought the party was just for potential VIP clients," he says.

"Old friends are always welcome and who knows, you might be in need of my services...old friends discount of course."

"I still couldn't afford you," Liam says with a laugh. "But sure. Why not? Not to the coaching, just yet, but the party sounds fun—a chance to see you in action."

"Great! It's Saturday night..."

"At 8:50. Because a true disruptor doesn't operate by customary, standard time slots."

I'm completely taken aback. "You really were paying attention." Maybe there is still a hint of something between us.

Liam pauses and turns to me with a look of admiration. "I always thought you were the most fascinating person I knew—of course I was paying attention."

Should I just kiss him now or...?

"I should go."

Right.

We turn the corner and walk toward a van with the faded "Jensen Pools and Lawns" logo on the side. I shake my head. "I remember great times in that van."

"I recall you weren't exactly thrilled when I drove it to pick you up for prom."

"I wouldn't mind being picked up in it...now."

My flirty laugh dies on my lips as a polished, beautiful woman, wearing a sundress that I know is Gucci because I've been eyeing it for months, trying to justify the price tag, climbs out of the passenger side and approaches us. She glances nervously at Liam to do the introductions.

Liam clears his throat and looks slightly frazzled, as though he'd been hoping to avoid this situation. "Sonia, this is Hailey Harris—an old...friend from high school."

Old friend? How many *old friends* had lost their virginity in the back of that van?

"Hailey, this is Sonia...my fiancée."

Okay, that's just some bullshit. Liam always claimed he wasn't cut out for marriage. His parents' divorce when he was twelve totally messed him up regarding the whole life-long commitment thing.

Reason number two for the breakup. His commitment issues made it impossible for me to feel vulnerable enough to trust him with who I am.

"Fiancée. Wow." I look closer and recognize his lovely bride-to-be. "Wait. You're Sonia Banks. Your family owns Banks Resorts, right?"

Sonia looks flattered that I know. She tucks a strand of pretty blond hair behind her ear and nods. "Yes. I'm a huge fan of yours. Your Monday motivational posts get my butt out of bed at four fifty a.m."

The fangirling was not expected. "Oh, thank you. That's kind of you to say." Though it does make me like her more than I want to.

Liam turns to her. "Hailey invited us to her influencer party this Saturday night."

Her hazel eyes light up. "Really? That's incredible."

My smile is so tight, I'm worried about my recent lip filler—again, done to secure a client, not because I have an issue with my lips. Neither had Liam at one time. Now I'm just an old friend in his version of our history. "Great, so you're both coming."

"Wouldn't miss it!" Sonia sends a sheepish look at Liam. "I actually didn't believe Liam when he said he knew you." She wraps an arm around him and grins up at him. They kiss and I'm not quick enough to look away. "Sorry, Hun-Hun."

Hun-Hun? The Liam I knew didn't believe in pet names. In fact, he despised them. And, oh Lord, how I tried. Baby, Sweet Cheeks, Honey Bear… Nothing. Refused to answer to anything other than Liam.

"So, you'll have a crew here tomorrow?" I say to interrupt the PDA in my driveway.

Liam nods. "First thing."

"Great. Thank you." I turn to Sonia. "Nice meeting you."

She hesitates, then holds out her cell phone. "Would a selfie be too bold?"

Yes. "Um, how about at the party? When I'm dressed properly." And I've had a team of stylists to help me stand a chance of competing with her breathtaking looks.

She laughs, embarrassed, and puts the phone away. "Of course. And I promise I'll rein in my fangirling by then."

Liam leads her away and I wave as they climb back into the van. Then my smile fades as they drive away.

That night, with a glass of wine in hand, I Google "Sonia Banks" because, naturally, this has become my new obsession. Internet pages load about the young heir to the Banks Resorts fortune, and photos of Sonia and Liam at a resort opening in the Caribbean only dampen my mood further.

But do I stop there? Hell no.

And the further I go down the rabbit hole of stalking, the more disheartened I am. Turns out Sonia is not some spoiled, rich bitch that I can reasonably dislike, but a wonderfully compassionate person who donates her time and money to charities. I scroll through the articles about her charity work, building schools in developing nations, hosting Christmas dinner at the local food bank and stop on one that reads: "Heir to the Banks chain of luxury resorts, Sonia Banks, donates kidney to stranger."

I drain the wine in my glass.

It's not like *I* wouldn't donate an organ to a stranger. I just haven't had the opportunity!

This shit is hard. Maybe I have had too many concussions to understand these complicated psychological theories.

Sitting on a barstool at Deek's, a quiet local pub, textbook on the bar in front of me, I read the same page over and over, trying to make sense of it. It's as though my brain can't absorb information that's not coming at me in a perfect spiral going sixty miles per hour.

Cliff was the smart one. Born with a heart defect, which was ironic because Cliff had the biggest heart of anyone I knew, sports were off the table for him, therefore he threw himself into academics for our impossible to please father. The lines were drawn very early in our childhood. Cliff was the genius expected to succeed in business. I was the athlete, expected to bring home championship trophies. We fell into our respective roles to give my father something to brag about and constantly struggled for his approval...

Until we didn't.

Liam enters the pub and I grin—my high school best friend live and in the flesh. The last time I saw him was at Cliff's funeral and I'd been far too messed up to appreciate the reunion. Liam had always been like a second brother to me and we'd drifted apart since he moved to New York. My weekly golf game with his father—the one I wish I'd had growing up—helps to keep me in the loop about what's happening in his life.

"Thought I'd find you here," he says.

"Hey, man, heard a rumor you were back in town." I quickly shove the book into my duffel bag—I'm probably going to fail this course, therefore keeping it to myself seems like the least embarrassing option.

We fist bump then share a manly one-armed hug.

Liam climbs onto the stool next to me and flags the bartender for a beer. "How's the team this year?"

"Going all the way to finals." If I can keep Marcus from staying out late before practice. He's been dragging his ass lately and I can tell the kid's not getting enough rest...enough of anything a professional athlete needs to function at his best. I know he's drinking despite my rules and I hope he hasn't crossed the line into other harmful substances.

"Wouldn't expect nothing less," Liam says. "And it appears you are in hot demand at high school career days."

I shake my head and take a swig from my beer bottle.

"Those fucking kids with their viral videos." If Liam, Mr. Anti–Social Media, has seen the video of Hailey and me going at it—and not in a fun, clothes off way—then the rest of the world must have. Not that I'm trying to protect my reputation these days, but looking like a jackass on the internet is something I try to avoid. Doesn't exactly send a good message to the impressionable teens on my team.

"I can't believe the two of you are still trying to slit one another's throats," Liam says with an amused chuckle.

"She destroyed my career and subjected me to an airport security search."

"In all fairness, she was banned from air travel for six months too."

"She started it." I refuse to feel bad that she missed an important event. Her career seems to be doing just fine. That billboard on the highway says it all.

"That's mature," Liam says, nodding his thanks to the bartender as a beer is placed in front of him on a coaster. He raises his bottle to mine and we cheers before he takes a swig. "Look, I'm heading to her party Saturday night. You should come."

"I'd rather have another cavity search."

"There's someone special I want you to meet."

I turn to look at him in surprise. Now it's getting interesting. "You're actually bringing a date to Hailey's?"

Liam shrugs. "She's cool with it. In fact, she and Sonia have already met."

I think about it then grin. "You know, I think I will tag along. Can't resist a good train wreck."

"Seriously, it's not like that," he says. "What Hailey and I had is in the past—we're cool."

"Okay, man, if you say so."

If there's one thing I know about Hailey Harris, she is absolutely not cool with the love of her life dating someone else. In fact, going to this party now serves a dual purpose—this Sonia person may need a bodyguard.

FOUR

HAILEY'S DAILY RULE FOR SUCCESS:
Never ignore your intuition—it's your
subconscious having your back.

LUXURY VEHICLES PULL UP OUTSIDE MY HOUSE and a valet parks them along the side streets. Guests from movie stars to business professionals to philanthropists, dressed in fashionable clothes, blinged out in expensive jewelry, arrive and join the crowd in my backyard.

The party is already in full swing, as I always invite my previous clients half an hour early to instill FOMO in those arriving later. The impression of maybe not getting here early enough to secure my services creates urgency. Everyone wants what they can't have.

Beautiful white lights, strung on swaying palm trees, illuminate the yard in a warm, welcoming, but sophisticated glow. A popular local DJ plays the latest hits, a bartender tends the outdoor bar, and servers, in black tie, rotate trays of champagne.

Only champagne is served at a Hailey Harris VIP party.

Guests mingle and chat around the pool deck. I zero in on one in particular and make my way toward her.

Alisha Jameeka, an up-and-coming, curvy-chic fashion designer whose TikTok shows featuring her creations are garnering close to a hundred thousand views. Not mind-blowing numbers, but enough to get my attention. Recognizing talent on the rise is one of my more natural gifts.

I also want to work with Alisha because I love her designs. They're fresh, fun, and fantastic. Like the jumpsuit she's wearing now. Classic black, off the shoulder, with a cinched waist. Stunning and shows off her natural curves.

"One of your designs, I assume," I say as I stop next to her. She's standing alone, clutching her champagne glass and looking nervous, slightly out of place.

She won't be for long.

Alisha does a shy spin, showing off an open back and slightly flared leg. "Can't find anything like this in my size anywhere in this city."

"These should be everywhere."

"I agree, but investors aren't convinced," she says with a hint of annoyance.

I move closer and clasp her hand in mine. "Investors will invest once the rest of the world does."

She stares at me with a hint of desperation. "How do I make that happen?"

I connect my lifeline to hers and my visionary powers are activated.

Inside a posh hotel ballroom, cameras flash as a line of curvy-chic clothing is exhibited on the runway. Alisha stands next to the stage, looks on with pride as the collection is well received by attendees— fashion royalty and luxury brand execs. The next day's style and fashion magazine sites have rave reviews.

I smile warmly at Alisha as I release her hand. "I can help you get to the next level."

Her demeanor changes and she waves a hand. "Honestly, the clothing line is just a passion project."

In addition to being super talented, she's adorably modest, which makes her the absolute best type of client. Unfortunately, everyone is wary of the price tag without some sort of guarantee. They'd rather downplay their goals than invest in them.

"We both know that's not true. You have dreams and you should chase them. I'm envisioning a collection at New York fashion week."

Alisha laughs, shakes her head, but then her eyes meet mine—a flash of her dream reflecting in their dark depths. "You think you can make that happen?"

There it is. The desire for success in her tone.

"No. *You* can. With the right push. That's where I come in."

Alisha hesitates, tucking a strand of gorgeous dark hair behind one ear. Normally, I'd bring out the tough sell—remind Alisha that she's posted her designs online to thousands of viewers and it's only a matter of time until someone else steals her fabulous ideas and becomes a huge success, but that approach won't work with her. Her confidence is still hanging in the balance—not quite at the level where she'll believe in herself.

"You know most people don't fear failure," I say. "They fear success. As women we've been conditioned not to let our ambitions soar too high. Balancing what society expects from us with our own desires keeps us in a paralyzed state of mediocrity."

Alisha breathes out as though I've just encapsulated her very existence. "You're so right...but what if I fail?"

It's times like these when I wish I could confide my secret—tell her with the utmost confidence that she won't—but I'm afraid without that self-doubt, without that uncertainty, my clients won't strive as hard to get where I've seen them.

That, and the fact that I'd be hauled off to the university science lab.

"Then we will fail fabulously together," I say, extending my champagne glass to hers. We clink and the deal is set. Though I will be getting a contract to her ASAP. "Now… as promised, let's record an announcement of our working partnership to your followers."

Alisha reaches for her cell phone and we move closer and go live.

As we wrap up moments later, Alisha heads off to get another glass of champagne and now that I've warmed up with an easy one, I scan the yard for my next acquisition.

I frown. None of the athletes I personally invited are here. What the hell do I need to do to get their attention? I offered a free introductory session through their coaches and got ghosted. I reached out to managers and agents and got the same old brush-off. I just need one client to commit and the rest will follow, but the people calling the shots tend to be old-school. The psychology of the sport isn't valued as much as the physical training.

Or…

I reach for my phone and open Spencer Stanley's socials.

That fucking guy!

I scroll through photos of his own event this evening—a VIP booth at a baseball game. Pro basketball, football, and hockey players all in attendance, eating pizza, drinking beer, and posing for selfies with Spencer. Why didn't I think of that?

Annoyed, I put the phone away, then spot Liam and Sonia arriving across the yard. Jealousy or longing? Not sure exactly how to label the emotion overshadowing my previous irritation. They both look fabulous—Liam in a suit, which has to be Sonia's influence as he always refused to wear one with me. She's dressed in a pale pink silk number with nothing underneath—not a trace of an undergarment anywhere. Elegant and fabulous. Liam's eyeing her as though he can't wait to get her out of here and out of the dress.

Definitely both—jealousy *and* longing.

"They make a cute couple, don't they?"

Startled by the voice so close to my ear, the warm breath against my neck, I jump and spill my champagne. I turn and glare at Warren, who's carrying a glass of whiskey on ice. "Who let you in here? And where did you get whiskey? It's a champagne-only event."

"I came with Liam and his adorable new fiancée, Sonia. And your bartender is a big football fan," he says smugly, sipping the liquid.

I roll my eyes and prepare an earful, but Liam and Sonia join us, arms wrapped around one another.

"Hope it's okay I invited him," Liam says.

I suspect he has an ulterior motive. Maybe wanting Warren and me to settle this feud once and for all. Not likely.

"Of course…like a high school reunion," I say with a tight smile.

"This place is fabulous. I can't believe I'm here," Sonia says excitedly.

Neither can I.

A popular song comes on and Sonia grips Liam's hand—tugs him gently toward the pool deck dance area. "Come on. This is my favorite song."

Liam resists and shakes his head. "You know I don't dance."

"Well, I do," Warren says charmingly. He forces his glass into my hand and he and Sonia head off. Liam smiles as he watches and I can't take my eyes off his handsome face. He's clean-shaven tonight and the smell of his familiar cologne lingers on the breeze.

At least Sonia hasn't changed one thing about him. Yet.

"She's really incredible," I say because it's true even if I don't love her being so incredible for *him*. Everything I've read online has only confirmed that she's as genuine as she is beautiful. Sure, not everything is as it appears and everyone has skeletons in their closet...but I'm not sure if I'm up to the challenge of discovering Sonia's. I'm still having trouble believing that Liam will actually go through with this lifelong commitment. How could one woman over five months reprogram a lifetime of anti-marriage views?

As lovely as they seem together, I give the relationship another three months before Liam freaks out and calls off the engagement.

"She's obsessed with you and she likes me more because I know you, so thank you for that," he says, sipping his champagne and grimacing at the taste.

"Does she know you're lying about the whole no dancing thing? I seem to remember your mom putting you in ballroom lessons." He'd hated every minute of it, but his football-obsessed mom had heard that dancing, yoga, and Pilates could make him a better player, so she'd enrolled him in all three. With the added bonus of pissing off her ex-husband.

"Actually, those will probably pay off," he says with a small nod. "I plan to surprise Sonia with my dancing skills at the wedding." Liam sips his drink as though he hopes the liquid has miraculously become something else, unaware of my panic.

"Wedding?"

He glances at me with a smirk. "Typically what follows an engagement, Hails."

"But not anytime too soon, right? I mean, you two just met." I know that from my cyber stalking. Sonia's relationship status changed around Christmas. I resist the urge to point out that relationships formed during the holidays are often influenced by the joy of the season—all the romantic songs and magical lights...and don't get me started on the effect of mistletoe.

"But when you know, you know, right? We want to get married before breaking ground on her family's new resort," he says but there's definitely a hint of resistance in his voice, confirming my suspicions. "We're thinking Labor Day weekend and we'd obviously love for you to come."

That's a big fuck no. "Wow..." Too fast but what can I say? We've only just reconnected. It's none of my business. "I'm so darn happy for you." I gulp Warren's whiskey and Liam looks at me with admiration.

"I'm really happy for you too. You did it, Hails."

"You sound surprised."

"It's just a wild industry... But I never should have doubted you." Liam touches my hand and I instinctively turn my palm to connect our lifelines. It's never worked in the past but maybe with time and distance...

Liam sits at a desk, divorce papers in front of him along with an employment contract termination from Banks Resorts. He looks destroyed and heartbroken. He picks up a whiskey bottle and throws it across the room. It shatters...

And so does my glimpse.

I stumble back slightly, shocked. I've never been able to see Liam's future before—not when we were in love. And the realization that the lingering attraction I have for him is more surface level than deep longing doesn't completely surprise me. But what does alarm me is what I saw in his future. To say I'm surprised that his current relationship is doomed would be lying, but actually seeing it...

Liam looks at me in concern. "You okay?"

"Um...yeah. Great."

I fight to calm my racing pulse as I stare across the yard at Sonia, laughing and dancing with Warren. Liam is enamored as he watches his fiancée glow in the string lights reflecting off the pool. The yard spins slightly beneath my feet as I'm spiraling in moral conflict. I should never have looked into Liam's future, but I did.

So, what the hell do I do now?

I have to admit, I was expecting a replica of Barbie's Dream-house complete with a topiary *H* near a swimming pool with a pink slide, but Hailey's home is surprisingly tasteful. At least the exterior is. And despite my dislike of the woman, I do feel a tinge of happiness for her. I know that her life hasn't always looked this way.

I'd always found it strange that she never had any family at school events or hosted a party as long as I'd known her. She'd kept to herself before she started dating Liam in junior year, and she wasn't like a lot of the other girls at school— rich, popular, privileged, and prissy. She had a down-to-earth vibe that intrigued me.

One day, walking home late after football practice, I saw her boarding a bus heading to the east side of town. So I jumped on and sat as far away from her as possible, just to see where she was heading and a bit because my protective instincts took over—the east side wasn't a place most sixteen-year-old girls liked to go alone.

When I saw her get off the bus and climb the stairs to a run-down apartment building, it confirmed my suspicion that there were things Hailey was desperate to keep hidden from her friends and school officials.

I never said a word to anyone.

I mean, do I think a five-bedroom, four-bathroom, four-thousand-square-foot home is a bit much for one single person? Absolutely. But I have to hand it to her, she does know a lot of influential people.

As I lead Sonia toward the poolside "dance floor," I spot a

local politician and his wife sitting with their feet dangling in the pool, and several actors I recognized but wouldn't be able to name if my life depended on it were standing near the bar.

"There are so many important people here," Sonia says, sounding almost giddy.

"*The* Sonia Banks is here, so I'd say so, yeah," I say with a wink as we start to dance to the hip-hop beat. I met her an hour ago and already I think she's fantastic. The fact that she's intimidated to be here says a lot about her. She's the heir to a luxury resort chain and yet she's unpretentious and sweet. Liam is a lucky guy. This relationship definitely fits him so much better than the one with Hailey.

I look across the yard and an odd feeling strikes my gut as the two of them laugh and chat together. According to Liam they haven't really kept in touch over the years, but they look a little too comfortable. The uneasiness is for Sonia's sake, obviously.

I mean Hailey's hot—especially in the knee-length, pale blue dress with a high neckline that accentuates her curves and shows off a classy, modest amount of fantastic legs, but she's far from my type.

Sonia catches my gaze and sighs. "I have a lot to live up to, don't I?"

Damn. Is that what she thinks? "Sonia, believe me when I say this—there's no competition."

She laughs gently as I take her hand and spin her around, sounding genuinely relieved to hear it. "You're Liam's best friend, so I'm going to trust you on that."

"You should. I've known Liam since we were five years old and I know he's totally in love with you."

My gaze locks on Hailey and the unsettled feeling refuses to subside. She's standing just a little too close and Liam's a little too fixated on her. I spin Sonia again so that she doesn't have a view of it.

"What's the deal with you two?" she asks. "I mean, I heard about the airport incident, but that was a while ago…"

Not long enough. "It's more than that… She just…" What? How do I explain my feelings about Hailey? I have every reason to be annoyed by her and dislike her, but it's almost deeper than that. I can't really understand the feelings she evokes and it's best that we steer clear of one another. "She's just aggravating and I don't know why. She's just like 'errrr.'" I clench my fists and shake them. "You know?"

"Honestly? No. I think she's so fantastic."

"Then her marketing is paying off," I say, sending another glance Hailey's way. She takes a sip of my whiskey and another wave of unlabeled emotions swirl through me. Primarily annoyance—get your own unauthorized whiskey. But also the same slight arousal I felt around her at the high school when I see her lick the rim of the glass to catch the drops. Apparently, my biggest turn-on is irritation.

"You don't believe she deserves all the hype?" Sonia asks.

"She's made a huge success of herself and good for her." I shrug. "I don't know, I just think this whole influencer, life coach thing is a scam. I mean, she's essentially helping rich people get richer."

Sonia eyes me with a hint of a sly smile. "That's what she portrays online."

"What do you mean?" I'm curious despite my better judgment.

"She only posts about her professional clients, but she's worked with a lot of people from all walks of life. She once helped a veteran who'd been living in Santa Monica and experiencing homelessness to launch a transition program."

Okay, so that's a little unexpected.

"And she helped a single mom start a daycare chain in Santa Clarita after her husband died. At no charge, by the way."

Sonia casts an admiring glance toward Hailey. "She doesn't publicize those things."

Damn, that's actually pretty cool of her.

I force away any admiration I might be inclined to entertain. Safer to keep my preconceived notions about her in check.

She may do some altruistic work, but it doesn't diminish the fact that she essentially manipulates people into believing they need some secret wisdom only she possesses to succeed in life.

We continue to dance, but as the song comes to an end, my gaze shifts across the yard toward Hailey and Liam again. They've moved slightly closer and their faces are illuminated by the white backyard lights overhead.

There's a moment—something—between them. Their gazes locked on one another, Hailey's hand resting casually on Liam's—a long beat...

Then Hailey swings her gaze back this way as though sensing they've been caught in a moment, and it's then that I see it.

The same look on her face from that day at the airport. Right before she blew up my life.

FIVE

HAILEY'S DAILY RULE FOR SUCCESS:
When in doubt, pro/con it out.

I SIT AT MY DESK FAR TOO EARLY THE NEXT MORN-
ing, clutching an espresso like a life raft. The document open
on my laptop is labeled "Pros/Cons of messing with my ex's
personal life."

Pro/conning is a simple yet effective exercise I have all my
clients do when making major decisions.

If the pro list outnumbers the con list, they're reassured
that the advice I've offered is in line with what they hope to
achieve and they go for it. Of course, the weight on both sides
of the pro/con equation needs to be balanced. Reasonings *for*
a decision can't be less impactful than the ones against, making them superfluous, just as the reasons against can't be intangible things like fear.

The blinking cursor on my laptop screen waits for me to
add something to the con side. The pro side is filling in quite
effortlessly:

–Stop Liam from heartache.

Obviously, the main objective.

–Stop Liam from damaging his career.

Also a big one.

–Help Liam and Sonia save money.

Weddings are ridiculously expensive.

–Ensure extended family aren't collateral damage in the
  eventual breakup.

I know firsthand the loss of the family unit can be as heart-breaking as the loss of the relationship.

–Liam will be single and available again.

I sigh and delete the last one. That would be more for *my* benefit than his. I need to remain a neutral third party and besides, that glimpse means I'm no longer emotionally in-vested in a future with Liam. Seeing him again after so long and the nostalgic feelings of once being head over heels in love with him had clouded my judgment temporarily. What Liam and I had is firmly in the past. Now I just want to help in the most platonic sense.

I click on the con side and think. Why *shouldn't* I interfere?

–It's none of my business.

Since when have I ever let that stop me? I delete the con. It's circumstantial, not based on fact.

I pause and think. There have to be other downsides...

–If I'm caught sabotaging, Liam will stop speaking to me.

Again, seems more about what *I* have at risk. I delete it.

I need at least one. Otherwise, it feels like I haven't tried hard enough. I always tell my clients that no matter how fantastic an idea is or how positive it seems, there is always a downside and if it's not acknowledged and explored early, it will no doubt be the thing that resurfaces to bite them in the ass.

Think, Hailey, think.

I tap my fingers on the desk and really dig deep. Why should I allow Liam to marry a beautiful, sweet, thoughtful heiress despite the inevitable disastrous outcome? Why is it better to sit back and be a silent observer in this volcano bubbling to the surface that will eventually erupt? Why would it be better to pretend I'm in complete support of this union, even though I know it won't work out?

All that's coming to mind is why would anyone do that?

I need to think of it a different way. What good comes from failure? What is learned?

I got it! I sit forward and type...

- Liam may not grow as a person if he avoids deep sorrow and regret. He may not learn from the life lesson this experience will provide.

I smile. There. No one could argue that's not a big one. Actually, that's technically two. I break the bullet points apart and count.

Four pros, two cons.

After much deliberation and sincere soul-searching, guess I have my answer.

Let Operation Breakup commence.

But first, I delete the document. You never—ever—keep the list, because as I remind my clients—things did not end well for Ross Geller.

★ ★ ★

Is it fair to say I'm taking out my hangover on the team? Absolutely, but they'll be better players for it.

Sunglasses on, head throbbing and feeling like death, I stand at the edge of the football field. Going to Hailey's party last night had succeeded in pissing her off and ensuring Sonia's safety, but the after-party drinks at Deek's with the happy couple had been a bad idea. Getting home after three and getting up at dawn to submit my final course paper before practice has me feeling my age.

I grab the whistle around my neck and blow three consecutive toots, then wince as the piercing sound hurts my brain. I wave a hand in the air, motioning for my eleven senior players to start the drill again.

Grumbles and profanity all around.

"Come on, Coach, it's like a hundred degrees out here," Marcus says, removing his helmet and pushing sweaty dark blond hair away from his forehead.

It actually is almost a hundred degrees out here. This spring has to be breaking heat records and the humidity is not helping my nausea. I could use five minutes in the shade.

"Five-minute break!" I yell to the team.

The teens rush off the field to get hydrated and I wave Marcus toward me. He grabs his water bottle and takes a swig as he approaches.

"What's up with you? You're slacking out there."

"Could say the same to you. Looking kinda rough today, Coach," he says.

"I'm not the one who has to impress scouts next month." I haven't had to impress anyone with my on-the-field skills in two years. Not sure I could anymore. The career of a professional athlete is even more fleeting than youth. Two years out of the game, I've gone soft—too slow, too uncoordinated, too unmotivated and I hate the nagging thought that maybe this would be where I am now anyway even if it weren't for Hailey's destruction.

"What's going on?" I ask Marcus.

"Late night, that's all," he says and what I hear very clearly is "get off my ass."

Not going to happen. My job as his coach is to push him even harder when I know he's not living up to his full potential. He entrusted me with that power when he signed up for my team. I peer at him. "Drinking?"

"Nah, Coach." He sighs and lowers his voice so his teammates won't hear. "Mom was working a late shift. Stayed up to meet her and walk her home."

"What's wrong with her car?"

He stares at the ground. "Crapped out."

I sigh and nod, lowering my voice. "Okay, well, call me next time, okay?"

Marcus nods, but I know he won't. I tap his shoulder and he hurries off toward his teammates.

I respect the hell out of him for his commitment to taking care of his mom, even if I know it's not helping his own future. Internal turmoil, external pressure, and every day not spent on this field is weighing on him and I'd like to help relieve some of that burden, but it's not my place. All I can do is hope people are right when they say tough times build character.

I reach for my bottle of Gatorade, take a swig, then nearly choke on it as I see Hailey walking across the field toward me, carrying two coffees. She's dressed in professional clothing—a slim-fitting pencil skirt and a loose blouse that blows casually in the wind to reveal just a hint of a lacy bra underneath. Her hair is pulled back in a messy bun, but several strands have come loose and fly across her face in the breeze. Completing the look are sky-high strappy heels. She looks like she stepped from the pages of *Forbes* magazine—despite this sweltering heat, she's not wilting one little bit. I glance at my sweat-covered shirt and quickly do an armpit smell check as she strides toward me...

...then stumbles on the grass. Coffee sloshes out of the cup as she quickly regains footing.

Underneath it all, still the same klutzy Hailey Harris from high school.

I hide a grin as I fold my arms across my chest and keep my gaze on the field as she stops next to me. "Aren't you afraid of ruining your shoes?"

"It's okay, I've worn these twice already," she says sarcastically.

I raise an eyebrow beneath my sunglasses. Up close, she's even more perky and polished. No sign of a hangover. I saw her consume copious amounts of champagne the night before—not that I was watching her, she just has an annoying way of drawing my eye. And after the exchange I witnessed between her and Liam, I was keeping an eye on things, so I don't know how she's so lively this morning.

"What do you want?" I ask when the reason she's here isn't immediately forthcoming.

Hailey extends a coffee cup. "Brought you a coffee."

With or without arsenic? "Why?"

She sighs at my suspicion. "Look, I know we haven't always seen eye to eye, but I thought it was time to kiss and make up."

I ignore the outstretched cup, despite the tempting scent of caffeine escaping from it. "I'll assume you mean figuratively."

"Obvs. Come on, Warren, our friend is getting married. Things don't have to be awkward," she says as though *I'm* the one being petty.

"I'm not awkward. And he's *my* friend. *Your* ex." Why they still talk I don't know. A breakup by definition means to break apart. They should be staying far apart, not pretending their history doesn't matter. This never works out...in my limited relationship experience. I can't shake the interaction between them the night before or my gut reaction to it.

But damn it, the coffee smells too good. I snatch a cup from Hailey and gulp, burning my mouth.

"Be careful, I asked for extra hot."

The warning comes a little late and I shoot her an annoyed look. She can't even pull off a truce gesture without fucking it up.

"Look, even though Liam and I are not together anymore, I still care about him and I'm worried." She pauses. "Does he seem happy to you?"

I turn to her and lower my sunglasses. "Happier than he's ever been," I say pointedly.

Her face twists into this mix of annoyance and a hurtful pout and damn if it isn't the most adorable expression I've ever seen. The thing about Hailey is she doesn't hide emotion. Happy, sad, frustrated, confident, or pouty, it's on display. I find it irritatingly refreshing that I always know what she's thinking, feeling, and where I stand with her at any given moment.

I've never experienced that with a woman before.

Not that I see Hailey as a woman in the datable sense. More like a walking red flag of what to avoid, but the transparency is something I wish for with the other women I date. Not having to be a mind reader would make the whole dating scene a lot easier. Although, truthfully, my ego probably couldn't handle what women were actually thinking of me.

"But isn't this whole wedding thing a little sudden?" she asks, sounding genuinely concerned.

There's an ulterior motive.

Sure, when Liam first told me he'd proposed to a woman he'd known less than a year, I was a little nervous, but having met Sonia, I can understand. And they say "you know when you know." I don't expect to ever get that kind of clarity, but it's the catchphrase for all lovesick fools.

"What's your problem with Sonia?" I ask. Besides the obvious—she's competition.

"Nothing! She's amazing," she says quickly and it sounds like she means it. "But Liam always wanted New York and skyscrapers and to make a difference with his architectural designs limiting environmental impacts—not luxury resorts. His plan was never to stay in California."

Ah. "You mean his plan was never to stay for *you*."

Hailey pouts again and damn, her mouth looks better in that position than any other. Maybe we should actually kiss and make up...

"This isn't about me," she says.

Ha! Since when? "Sure, it is. You thought you were getting a second chance when he came back. The reality is Liam has moved on. Don't mess this up for him."

Hailey rolls her eyes and scoffs. "How on earth could *I* mess this up?"

"I don't know. It's just a gift you have," I say and notice that the team are staring at us from across the field. I can hear their dirty teenage minds at work as they grin and check out Hailey.

I check my watch and call them in. "That's it for today, guys! It's hot as hell—go cool off. See you all on Tuesday."

They all looked thrilled by the practice being cut short and start casually tossing around the football and play tackling one another.

Sure, *now* they've got energy.

I turn to Hailey as the teens mess around on the field. "As much as it's been a pleasure seeing you three times in one week, I gotta go."

"Who's the lucky lady about to be left disillusioned and disappointed?"

Ah, there we go. Back to insults. It's a relief to have the

universe's balance restored. "Actually, I'm meeting the perfect couple for lunch."

I bend to gather my things and out of the corner of my eye I see it…but I'm too late with a warning.

A football flies through the air, sailing straight toward the side of Hailey's head. As if in slow motion, I see Marcus run and dive…

He catches the ball just before it hits her but bodychecks her straight off her feet in the process.

Shit.

I move toward her limp, flailed body on the grass. Her coffee cup was luckily launched three feet away otherwise she'd probably have third-degree burns. Her eyes are closed and her face is slack.

"I think she's dead," Marcus says, holding the ball under his arm.

"She's not dead. She's dramatic," I say, gently kicking her outstretched arm. "Hailstorm, get up."

Marcus shoots me a look at the insensitivity, then bends next to her. He shakes her shoulder gently. "Hey, lady. You good?"

Hailey's eyes flutter open. She blinks several times toward the sky, then sits up slowly.

Marcus looks relieved. "Shit, sorry 'bout that." He stands and extends a hand to help her up.

Hailey reluctantly accepts it as she gets to her feet. She still looks slightly dazed as she stands there, almost in a haze-like state, but then she drops Marcus's hand as though she's been torched. Her expression is suddenly one of conflict and…fear? She takes several steps back.

"You cool?" Marcus asks her.

"Fine," she stammers awkwardly. She stares at him for a long beat, an odd look on her face. "Um…stay out of trouble," she finally mumbles.

ALL SIGNS POINT TO MALIBU   77

"O-kay," Marcus says slowly, then hurries off across the field.

Hailey watches him with a seriously weird expression on her face and I study her. "If you're thinking about pressing assault charges, the ball would have done a hell of a lot more damage if he hadn't caught it. That thing was going like sixty clicks."

She finally turns to look at me and shakes her head quickly. "No...yeah, um...okay," she says rambling and incoherent.

Maybe she did actually die for a moment.

A rare moment of concern for her strikes and I move a step closer. I peer into her eyes for any sign of concussion. "You sure you're okay?"

"Fine," she says brusquely. "Don't you have somewhere to be?" she asks, and my spidey senses tell me this won't be the last of her I see today.

Inside my sweltering vehicle, I struggle to shake off what just happened. Not the body-check that nearly knocked my soul free of my body, but the glimpse I'd had of that kid's future when he helped me to my feet.

Correction: *Glimpses.* Plural.

That alternate universe thing has never happened to me before—maybe it's because I try to avoid glimpsing the future of anyone under twenty-one, or maybe because all my senses had been rocked, or maybe it was because his future is still undefined, but I'd seen two variable futures for this kid. One fantastic. One not so much.

I wonder if Warren knows...

He climbs into his Jeep across the gravel lot and when he pulls into traffic, I follow close in my convertible.

What would I even say to him? He'd never believe me anyway.

I struggle with the moral dilemma as I follow him. The

kid could obviously use some guidance, but I don't take on minors for good reason and the dual glimpse has me freaked out. I'm hoping it's a one-time occurrence, so I shake it off and focus on keeping Warren's Jeep in sight through the traffic.

Right now, I have enough to deal with. One problem at a time.

I've decided meddling is the right course of action, but Liam and I aren't all that close anymore. After my party the other night, who knows when we'll see one another again. Now that he's engaged, hanging out with me is probably last on his agenda. Sonia likes me, but let's be real—no woman truly loves the idea of her fiancé being besties with his ex. So, getting on the inside to stop his wedding poses a bit of a challenge. I was hoping with Warren on my side, he could help me talk sense into Liam…but apparently he's team Sonia.

No surprise there.

At my party, the two of them had danced and laughed the night away. Not that I was watching, but Warren's annoyingly loud laugh seemed to fill my yard, and there was no escaping him. *He* seemed to be keeping an eye on *me*. Anytime I was near Liam or Sonia, he was there too—like a shadow. It was difficult to get a read on the couple with Warren so close.

To say my game had been thrown off after my glimpse into Liam's future would be an understatement. I totally neglected the other potential clients in attendance. At least I'd verbally signed Alisha before everything went to shit.

A few moments later, Warren's Jeep pulls into the parking lot of Malibu Moon, so I pull my convertible into a space several feet away. I see him remove his T-shirt and my mouth dries slightly at the sight of his tanned, muscular body. So, the forearms aren't the only noteworthy feature. He may not be a pro-athlete anymore, but his body sure as hell didn't get the memo. I eye the toned chest, wide shoulders, and the six-pack abs—it's easy to see why women could overlook his personality. He reaches into a bag for a new shirt and puts it on, then he gets out and goes inside.

I wait a second before doing the same.

Inside the hip café full of Gen Z ordering elaborate drinks over blaring pop music, I see Warren slide into a booth across from Liam and Sonia.

I pretend to scan the drink menu at the counter, then casually glance around. I "spot" the group and approach the table.

"Hey, friends! What a coincidence!"

His arm draped against the back of the plush booth seat, Warren sighs as he glares up at me. "Did you follow me?"

I scoff laugh at the ridiculous—true—suggestion. "Don't flatter yourself. Needed a caffeine fix after my coffee got knocked out of my hand by a wild ball," I say tightly.

"Well, if you hadn't been standing in the way, it wouldn't have happened," he counters.

Across the booth, Sonia looks mildly amused by our heated exchange, as though she senses chemistry. She's totally, a hundred percent wrong, but I can't even be bothered to entertain the thought right now—I'm on a mission. I need to get myself invited to this lunch.

Liam looks back and forth between us. "What's going on?"

"Hailey's suddenly obsessed with me," Warren tells them.

My mouth gapes. "Hardly."

"Hailey, why don't you join us?" Sonia says politely, gesturing for me to have a seat next to Warren.

That was easy—thank you, Sonia. You may be an ally in your own demise yet.

A stunning ally. She's wearing another pale-colored sundress that accentuates her tanned skin to perfection. Fresh-faced, hair in a messy bun, her casual Sunday brunch look is arguably her best look. I bet her messy bun is actually a messy pulled-together look and not the twenty-minute exercise mine was.

"Oh, I'm sure Hailey's rushing off to a meeting with a client. No rest for the wicked," Warren says, sending me a look that says "beat it."

I refuse to let him throw me off course. If he won't help me save Liam from making the biggest mistake of his life, then I'll find a way to do it on my own. "Actually I am…but I have a few minutes."

I motion for Warren to slide further into the booth. He begrudgingly moves less than an inch. I sigh and place half an ass cheek on the edge of the seat, struggling not to fall out. I place my forearms on the table and lean forward, my thighs burning in the half squat position. I hide my pain as I smile brightly. "So…what were we talking about?"

"Warren has generously offered to throw us an engagement party," Sonia says excitedly, wrapping one arm through Liam's and cuddling closer. The two share a look of love that if I didn't know better, I'd swear was the real deal.

But I do know better. They may seem happy now, but it won't last.

I frown, turning to Warren. "You're hosting an engagement party?"

"Yes."

"You?"

"Yes."

"Mister 'I hate all things commitment'?"

Warren swings toward me and I nearly fall out of the booth. "For the last bloody time—yes! Isn't your business built on you being a good listener?" His gaze burns into mine.

I glare back at him. Damn, his eyes are really blue and the color seems to intensify when he's all charged up like this. Do other people have this effect on him or am I the only one? He's usually so chill and yet, I seem to be particularly skilled at bringing out this version of him. Should I take it as a compliment?

As our gazes lock for far too long, something in his expression changes and while I can't define it, I'm definitely uneasy enough to be the first to look away.

He may have won this silent battle of wills, but he won't win the war.

I turn my attention to Sonia and Liam. "Why don't I help him?"

"No thanks," Warren says.

I ignore him and continue my pitch to the couple. "We can host it at my place."

Across from me, Sonia's face lights up.

"I have a house," Warren says.

"A sad and pathetic smelly man cave doesn't exactly scream happily ever after," I say with a wild, dismissive wave that nearly smacks him on the cheek. It forces him to slide in a little further and I take the opportunity to move in a bit more. "My place is…"

"Over-the-top, like you." Warren turns toward me and for what feels like the millionth time, we square off. I grip the edge of the table so as not to fall out of the booth, refusing to back down.

"Why? Because I have matching dishes and don't use a Ping-Pong table as a dining room set?"

From the corner of my eye, I notice Sonia sending Liam a worried look.

"I'm sure she's kidding," he whispers in reassurance.

"It's called multipurpose furniture," Warren says to me.

"Okay, maybe not," Liam whispers to Sonia.

"It's called cheap and sophomoric," I tell Warren.

Another sizzling stare down. I wonder what it would be like to spend five minutes with Warren when we weren't bickering. Probably not as exciting.

Sonia squeezes Liam's arm. "We think it's a good idea,"

he says quickly. "It will be a great way for you two to figure out how to get along before the wedding."

"Fantastic," Warren mumbles, knowing I've won this one.

"Fantastic," I say with a beaming smile, because well, I won.

Though moments later it's tough to keep the smile plastered on as Sonia recounts the story of how she and Liam met.

"There I was soaking wet on the side of the street, when this taxi stops and Liam rolls down the window and offers to share his ride," she says.

I lean my elbows on the table, my thighs completely numb by now, and look completely engrossed in the romantic meet-cute story.

Liam stares lovingly down at Sonia. "What could I do? Couldn't leave her out in the downpour."

"Only turns out we were heading in different directions," Sonia says as though it's the cleverest twist of fate ever.

"Obviously, I missed my meeting," Liam says and there's a hint of regret only someone who knows him well could decipher.

I frown, doing the math in my head to calculate when this union might have occurred. "Is that why you lost the build contract you were working toward before Christmas?" As I said, Mr. Jensen keeps me posted.

Liam looks surprised that I know about the long hours and incredible work he put in to secure a meeting with his dream firm in New York to design a city community space.

Not only do I know about it, I may have asked a former client of mine who's in business development to put in a good word for Liam to help secure the meeting. It may have been somewhat counterintuitive to the possibility of a second chance, but if my ex wasn't happy here in California, I still wanted him to be happy and successful following his dream across the country.

Liam's smile is definitely forced as he says, "I didn't lose it—I backed out."

Sonia squeezes his arm and sends him an almost grateful look as he continues, "Once Sonia and I started dating, her father's company offered me a contract I couldn't refuse."

To build resorts. All makes sense now...

"Best decision I ever made," Liam adds quickly.

I call bullshit.

I go to speak, but Warren interrupts. "Got the girl and the amazing career opportunity. Win-win," he says in an attempt to wrap this up.

Sonia's phone chimes and she glances at it then turns toward Liam. "Oh, we have to go. We have an appointment at the jewelers," she says.

Liam's expression is slightly tense as he nods. I know he's still thinking about that contract he gave up.

"Rings. Wow. Really committing."

Everyone looks at me and I laugh.

"Kidding."

As we all get up to leave, my legs nearly give out thanks to painful pins and needles as blood returns to my lower limbs. I hold the table for support as I try to shake feeling back into them.

"I'll pay the bill," Liam tells Sonia and he and Warren walk away toward the counter.

Alone, Sonia approaches me and lowers her voice. "Hey, I was...uh, wondering if you might have any openings?"

I frown. "For coaching?"

"I could use some advice," she says nervously.

I doubt that. Sonia Banks is the most polished, confident, put-together woman I've ever tried not to like. Besides... "As the heir to the Banks Resorts family legacy, I'm sure you have things pretty well figured out." Or things have been perfectly figured out for her since birth. Either way, she'll be fine without my help.

"Ha! Believe me, I don't," she says and damn it if I don't like her even more for her sincere vulnerability. Why does she have to be marrying and divorcing my ex-boyfriend?

"Oh, um, my schedule's a little full." I obviously can't coach her. Too much of a conflict of interest.

"I get it," she says, nodding disappointedly. "You're in high demand."

I hesitate. Conflict of interest or just another step in my plan to stop the wedding? It might be challenging to get close enough to Liam without raising any red flags, but Sonia was coming to me...

"You know what? I can fit you in," I say as though I'm doing her a huge favor. Let the record show, this is not my fault if it backfires.

Her eyes light up. "Really?"

"Absolutely." Glimpsing Sonia's future might shed some light on the situation, and on another level I'm actually curious to see why Sonia Banks could possibly need my career advice.

She links her arm through mine and from the corner of my eye, I see Warren watching us. Suspicion appears on his face and I need to be careful. I can't let him figure out that I'm getting involved with this wedding simply to destroy it from the inside.

SIX

HAILEY'S DAILY RULE FOR SUCCESS:
Treat your competition with the respect they
deserve. They are challenging you to be
the best version of yourself.

Big congrats on the Laywood deal! Keep hustling—you'll get
there!

I TYPE THE COMMENT ON SPENCER STANLEY'S
social media page under his post announcing the partnership.
Waiting a week ensures he doesn't think I'm stalking his page
and paying attention to his every move but shows industry
respect with just the slightest hint of condescension—to let
him know I'm not threatened.

I hit Post then turn my attention to life coaching conference prep. I may not be threatened by Spencer Stanley yet,
but I have to be a bigger presence at this conference. Heading online to the conference's networking platform, I immediately search for attendees I want to connect with and send

"meeting invite" requests. Confirmations pop up almost immediately from local business owners and any nervousness I may have felt about my competition evaporates. I'm Hailey fucking Harris—of course people want to meet with me.

I wonder if success ever dilutes imposter syndrome?

Time passes as I work on my presentation notes and two hours later a nervous-looking Sonia sits across from me in my office. She's dressed in a black business suit and white blouse, her hair coifed in a tight bun—professional. I too dressed for the part today in my favorite charcoal suit, electric-blue blouse and matching sky-high power heels, which my feet are regretting, but they've already done their job. Sonia's been eyeing them as she's been waiting for me to shut down my conference prep—shoes are like a secret language between women. Not just an accessory, but a way to connect through fashion.

Similar taste in shoes indicates compatibility like no extensively researched test can measure.

"How can I help?" I ask.

"This feels silly to say out loud," she says, playing with a tennis bracelet on her wrist. I recognize the power move and applaud the effort—toying with the expensive accessory indicates she's humble enough to seek my advice, but a quiet reminder that she probably doesn't truly need it.

Say the wrong thing and my value will quickly be diminished in her eyes.

"The first step in manifesting is putting the desire out into the universe." I wave the words out of her as though I don't have time for lack of confidence.

She sits straighter, chin raised, and announces, "I want to be an actress."

Definitely not what I was expecting. Not that she's not stunning and enigmatic enough to be a star, she just seems a little...naive, which is odd for a woman surrounded by mega successful professionals her entire life. Hollywood would eat her alive with her current sweet, genuine nature.

"An actress…okay," I say slowly.

Sonia lets out an incredulous laugh as though vocalizing it has highlighted the inherent flaws in this plan. "I know—it's cliché. Who in this city doesn't want to be an actor? Right? It's a bad idea, right?"

She wants me to talk her out of it, but I refuse to let my clients put that burden on me. I can shed reality on the dream and if they waver then it wasn't that strong of a desire to begin with, which would jeopardize their chances of success.

"Do you have any acting experience?" I ask.

"A few plays in New York after graduating from a theatre program. Off Broadway, obviously. It was more of a hobby… or at least that's what I told everyone."

Hold up. "No one else knows about this goal?"

"No."

"Not even Liam?" Seems like a third date discussion to me. Not that I'm an expert on dating, but after six months together, wouldn't the hopes and dreams conversation have happened by now? Definitely an important one to get to know someone on a deeper level and ensure life goals align.

"I don't want to tell anyone in case I fail," she says.

I hear that a lot and I can totally appreciate and even encourage chasing your goals in silence (when it makes sense and the person's goals won't impact others). Plans spoken out loud can often diminish motivation and people have a way of dashing dreams they can't understand.

But with all they've accomplished, her family seem like big dreamers. "I'm sure everyone would be supportive."

"I'd just like to keep it to myself," she says quickly and I detect that there's more to this secrecy.

"It's the reason you wanted to move back here, isn't it?" This wasn't just about being involved in expanding her family's resort chain. Sonia had another motive for being back here in California.

"Yes," she says, then quickly, "And of course the amazing opportunity for Liam's career with the resort build."

"Of course," I say with a smile and a pause. First things first. Let's see if a career in the spotlight is in Sonia's future. "One thing I like to do with new clients is some breathing exercises to manifest a mutual connection. It helps me help you better." I've yet to discover a less new agey way to pitch this. Luckily most clients open to working with a life coach are open to the idea of divine intervention, manifestation, fate, and other intangible paths to success.

I stand, move around the desk, and motion for Sonia to join me.

She looks almost giddy as she does. "You're so incredibly cool." Professionalism gone. Fangirling back.

While I appreciate the ego boost, I send her a look. Fangirling won't help her be taken seriously in the film industry, where she'll be surrounded by people a lot more impressive and influential than me.

Sonia nods her understanding at my unspoken warning. "Sorry, reining it in." She raises her hands and presses down her excitement with a deep breath. Then she stands across from me—serious and focused on doing whatever I say.

I extend my hands, palms up and Sonia places hers on mine. Hers tremble slightly and I work to keep mine rock steady. I'm the one who should be nervous about what I'm going to see. I've never done this before—view two life paths that are connected in a meaningful way. That's one reason I refuse referrals. If I've helped one person, I need at least six degrees of separation to avoid crossover and possible mayhem. I close my eyes and pretend to breathe in and out deeply as our life-lines connect, the energy flows through us and I see into my ex's fiancé's future.

Sonia walks down a sandy shoreline hand in hand with a tall, dark, and handsome man—not Liam. Shoes off, feet in the waves, she looks happy and vibrant. The two pause and the man takes her into his arms. The sunlight reflecting on his face hides his identity, but his affection is obvious as he lowers his head and kisses her.

Clearly Future Sonia is not hurt by the breakup with Liam. Though, I am a little confused about why I'm seeing a relationship update on Sonia instead of the career one we were vibing with. Is she doubting the relationship with Liam? Is it weighing heavy on her heart and subconscious? Or maybe like Amelia, there is no career to see.

Either way, I feel validated in my decision to try to stop the wedding. I release Sonia's hands abruptly. "I think you should go for it." Can't hurt and what else am I supposed to say? This meeting has served my purpose and, with her family's bajillion-dollar fortune behind her, Sonia will be just fine—succeed or fail in her acting endeavor. I saw the happiness on her face in my glimpse.

Sonia's eyes open and she frowns. "That's it?"

Obviously, that won't fly.

"Of course not," I say.

She laughs in relief. "Thank goodness."

Should I remind her she's not paying for this incredibly valuable session? I've offered it as an engagement present. Had to do something to balance out my karma.

I head back to my desk, open the contact list on my computer, and refer to it as I grab my cell phone and type quickly.

Sonia's phone chimes a second later. She pulls it out of her Gucci bag and sees the new message I've sent.

"That's a list of contacts—agents, managers, and acting coaches. First assignment is to send out your headshot and résumé to these people." I know she has professional photos of herself from various events and publications she's been featured in. No sense doling out cash for new images in case this thing is a bust. I always encourage my clients to spend as little as possible in up-front start-up costs.

She scans the names on the list and her eyes widen. "These are major players in the industry. I can't thank you enough," Sonia says excitedly but with a hint of nervousness.

"This is what I do." I've set her up with a contact list that would normally take new actors six years living in LA and slugging it out as assistants, waiters, and Uber drivers to build—now it's up to her. It eases my conscience a little for messing with her other life plans.

She takes a deep breath and leans forward. "I also meant for stepping in to help plan the engagement party. Warren seems like a great guy…"

"'Delightful' some might say."

Sonia laughs. "But I think his idea of a formal event and my family's are a little different." Sonia looks around my impressive office. "Your taste is a lot more…on brand."

"It's really no problem," I say and stand again. Especially if it never happens. I check my watch for effect when Sonia remains seated.

"Right. We're done," she says, collecting her things and standing again. "I'm sure you have a full schedule."

Actually, the rest of my day consists of reaching out to every contact I have to try to secure tickets to the World Golf Championships coming up so I can host an athlete VIP event before Spencer Stanley beats me to it, but I nod.

I walk her toward the office door and she turns to face me with a hesitant look. "Oh, and I have one more request."

Should I remind her I've just given her a free consultation and a contact list worth millions? I smile expectantly—ready to grant her one last wish.

"Will you be my maid of honor?"

Fuck no.

I try to stop my eyebrows from rising, but they have a mind

of their own. "Oh, um…we don't really know one another."
She can't be serious. There are so many reasons why this is a
ridiculous request.

Sonia steps forward and reaches for my hands, but I shove
them into my pockets. The conversation has now turned to
my potential involvement in her future and anytime that's happened in the past, the glimpse turns out to be a sharp, bright,
loud blast of noise and light that messes with my equilibrium
for days, as though I just got off an out-of-control teacup ride.

Sonia frowns at my abrupt rudeness but pushes on. "You
are important to Liam and you're the first person I've even
told about my dreams. That puts you high on the list of prospects to stand next to us on our special day."

"There has to be a family member who'd be a better
choice." A cherished family pet for that matter.

Sonia shakes her head. "I'm an only child. I have eight female cousins and if I choose one of them, the others will riot.
It's safer to have them all bridesmaids."

"*Eight* bridesmaids? This is going to be a big wedding." I
should have guessed. It's a Banks wedding. There will likely
even be press and they'll need security to keep paparazzi at
bay. *If* it happens, and I'm even more hell-bent on ensuring
it doesn't now that there could be a hideous maid of honor
dress in my future.

"Huge." She nods. "I'll get you the invite list for the engagement party—" she waves a hand "—but please say you'll
do it?" Sonia folds her hands pleadingly and gives me a puppy
dog look.

I can see why Liam proposed. Here I am determined to
stop this wedding and yet I'm envisioning the most epic bach-
elorette party she more than deserves in addition to the engagement event.

Right now, I feel cornered and there's no harm in agreeing. "Of course."

Sonia squeals in delight the same way I'm sure she has since she was two years old, getting her way with her impossible to say no to demeanor. "Thank you!" She steps forward and hugs me tightly. My arms remain limp at my side, squeezed against my body.

Operation Breakup needs to launch as quickly as possible—before I offer to help her make wedding favors.

A *B-*?

I stare at the grade posted on the sports psychology course site and feel a sense of pride I've never gotten from academics. My self-esteem always centered around sports. Classes and studying were just mandatory pain in the ass requirements to play football.

But seeing this grade—one I busted my balls for—fills me with pride.

Instinctively, I reach for my cell phone, then stop.

It's been two years, when will that urge to text Cliff stop hitting me out of nowhere? For brief instances I forget he's gone and there's a new voice at the other end of his old phone number.

I learned that the embarrassing way when I called to listen to his voicemail message six months ago and a woman answered. To say it was a shock to the system would be an understatement.

Grief is weird. It holds so many layers and presents itself in unusual ways.

I stare at the grade and deep remorse replaces the pride. Maybe if I'd been quicker to start a program like this, I'd have been able to see the warning signs of stress and burnout in Cliff. Maybe if I hadn't been so caught up in my own career and the stardom that came with it, I'd have noticed something was off. If I hadn't been so caught up in my own life, I would have realized Cliff wanted to end his.

The grief counsellor I saw once after his death said there was absolutely nothing I could have done for him. People at that stage in their decision would find a way. They've made peace with the choice and aren't open to other options anymore.

But it's hard not to call bullshit on that.

Cliff was stressed and the pressures put on him by his job as a stock broker, the pressure put on him by our father, got to be too much, so he turned to alcohol, drugs, gambling... So many signs that he needed help and I would have spotted them if I'd cared enough to make time to look.

Check in on him more.

Now I'd give anything to check in on him and it's too late.

But I know he'd be proud of me. He always said I was more than just my play stats. He was the only one who saw me as more than a championship. The only person who was happy to just watch me do what I loved to do.

My cell phone chimes and I pick it up and read a text from Marcus:

Don't need a ride today.

Maybe his mom's car is fixed. I hope that's the case. If one of his friends is giving him a ride, it means they'll stay to watch the practice and that always throws him off his game. He starts showboating and trying to impress and ends up pissing everyone off.

I close the computer and grab my gear, then head out.

At the football field twenty minutes later, I scan for Marcus but don't see him warming up with the others. I text him:

Dude, you're late.

I see the message is read a second later...but no response.

I may not have seen warning signs that Cliff was in trouble, but I damn well won't be ignoring them in Marcus.

After practice, I drive straight to the Kent home. Maureen's car is parked in the driveway and I eye it as I climb out and head toward the front door. I wonder if she'd let me take a look at it. I don't claim to be a great mechanic, but it could be something simple. At this point, I'm willing to try anything to eliminate excuses for Marcus to miss practice. We're weeks away from scouts coming and he needs all the training he can get.

I ring the bell and hear the sound of footsteps approaching from inside. I tug the sweaty fabric of my shirt away from my body and run a hand quickly through my hair. Probably should have showered first, but she lives with a stinky teenager, so I'm sure she'll let it slide.

She looks surprised when she opens the door, still dressed in her convenience store smock. "Hey, Coach."

"Hi, Maureen—good to see you. Can I come in for a minute?"

She hesitates, glancing inside the house. "Wish you'd called first..."

"My house looks like a bomb went off inside, I promise not to judge."

She still looks uneasy but stands back to let me enter.

The house is spotless so I'm not sure what she was worried about. Not a thing out of place and I know Marcus isn't exactly tidy.

"Coffee?" she asks.

"That'd be great."

In the kitchen a moment later, she pours two cups of coffee and sets one in front of me with a yawn before sitting across from me. "Sorry, excuse me," she says.

"Late shifts this week?"

"Double shifts," she says with a nod, picking up her coffee cup and taking a sip.

I feel bad for taking up her time, so I get straight to the

point. "The reason I stopped by is Marcus wasn't at practice today. It's not like him to skip. Especially so close to scouting season." I pause. "I wanted to make sure he was okay."

Maureen sips the coffee again and nods. "He had to work."

I frown. "He's working now?"

"At a grocery store, stocking shelves."

News to me. Not that my team are under any obligation to keep me posted about their personal lives, but I thought we were all on the same page regarding Marcus's focus.

School. Study. Football. Repeat.

"He didn't tell me."

"It was news to me too," Maureen says with a shrug. "But we could definitely use the money, Coach, and you know as well as I do, trying to talk that boy out of anything is useless."

"How often is he taking shifts?"

"They guaranteed him thirty hours a week," she says.

"What about school?" I'm definitely overstepping, but I care about this kid's future. Stocking shelves would be a waste of his talents and not finishing high school will limit his future options. Maureen knows this too and it's not my place to say anything at all, but I feel like the family has entrusted me with Marcus's future in football and they technically did sign a commitment to the team.

"He says he can keep the grades up, even if he skips a few classes. I have a meeting with his teachers next week to discuss remote learning for the rest of the year."

Damn it. Still doesn't solve the issue of football. I can't move practice times for one player.

I sigh and clear my throat. "I understand the job is important, but is there some way he could take fewer hours? He has a real talent and he's so close..."

She straightens slightly. "Look, Coach. I appreciate what you've done for him, but bills aren't paid on dreams."

I take a breath. She's right, but... "It's not just a dream.

The kid's incredible." If it was any other player on my team, I wouldn't be sitting here now making this statement, but Marcus is the exception. "He really could make it," I say and feel it in my gut, otherwise I'd never raise their hopes. I don't want to argue with her or push, but... "It's just another month and Marcus could be scouted. A few more weeks..."

She stares into her coffee cup, conflicted and tired.

I'm asking her to help me with something that could change her life too. Alleviate some of the pressures she's under. "He won't listen to me. I need your help with this."

She hesitates, then nods. "I'll tell him to reduce the hours so he can make it to practice."

My gut twists, knowing what that will mean for her. "If there's anything I can do..."

"Keep coaching my baby and make sure this dream of his becomes a reality," she says pointedly and I hear the note of warning in her voice—she's trusting me and I better not fuck this up.

SEVEN

WITH ITS MEDITERRANEAN FLAIR, THE BANKS RE-
sort Hotel in Santa Monica is one of the most impressive
family resorts along the coast. Whitewashed buildings with
terracotta tiles and vibrant color accents, lush greenery, six
outdoor pools, a swim-up bar, an upscale restaurant serving Mediterranean cuisine, and luxury all-service spa. The
kind of place my mom and I would walk through, hoping no
one would kick us out. She'd say, "Someday, Hails, you and
I will go on vacation and stay in a resort just like this one.
We'll swim in the pool and drink pretty colored drinks with
umbrellas and we'll order room service and eat in bed while
watching *Sleepless in Seattle*." It was her favorite movie. Without cable, we must have watched it four hundred times on an
old DVD player previous tenants had left behind.

Wearing oversized sunglasses and a wide-brimmed hat, I
approach the front entrance. No fear of being kicked out now.

And yet, the same feeling of not belonging shadows over my confidence as I near the rotating doors.

A doorman greets me with a warm, courteous nod and holds the door open as I step into the lobby. Large chandeliers hang from the ceiling. Old black-and-white photos of celebrities are featured on the walls. A faint smell of flowers and decades-old cigar smoke has embedded itself in the material history of the place. Elevator music plays and I recognize the tune as a death metal song slowed down and played softly on a piano. It gives the hotel an even cooler vibe.

Banks Resorts are known for their luxury, but they're also on the cutting edge of new hospitality trends. One of the first hotel chains to switch to digital key entry sent directly to the guest's smartphone for access to rooms and suites. Self-check-in stations are in the lobby, but they haven't lost the personal touch as an attendant lingers nearby carrying a tray of champagne and assisting guests with the process.

I walk through the lobby toward the restaurant. The Koi Reserve has three Michelin stars. Rumor has it that the chef turned down an offer to work in Paris after the Bankses promised him a baby Bengal tiger. Photos of Pascal LeCroix and the amazing beast hang in the entryway of the restaurant, where a hostess greets me. I carefully check around me before removing the hat and sunglasses. While I have a legit reason to be here, I don't want to run into Liam or Sonia just yet.

"Reservation for Harris," I say.

The young woman with a nametag that reads Emily—with flags from eight different countries, indicating how many languages she's fluent in—checks the reservation system and nods. "Welcome Ms. Harris. Table for two near the koi pond. Your guest has already arrived."

"Wonderful."

She leads the way through the restaurant's interior, past dark mahogany furniture, plush velvet booths, and bar-height tables. A grand piano is in the corner and the bar features a champagne waterfall and only top-shelf liquor bottles. The smell of their award-winning (and astronomically priced) seafood dishes wafts from the kitchen.

Growing up, I never liked fish, but my mother insisted I learn to eat it.

Rich people eat fish. Classy people eat fish.

I never knew where she got that from other than the fact that we could never really afford the nice fish at the seafood counter and always bought cheaper breaded filets or imitation crab meat. While I can afford to buy any variety I want now, I still don't like it.

Outside, near a koi pond I spot Alisha sitting at a table for two. A water jug with lemons and limes sits on the table in front of her. She's been here a while as it's half empty and condensation covers the exterior of the jug and the wineglass in front of her.

Being late is on purpose this time.

Once a person reaches a certain level of success, being early or even on time is often viewed as a weakness. Not my rules— I didn't make this up. People view lateness in the highly successful as a power move. I'd personally rather respect my clients' time, but I can't give any hint that I'm not part of that elite class who think they're superior.

"Right over there," the hostess says.

"Thank you."

I make my way toward the table and Alisha looks up and smiles nervously in greeting. "Hi…"

I smile, bend to kiss her cheek, then sit across from her. No apologies for keeping her waiting. "Great to see you. How fantastic is this hotel?"

"I wasn't sure they'd let me in," she says and my adoration of her increases.

"Me neither," I say a hundred percent honestly with a wink.

She laughs as though anyone would ever turn me away, then looks completely overwhelmed as she scans the restaurant. "You really know how to treat your clients," she says.

"About that," I say, reaching into my bag to pull out my official life coaching contract. I'd been so preoccupied after the VIP party, I'd forgotten to formally seal the deal. This recon mission is serving a dual purpose.

I slide it across the table and Alisha looks slightly nervous as she scans the first few pages. "Should I have a lawyer look this over?"

"You can," I say, "but you will notice the terms are six months only—much shorter commitment than most." My gift allows me to jump ahead a few steps. "And clause eight guarantees my services. If things don't work out the way I promise, you get a full refund." It's a fairly safe bet on my part. I've only had to return money once and it was by choice, because the man died and his family needed the funds for his funeral expenses. Unfortunately, he hadn't been attending our weekly meetings or perhaps I'd have seen the skydiving incident.

Alisha flips through the pages and reads. "I guess that's really all one can ask." She picks up the pen and signs the contract. With an eager smile, she slides it back. "So, what do we do first?" she asks.

From the corner of my eye, I see Sonia and her father, William Banks, enter the patio area. I recognize him from the online photos, but he's even taller and has a more commanding presence in real life. A silver fox who obviously takes care of his health, he's a great-looking man, dressed in expensive, but business casual attire. Next to him, Sonia wears tailored slacks and a crop top, strappy sandals, and gold bangles around her wrist. Her hair is pulled back into a high ponytail and her makeup-free face is perfection. Side by side, they are easily

identifiable as father and daughter with the same bone structure and complexion.

My heart flutters slightly as I pick up the menu and cover
my face from their view as they are shown to a table just feet
away from us. "We should order first, then talk business," I
say quietly to Alisha.

"Okay," Alisha says, picking up her menu.

I peek around mine to see that luckily, Sonia has been
seated with her back to me. This might be easier than I expected. I'd been prepared to snoop around the hotel, talk to
the staff and eavesdrop on boardroom meetings, using my
lunch meeting with Alisha as cover, but maybe the intel has
just come to me.

I'm desperate to learn more about the Bankses and their
plans. The family has been in the public eye for years, but the
coverage has always been favorable, and I struggle to believe
anyone this wealthy with such a successful, profitable company doesn't have a few skeletons in the closet.

Better for me to discover them than Liam.

William reaches into a briefcase and places documents on
the table between them.

A business luncheon? Odd that Liam wasn't invited.

"What do you recommend?" Alisha asks from across the
table.

I blink. "Huh?"

"From the menu. You've eaten here before?"

"First time actually," I say. "I'm sure everything is delicious."

"These are Liam's latest drafts," William says to Sonia. "I
want your thoughts." He presents several architectural designs.

Strange that Sonia wouldn't have already seen these. Wouldn't
Liam show her what he has planned for her family's resort?

I strain to hear the conversation.

"They look fantastic. I see he's incorporated the extra three
floors for executive level guests," Sonia says.

"I'm thinking it's not enough. Five would be better," William says.

"Salmon or chicken—both sound tempting," Alisha says across from me and I miss Sonia's reply. "What are you having?" she asks.

I really should decide. I scan quickly, then set the menu aside. "Shrimp cocktail."

"Ooooh, that sounds delicious," Alisha says. "But I'm actually starving..."

Her voice competes with the conversation at the Bankses' table and I miss part of it.

"Order whatever you like." And please stop talking.

"Liam said the regulations for height in that area of the coast forbid us going any higher," Sonia is telling her father.

William waves a dismissive hand. "A technicality. He'll figure it out."

"Dad, it's not something he can just decide on his own."

William shrugs as though he's appeasing her. "Look, he wanted more say in the process and I'm allowing him to have that."

So they can pin this unsanctioned design on Liam if the resort doesn't meet height regulations?

"Daddy, you can't insist Liam adjust the designs, knowing this will be problematic."

William leans in and his expression is so serious that even I feel like a child being disciplined. He opens his mouth and I still, waiting to hear what he's about to say...

But the waterfall next to us turns on. Crashing water cascades over the rocks into the koi pond below, drowning out the conversation.

Shit. I need to know if William is actually going to insist Liam redesign the building so I can somehow warn him about the height restrictions. Or is Sonia going to step up and fight against her father's wishes?

"Excuse me for a sec," I tell Alisha. "Ladies' room."

She sets her menu aside. "I've had so much water, I'll come with."

"No!"

She looks taken aback.

I force a strained laugh. "Sorry, I just mean, maybe you should stay in case the waitress comes to take our order. If we miss her, we'll probably be waiting forever for her to come back."

Alisha nods. "Good thinking."

I stand and put on my hat and sunglasses.

"You're taking your things to the bathroom?"

"It's the sunlight. I'm supersensitive."

She gives me an odd look.

Great, I'm acting like a weirdo in front of my new client.

"I'll be right back. Shrimp cocktail for me if she asks," I say and hurry away from the table and the noisy waterfall. I reach into my pocket for my lipstick and my wide-brimmed hat hits a diner in the head. They turn to glare at me.

"Excuse me. Apologies," I whisper and keep going.

I move closer to the Bankses' table and pretend to drop the lipstick. Luckily, the large brim on the hat covers my face as I bend to retrieve it, linger and listen.

"Three resorts in a year seems ambitious even for you, Dad," Sonia says.

Three? Liam only mentioned one.

"Competition is rising," his deep voice responds. "We want to be first to market on some of the newer, innovative concepts. Do you think Liam's up for the challenge?"

I move closer, listening intently. Will she have Liam's back?

"Of course... Though we may need to move up the wedding date," she says.

My heart pounds. What the hell? Three months was al-

ready too fast. Pushing back the wedding date would make
more sense.

"Whatever you have to do sweetheart," William says.
"Business first, remember?"

"Business first," Sonia agrees.

I knew there was something I didn't trust about the Bankses. Now if only there was some way to warn Liam…

"Whoa!"

I hear the voice behind me but it's too late.

In my crouched position, a waiter carrying a tray of food
doesn't see me. He stumbles over me and the tray launches out
of his hands and across the restaurant. It crashes to the floor a
few feet in front of me and the clanging of metal and breaking of glass catch the attention of everyone in the restaurant.

I cringe as I slowly glance up at him.

Unimpressed, he glares down at me.

I slowly get to my feet with an apologetic look. "Dropped
my lipstick," I say lamely, holding it up.

"Hailey?!"

Great.

I turn toward Sonia and her father at their table, plastering
a look that suggests this is the biggest coincidence of all time.
"Sonia! Great to see you."

She smiles, but there's a hint of unease in her expression as
she scans the restaurant. "You're dining here?"

"Yes! A client lunch meeting. You've spoken so highly
about the resort, I thought I'd come check it out."

William is eyeing me, annoyed by the interruption, and I
turn toward him with my most charming smile. "You must be
Mr. Banks," I say politely, extending a hand. "Hailey Harris."

Sonia nods quickly as though she's forgotten her manners
in her surprise at seeing me. "Sorry, yes, Daddy, this is Hailey—she's a good friend of Liam's."

"I know who you are," he says to me.

He what now? My smile shifts slightly as it's hard to detect the emotion behind the comment or the steely locked-on gaze.

"I Googled you when Sonia mentioned going to your party," he says to Sonia. To me, "It's a parental thing. Can't have my daughter attending parties hosted by strangers," he says with a chuckle, but it's mirthless as the waiter cleaning up the mess wipes a blob of tahini from William's shoe.

"Sorry about that," I say sheepishly, casting another apologetic look at the poor guy cleaning up the mess. I'll be sure to leave a big tip. "Lipstick," I say, holding it up again. My hand shakes slightly and I quickly drop the lipstick back into my pocket.

"Hailey is planning the engagement party, so it's great that you two are getting an opportunity to meet," Sonia says to her father. "How's that going, by the way?"

Not at all.

I force a wide smile. "Totally under control."

"Thank you again for everything," she says, and I know she's referring to our secret working arrangement.

I wink at her. "My pleasure. Anyway, I'll let you two enjoy your lunch."

As I walk away, I slowly release a breath.

That was close.

"Hailey." The sound of William's voice behind me has a shiver dancing down my spine. I resist the ridiculous, overwhelming urge to flee and turn back toward him.

He holds out a business card. "Send any engagement party receipts to my assistant."

Absolutely not, but I can't find my voice to argue as I nod and accept the card. I just want to be away from him.

My interaction with William Banks has me severely on edge. He looked at me with a hint of distrust, as though he knew my every last secret…which is impossible, but still un-nerving.

I wave bye and pick up my pace as I walk away, aware of his gaze lingering.

As I continue toward the restroom, I pull out my cell phone and scroll to Warren's number. Until I can find a way to stop this wedding, we're going to have to actually start planning an engagement party.

I climb out of the Jeep and head toward a row of trendy businesses in the arts district. Hailey stands on the sidewalk outside Frost God Bakery, preoccupied with her cell phone. She's dressed in casual jeans, ripped at the knees, and a crop top under a loose white button-down. I can't remember when I've seen her dress so casually, but she looks…cute. Until she glances up, sees me, then taps her watch as though I'm an hour late.

Different wardrobe. Same annoying Hailey.

It's actually only *ten* minutes and I would have been on time if there'd been any available parking in this area of town midday. Of course, I'm not going to tell her that. I have a reputation as a sloth to uphold.

"Okay, Hailstorm, let's get this over with," I say, stopping in front of her.

"Pretty sure I've asked you to stop calling me that."

"Pretty sure I don't give a shit." It's our natural, familiar banter and her over-the-top dramatic eye roll shows me she loves it as much as I do.

"Thank you for meeting me here," she says tightly. "I was thinking we'd start with the easiest and most important thing on the list for the engagement party—food."

I nod. "I'm thinking hot dogs, hamburgers…you have a grill, right?"

Hailey looks at me like I've suggested we eat the family

pet. "Yes, I have a grill, but this isn't a sorority mixer. It's an engagement party for a wealthy hotelier's daughter."

"I suppose you want a fully catered meal?" We've yet to work out who's paying for this party. I was all in to cover the costs of a low-key barbeque in my yard. But if this is turning into a coronation, she's going to have to pony up her half. It was her idea that we do this together after all.

"Actually, I was thinking desserts. Hence meeting at the bakery." She nods toward the building as she checks her watch again. "We have a tasting appointment in five minutes."

"You told me to be here at one."

"Because I knew you'd be late. Which you were."

I hate that I've given her a reason to be smug. "A tasting appointment?" That's a thing? "Really thought you'd get your way on desserts, huh?" I ask, reaching for the door. I open it and the amazing scent of baked goods makes my stomach rumble.

Hailey strides in ahead of me and glances over her shoulder. "If we're going to work together, you should know—I always get my way," she says as I follow her inside.

Something tells me she's right about that.

Inside the busy bakery, over-the-top desserts and cakes are on display. A couple sit at the counter and flip through a binder of wedding cake designs. The groom-to-be looks slightly pale and overwhelmed—no doubt by the price tag on the five-tier cake his fiancée seems to have her heart set on.

Wedding cakes always seemed pointless to me. No one ever eats it. The cake is just a photography prop for that pathetic smearing frosting on one another pic. Why not just hand the bride and groom cans of whipped cream and let them go at it? Problem solved.

"This place seems a little expensive," I say, noticing the prices on the elegantly decorated cupcakes in the display case.

What the hell is gold leaf? And does it really taste good enough to warrant the twenty-six-dollar cost?

Hailey shoots me a look. "You'd prefer supermarket day-olds for your best friend's engagement party?"

"Overpriced cake tastes better?" It's sugar. Hard to mess up.

"Well-made desserts with quality ingredients made by a trained pastry chef and not a teen with a summer job do—yes."

"If you say so." I shrug. She's covering this bill.

Hailey sighs as though I have zero class and maybe, when it comes to desserts, I do. As a professional athlete, refined sugar wasn't on my diet. Of course over the last few years, I haven't been as restrictive, but I still don't think something you eat when you're already full should cost as much as an entire meal.

But damn, if I'm not suddenly wondering what gold leaf tastes like.

We approach the counter and the owner, Yates Carmicheal—an energetic pastry chef I recognize as a judge from several baking reality TV shows—approaches with a wide smile. He wears an apron that says "Lick My Frosting."

Respect.

"Hailey! Nice to see you! I'll be with you both in a moment," he says.

"Take your time," she says.

"Client of yours, I assume?" I ask as she zeroes in on the display case.

"Yates came to me four years ago with the idea of opening a—" she lowers her voice slightly "—erotic dessert bakery."

Explains the apron.

"And while I personally found the idea of vagina pops fascinating, I didn't see the market embracing the concept enough to be lucrative, so I encouraged him to keep the X-rated of-

ferings as a side hustle and open a high-end patisserie instead."
Hailey peruses the display case. "And he's a *former* client."

I snap my fingers. "That's right. You have a timeline to
your helpfulness."

She turns toward me. "I get clients started on the right path
and then it's up to them," she says with a hint of exasperation,
and I can tell I've hit a sore spot.

Still, I can't help myself from poking the bear further. I
seriously get off on irritating her. "Translation, you abandon
them for the next dollar sign."

She looks murderous as she opens her mouth, but Yates
approaches, interrupting what was sure to be a well-articu-
lated telling off.

One I would have liked to hear.

Her business model has always intrigued me. Not that I've
spent a lot of time thinking about it—or her—but after the
airport disaster, I did go down a dark hole of cyber stalking…
more to see who else had their life derailed by Hailey. Turned
out, all I found were success stories.

Every. Single. Client.

People had only great things to say about her services.
Didn't matter the industry, her advice was somehow spot on.
It was baffling. And her six-month terms are even more so.
Wouldn't it be easier to continue milking one happy client
for years instead of always having to drum up new business?

Unfortunately, asking those questions will only give her
the impression that I give a shit, and I absolutely do not.

"Your tasting sampler," Yates says as he slides a tray toward
us with six delicious-looking bite-sized samples of cake, each
labeled. Lemon surprise, cocoa bliss, espresso love…

Gotta admit, they look great and this definitely beats select-
ing something from the supermarket bakery counter. "You
don't mess around," I say to Hailey.

"What's the point of choosing desserts if we can't reap the benefits of tasting them first?" she says and for the first time ever, I can't fault her logic.

She beams at Yates. "Once again, you've outdone yourself. How's business?"

"Good. Great, actually," the man says with sincere gratitude. "I still don't know how you knew this location would be so perfect back when there wasn't much around, but with that dog park opening up across the street last year and the co-working artist space a block away, I can barely keep up with the business."

Hailey looks slightly embarrassed by the praise, which is unexpected.

Humble? Hailey?

She's actually cute when her cheeks go bright red like that. I have to stop finding things about her cute if I'm going to continue our feud.

"I know a lot of people in this city," she explains with a shrug. "And it's more than the location. People would drive to the middle of nowhere to get your desserts."

Giving credit where it's due. Is it possible I've misjudged her slightly?

Across the counter, the couple glance our way and flag Yates. Obviously, the bride-to-be has won the argument over the cake design. The groom looks physically ill.

"I'll let you two taste and let me know when you're ready to place your order," Yates says to us. He taps the counter, then moves back to the couple.

I chuckle as I see the poor dude pull out his credit card.

"What's funny?" Hailey asks.

"The debt people are willing to go into for some elaborate party."

"Be sure to add that to your best man speech," she says.

I grin despite myself.

"Shall we?"

Don't have to tell me twice. I scan the options then pick up a piece of carrot cake and take a bite.

Hailey reaches for a piece of chocolate cake and pops the whole thing into her mouth.

I nearly choke on mine as I laugh.

Okay then.

I pop the rest of mine into my mouth and have to admit—she's right. This thing has to be the best carrot cake I've ever had. Moist, decadent, with hints of pineapple that I would normally consider gross. Flavors blend on my tongue and I don't even want to swallow.

"So...you're really okay with this?" I ask Hailey when I finally do allow the cake to go down my throat.

"Okay with what? Oh my God, this one is so good." The words come out almost like a groan as she closes her eyes and savors the chocolate.

I'm momentarily distracted by her near orgasmic reaction. My eyes land on her lips, where there's chocolate frosting, and the temptation to lick Yates's frosting alright comes out of nowhere. Okay, maybe not nowhere. I've admired her lips before, but I've never wanted to taste them. I still don't. I just want the chocolate.

Keep telling yourself that, man.

"What were you asking?" she asks in my trance.

I snap out of it and look away from her mouth. "Liam marrying someone else. You're cool with that?"

Hailey scoffs as though it should be obvious. "Liam and I broke up years ago. I'm totally over him." She pops a piece of the carrot cake into her mouth. "This one's delicious too."

"Except you're not," I say, not done with my questioning.

"If I was still in love with him, why would I have offered to throw the engagement party?"

"I'm still trying to figure that out."

"Don't hurt yourself." Hailey reaches for the other piece of chocolate cake and extends it toward my mouth. "Try this one."

I open my mouth and she pops it inside. Instinctively, I close my lips around her finger and lick the frosting free. Our gazes lock and we simultaneously realize she just fed me. And that my mouth is still holding her finger captive.

Awkward tension simmers between us. She doesn't immediately retract the finger and I don't immediately release it. Instead, my tongue actually circles it and Hailey's expression looks like she's not exactly hating the unexpected gesture.

"Decided?"

Jesus. Where did he come from?

At the sound of Yates's voice, I open my lips and Hailey steals her finger back. She looks slightly embarrassed as she turns her attention to the Frost God. "I think so...the carrot cake, the chocolate and maybe the lemon for variety?" She turns to me and I nod, no longer giving a shit about the dessert choices. Hailey Harris's finger was just in my mouth and all I can think about is tasting other parts of her.

Which blows my mind for so many reasons.

She places the order and although I insist otherwise, pays for it.

Moments later, we say goodbye to Yates and head toward the door, a lingering awkwardness still simmering between us. I need to say something. The last thing between us can't be a sexually charged finger licking.

Keep it caszh.

I clear my throat as I open the door for her. "Did we just agree on something?"

Hailey glances up at me with a look of relief that I've broken the weird vibe. "To deciding on desserts without bloodshed," she says, extending a fist.

I bump it and we exit.

Outside, I check my watch. "Well, I have to get to practice."

Hailey nods, then hesitates before asking, "Hey, there's a kid on your team—I think his name is Kent? That was the name on his jersey."

"Marcus, yeah, what about him?" I haven't forgotten the way Hailey looked at him that day when he saved her from the flying ball, then crushed her with the body check.

"Is he...um...good?"

I nod. "Fantastic player. Great potential, but he's going through some stuff at home." He's missed two practices because of his new job, but he's trying to juggle everything—all the responsibilities on his plate—the best he can, so I'm cutting him some slack. At least working keeps him off the street and away from the negative influences of the crew he desperately wants to fit in with. "Why?"

Hailey shrugs casually. "Just saved me from a wild football, so figured he must be good, that's all."

That's definitely not all, I can tell, but I need to get to practice, so I have to let it go for now. "I'll meet you at your place later tonight to go over the rest of the planning?" I ask as I walk backward down the street to the Jeep.

Hailey looks surprised. "Tonight?"

"Or I can just handle the rest of the party planning on my own." Probably safer... Dessert choosing already took a weird turn. I'm afraid what other antics could go sideways. And spending time with Hailey is having an unsettling effect on me. Seeing different sides of her is making it harder to remember I despise this woman. I don't want Hailey Harris to be three-dimensional. I prefer her to be as one-dimensional as her photo on that billboard I continue to drive past, despite the crater being fixed on the alternate (faster) route.

"Not a chance," she says, and I hate that it's relief or potentially excitement I feel. "See you tonight." Hailey puts on her sunglasses as she heads toward her car.

I head in the opposite direction, but several feet away, I glance over my shoulder at her.

Of course, she doesn't look back. Why the hell would she?

Get a grip, Mitchell. It's Hailey Harris. You can trust that woman about as far as you can throw her.

And now all I can think about is scooping her sexy little body up into my arms.

What the hell just happened?

I felt the earth shift more inside the bakery moments ago than during the tremor last week. My finger in Warren Mitchell's mouth—gross!

Only not exactly gross.

Physical attraction to Warren was never a problem. In fact, in high school, before Liam and I started dating, I'd had the tiniest crush on Warren. I'd been hoping *he* would ask me to winter formal the year my gift made me popular, but Liam asked first and he was my science partner and friend...and I have no regrets. Liam and I were absolutely the better fit. And I never thought of Warren that way again.

Until five minutes ago.

My phone chimes with a text and, taking it out of my pocket, I see a message from Sonia that reads:

Crisis. Need your help asap!

Trouble in paradise? My fingers fly over the keys.

Meet me at my place in fifteen.

Thirty-seven minutes and a speeding ticket I couldn't sweet talk my way out of later, I sit across from a frazzled-looking Sonia. "I'm rethinking all of this," she says, definitely flustered, blowing her nose into a tissue. This is the first time I've seen her look unpolished and slightly unhinged. Her voice sounds scratchy. There are definite mascara tracks on her cheeks and the skin around her eyes looks puffy. She's been crying and I feel bad, but also a little hopeful. I mean, sure, I just spent five hundred dollars on desserts for an engagement party, but I could find another use for them.

I'm going to hell. There will be no resetting my karma after this.

"The wedding?" I say gently, knowingly, as though she's finally come to her senses.

She looks up above the snotty tissue. "No," she says as though that was never a consideration. "The acting thing."

Oh, right…

My own hopes dashed, I take a breath and reset. "Why? What happened?" Did she tell her father about it and he threatened to disown her, cut her from the will? He seems more than capable of that kind of overreaction and based on my brief interaction with him, he's certainly still controlling aspects of Sonia's life.

One kink in the Banks family armor.

"I reached out to that contact list you gave me and I didn't know there were so many different versions of 'fuck off,'" Sonia says instead.

Oh hell, if she's going to let a few "no's" stop her from achieving her goals, she's in for a rude awakening.

Though, I could have predicted this outcome. Under normal circumstances, I would have given my previous clients on that list a heads-up, paved the way for Sonia reaching out, but I've been single-minded in my focus on Operation Breakup. Not exactly doing my best to help with her career.

"Maybe I'm not cut out for this," she says. "My skin's not thick enough for rejections."

Probably because she's never had to deal with one in her entire life.

"Just relax," I tell her as I reach for my cell phone and dial a number.

The call connects after the first ring and I put it on speaker.

"Go for Jay." Jay Ashley's thick Southern accent competes with the sounds of wind and traffic.

He must be in his convertible—the dream car he'd had on his vision board for six years before he reached out to me for coaching. He could finally afford to buy it after our six-month partnership. I was the first one he took for a spin the day he bought it.

"Jay, it's Hailey Harris. I have someone you should meet—an aspiring actress who is the next Cameron Diaz."

Across from me, Sonia shoots me a look.

"What's she done?" Jay asks.

"Nothing yet, but there's interest."

Another look from Sonia. If she's going to be successful, she needs to understand that the lightning speed way to achieve her goals is to pretend she already has.

"Like to help, Double H, but my roster's kinda full right now," Jay says dismissively.

Oh, how quickly people forget what it's like to be new to town, with limited experience and contacts, and be shut out of every opportunity. When Jay first came to me, his non-Californian upbringing was hindering his ability to secure meetings with potential clients. The big agencies wouldn't touch him despite a mediocre client list in the Atlanta film industry because he wasn't part of the Hollywood boys' club.

Appealing to his good nature won't work and I'd never make my clients feel as though they owe me one, so...

"Okay, no problem. She's meeting with Executive Talent but I thought I'd do you the solid of seeing her first," I say.

Sonia's eyes widen at the white lie, but I gesture for her to just wait.

After a brief pause on the line, "When can she come by?" Sonia's jaw drops to the floor.

I grin. "Let me check with her." I put the call on mute and turn to Sonia. "Now we let him wait."

Her eyes bug out of her head. "Wait? What? No! Tell him I'm free anytime! I'll go right now!"

I eye her disheveled state and send her a pointed look. "Just take a breather."

She takes half a breath, then asks, "What if he hangs up?"

"He won't." I gesture for her to drag her chair around the desk. "Come check this out."

She reluctantly does and I click on my favorite online makeup tutorial. "Have you seen this vlogger? She's fantastic."

Sonia's knees bounce as she glances at the time ticking away on the call, but as AirbrushQueen45 demonstrates the latest contour and highlight tricks to elongate and accentuate the neckline, Sonia relaxes, engaged in the tutorial. "That's incredible." She pulls out her phone and immediately subscribes to the page.

I check the time on the call. It's been four minutes. He's waited long enough. I motion for her to stay quiet as I resume the call. "Jay? She can do tomorrow morning."

"Ten? My office?" he says.

Sonia nods eagerly.

"Nine forty-five. Her name is Sonia Banks." I disconnect the call with a smile at a mesmerized Sonia.

"You. Are. Amazing," she says.

I'd love to accept the praise, but I can't in good conscience.

"Jay's great," I say. "He's experienced enough to get you some great auditions while new enough to still be hungry." He really is a fantastic agent and I think the best fit for Sonia.

He'll boost her confidence if she can act, but give it to her straight if she can't.

"Thank you," she says gratefully.

"You're welcome," I say and I find I truly mean it. What's the worst that could happen by actually helping her with her acting career? It's the least I could do given the circumstances.

Sonia checks her watch. "Shoot. I have to run. I'm meeting my father at the resort."

And...there's the perfect segue into the conversation *I* need to have.

"How's the new resort design?" I ask casually.

She looks slightly frazzled. "Designs. Plural," she confides.

I lean closer. "More than one resort?"

She nods. "Personally, I think we've bitten off a bit more than we can chew, but my father is adamant."

"And Liam's cool with it?"

Her face clouds slightly, but she nods. "No one's very effective at saying no to my father." She stands to leave and reaches into her purse. "Oh, almost forgot. Here's the invite list for the engagement party." She extends it toward me.

I take it and scan the names on the two-page printout.

Single-spaced. Double-sided.

"Long list." May need to triple the baked goods order. I frown when I notice... "Liam's parents aren't on here."

Sonia sighs and looks truly devastated. "They aren't exactly on board with all of this. Liam says it's ironic that it's the only thing those two have agreed on in twenty years. The engagement took them by surprise."

Naturally, since Liam had been vocally anti-marriage up until six months ago.

"He's hoping they'll come around before the wedding," Sonia continues.

So, I'm not the only one who thinks this is rushed and perhaps not the best idea.

"Between you and me, I'm kinda okay with them not being involved. From what Liam says they can't stand to be around one another and I don't want those negative vibes on my wedding day, you know?"

Actually, I don't. Unless WrestleMania 1000 was about to break out, I could never imagine not wanting the love of my life's parents involved in my special day. Without parents of my own, the thought that Liam could possibly have this big life event without the support of his family breaks my heart.

But I force a smile. "I'm sure your day will be perfect," I say. But hopefully there won't be a day for the Jensens to miss.

I see her out and, in a much better state of mind, Sonia exits with a wave. I stand in the doorway, processing this new information. If Liam's parents think this union is a bad idea, then I'm totally justified in feeling the same way. They know their son better than anyone.

But if Liam won't take his parents' feelings on the matter into consideration, what are the chances he'll take my concerns seriously? He'll likely only dig in even more out of stubbornness and an unwillingness to listen to advice with all of us seemingly teaming up against him.

The only way Liam is going to realize he's making a big mistake is if he arrives at that conclusion on his own.

I just need to help him get there.

After ringing the buzzer on the front gate, I pull my Jeep into the circular driveway of the Mediterranean-style mansion and park near Hailey's front door. This house is big enough for two families and Hailey lives here alone. I don't judge her for her extravagant lifestyle. If this house gives her the safety and security she never had growing up, that's her business.

I'm not sure why I've suddenly softened in my opinion of her, but I need to keep it in check.

I climb out with a bag of take-out food, go to the door

and ring the bell. A melodic tinkling sounds within. A few seconds later, Hailey answers, dressed in yoga clothes—a bra top and shorts. I'm annoyed that I like what I see. I didn't know she worked out, but those abs don't create themselves.

Hailey eyes the take-out bag. "I already ate."

"Good, 'cause I didn't bring any for you."

Hailey sighs and stands back to let me in.

I step inside and take in the elegant house. A spiraling staircase leads to the upper two floors. A big chandelier hangs in the foyer. Expensive artwork adorns the walls. Beautiful home. Again, not exactly what I'd been expecting. Guess I thought Hailey would have self-portraits of herself everywhere—a Romanesque statue in her likeness or something—but the house is tasteful and classy, lacking the usual pretense a home like this usually holds.

Next to me, Hailey sniffs and covers her nose. "Why do you smell?"

"Just came from a late football practice," I say sniffing my shirt, then immediately wish I hadn't.

"You don't shower afterward?"

"I do when I'm going somewhere important," I say, but I actually wish I had showered. The smell of the take-out and salty ocean air as I'd driven along the coast with the hardtop down had masked the scent of sweat in the Jeep, but inside her house, it's a little much. I hadn't planned on practice this evening, but Marcus couldn't make the regular time slot, so we worked one-on-one. Not great, but at least it was something. The kid's trying.

And he'd kicked my ass all over the field—which admittedly wasn't saying much these days.

"Well, let's get this over with so I can breathe again," Hailey says, her voice nasally as she's pinching the bridge of her nose.

I eye her lack of clothing. "You wanna get dressed first?" Not sure I'll be able to focus with her in that. Unlike me, if she's just finished a work-out, she doesn't look or smell like it. In fact, she smells like coconut rum and pineapple—an in-toxicating Caribbean cocktail. And she looks good enough to have the same bad decision-making effects.

"Not really," she says, gesturing the way to her office off the front of the house.

Great, so I'll be staring at her tiny waist and sexy curves while I try to eat. Disgusting.

I follow her into her office. It's painted a shade of dark denim blue and the light pinewood furniture stands out against the coloring. Two large bookshelves host her own awards and achievements, but also those of her clients'.

Okay, so kinda cool. Maybe dropping them after six months is a business tactic and not because she's cruel and heartless the way I always wanted to believe.

Framed magazine covers are leaning up against one wall, the glass broken. But there's the definite fading of paint on the wall where they used to hang. I motion toward them. "The tremor?"

She nods. "Haven't had time to rehang them yet."

Do not offer to—

"If you have tools, I can do it for you."

She looks just as surprised as I am by the offer that escaped my lips without my conscious blessing. Then her expression changes to slightly unreadable as she stares at them. "Actu-ally, I haven't decided if I will just yet."

Odd, but none of my business, so I shrug.

She reaches for a sweatshirt from the back of an ergonomic desk chair, pulls it on over her head—thank God—then sits at her desk.

I sit across from her and empty the take-out bag.

Hailey eyes the French fries with longing. "How do you eat this junk and still stay in shape?" she asks.

"You checking me out?"

Hailey rolls her eyes and ignores the question, instead getting straight to work. "I have the engagement party guest list." She slides it across the desk toward me as I take a bite of my double-decker sandwich. I lick mayonnaise from my lip and scan it. Two pages? Single spaced? I quickly tally. "Eighty-six people?"

"Yep."

She stares at me expectantly.

I blink as I chew. "What?"

She huffs in exasperation. "See anything odd about the list?"

I look closer, flip the pages over. I recognize none of the names. "Where's Liam's family?"

"Not coming. Apparently, they don't support this," Hailey says, leaning forward with a self-satisfied look.

Great, she thinks she's right about this wedding being a mistake. I'm sure there's more to it. "Sure, they do."

"Nope," she says, as though she's got hot gossip. "Not according to Sonia."

Now she's caught my attention, but not in the way she was hoping. "You've been spending time with her?" Hailey and Sonia hanging together makes me uneasy and it should *really* make Liam uneasy. Dude is too trusting of his ex, which I know in my gut is going to come back to bite him in the ass. Thank God, I'm not about to let *my* guard down anytime soon—body like a temptress or not.

Hailey looks away. "Had to get the guest list," she says, but she's definitely hiding something. "Anyway, his parents must not be happy that he's given up his own dreams of skyscrapers in New York to build hotels here on the coast."

"That's quite an assumption…" I stop. "Wait. *Hotels?* Thought it was one resort?"

"Nope. Three."

That's quite the ambitions plan. The night we had drinks together, Liam made it seem as though he was doing this as a one-off favor to Sonia but had no plans to design resorts the rest of his life. He'd alluded to going back to New York and continuing to work with bigger developers on the cityscapes he was passionate about.

Maybe those plans had changed? Maybe he decided the Bankses' family business was a better fit? Either way, I refuse to speculate about something I know nothing about. "Don't look so smug," I say over another bite of my sandwich. "Liam wouldn't be doing this if he didn't want to."

"I'm just stating for the record that I'm not the only one with concerns," she holds her hands up innocently, but she does not pull off the look. She looks quite naughty indeed and she's definitely scheming. I can see the wheels turning in that pretty little head.

"Well, keep them to yourself," I say, popping a handful of fries into my mouth. "Let's get to it. Do you have the invites?" I glance around.

Hailey sighs and opens her laptop. "It's too late to send out invites by mail. We'll have to email the guest list."

"Email invites? Seems off-brand for the great Hailey Harris."

Hailey shoots me a look as she sets up her tripod and selfie light. "We're not sending a regular email. We're going to record a fun video."

I shrug. Have at 'er.

She reaches up and pulls her hair free of the messy ponytail. A few swishes and pats and it looks camera ready. She definitely did not work out before I arrived.

I sit back and continue to eat as Hailey gets ready to record, but then she gestures for me to join her on the other side of the desk.

I shake my head. "No way. This is your thing."

"If you insist on being on the planning committee, this is part of the job."

Hailey leans around the desk, reaches for my chair and with a surprising show of strength pulls it closer into the camera's view.

This is not my scene. After-game interviews used to freak me out. My nickname from the team was "Flash Fumble Mitchell" for how I used to freeze once the cameras were pointed at me and there were mics shoved in my face. This is different, arguably less pressure, but I'm still sweating at the idea of going on camera with her. Definitely should have showered.

Hailey glances at me. "Just follow my lead...and maybe wipe your face."

I do quickly with the arm of my shirt as Hailey starts the recording.

Bright white-toothed smile on her face, she starts, "Hi, Banks family and friends! This is Hailey Harris and..."

She turns to me, but I'm just staring at her.

"Your cue," she whispers.

"What's that voice?"

Hailey sighs as she stops the recording. "What voice?"

"The one you were just using."

"Mine."

"Nope. It was more like this..." I take a breath then mimic the higher-pitched, perky voice she just used. "Hey, Hustlers, it's three twenty-six a.m., time to hit the gym before spending twenty hours at the office."

Hailey's eyes narrow. "I don't sound like that."

"You do."

She huffs. "Okay, well should I sound more like this...

Hey, bros, it's after noon, time to hit the iron before hitting the club to troll for bitches," she says in a deep frat-boy voice.

I grin and shake my head. "That sounded just like me. Nailed it."

Hailey's face cracks into a smile and for a moment, we share a rare beat of connection almost like friendship.

Guards down. Rivalry forgotten.

She reaches for a French fry and pops it into her mouth and I watch it disappear with irrational jealousy.

"Can we just record this? We need to get it out tonight," she says.

Obviously, I'm not getting out of this video without backing out of the whole engagement party planning thing and I refuse to let her out of my sight. We may have had a brief moment of knives down, but I still don't trust her motives.

"Okay. Fine." I can do this. It's just a party invite.

Painfully…somehow…we record the video. Hailey miraculously refrains from using "the voice" and I only turn a light shade of crimson as I say my name and my one line—"Bring your dancing shoes."

She stops the recording and turns to me. "All done. See? Wasn't that hard."

"Maybe not for you. You do this every day."

She eyes me.

"What?"

"Nothing."

"Since when do you hold back at taking a shot?"

"No shot," she says then pauses. "I guess I didn't realize someone like you would be nervous or insecure about anything."

"Anything is a really big range," I say. If only she knew the things I'm insecure about. Commitments. Real relationships. Being vulnerable. Being enough for my narcissistic father. Never measuring up to expectations. All things I'm not willing to share with her and yet, the urge to be honest throws me off guard.

I clear my throat and look away from her penetrating gaze. "Cameras freak me out, that's all. Just seems intrusive and nine times out of ten I'm going to say the wrong thing." There. That's all she's getting.

She seems surprised I shared *that* much. "Well...we're done."

Uh-uh. Nice try, lady. I nod toward the recording. "You haven't sent it yet."

She scoffs. "What? You think I'm going to go through the trouble to plan a party, then not invite anyone?"

"That's exactly what I think you'd do."

"Why? What would be the purpose?"

"Have Liam and Sonia think *no one* supports their union."

"That would be petty."

I shoot her a look.

"Fine." She opens an email, types in a contact list she's already created, attaches the video and hits Send. "There. Done. Happy?"

"Immensely. So, what's left?" I ask.

"Booking a DJ, but I have a guy. I'll swing by the bar tomorrow and secure that."

"I'll come with."

"That's really not necessary."

"In it together, remember?"

She sighs. "Fine. Suit yourself. We also have to decorate... but I can hire someone for that too," she says, consulting a to-do list on her desk.

For someone not fully in support of this whole thing, she's impressively organized, and I'd die before admitting it, but I'm glad she stepped up to help plan this. I'd never think of DJs or decorations. But the cost is definitely starting to climb. "Nah, we can handle the decorating." And I'm not sure when the idea of spending that much time with her didn't instantly make me break out into a rash, but here we are.

She raises an eyebrow.

I shrug. "How hard is it to blow up some balloons and hang some streamers?"

Hailey stares at me like I have two heads. "First of all, this isn't a three-year-old's birthday party and second, I can handle hiring people by myself."

I lean closer. "Look, say what you want but I know you're up to something, so I insist on being part of all the planning. Until Liam and Sonia have said their 'I Do's,' expect me to be around. A lot. Close." With each word, I've moved closer until our knees are touching. I stare her down and she glares at me.

Knives back up. Among other things.

I shift in the chair hoping she doesn't notice the semi I'm sporting as our gazes meet and hold.

She backs down first. "Okay, suit yourself," she says as she stands.

I'm not sure it's safe for me to.

Think about baseball or grandma's underwear...

I reluctantly get to my feet, happy my shorts hide the evidence of the impact she suddenly has on me.

And it's not disappointment I'm feeling now that the night is over...it can't be. Just in case, I head toward the office door before I can suggest something seriously dangerous like a nightcap. "You can have the rest of the fries," I say over my shoulder as I exit her office.

"I wasn't planning on letting you take them," she says in that smartass tone of hers, and the semi's back.

Outside her house not a second too soon, I climb into the Jeep and start it. I can see Hailey through her office window. I watch for a second.

Maybe we should talk decoration colors...

What the fuck's wrong with me?

I shake my head and tear out of the drive, unable to comprehend how, suddenly, I want to spend time with Hailey Harris.

What the sweet hell is happening to me?

EIGHT

HAILEY'S DAILY RULE FOR SUCCESS:
Women supporting one another is the only way we
will secretly take over the world—so fix those tiaras!

I'M ALL FOR FIXING SONIA'S TIARA IN A PROFES-
sional sense, but on a personal level, I'm still concerned about
Liam.

Knowing Sonia is meeting with Jay this morning, I head
to the Banks Resort. I want to check in with Liam and see
if Sonia has told him anything about, well...anything. The
fact that he's being kept in the dark about so much fuels me
in my mission.

Inside the resort, I don't have to go far to find him. He's
pacing the lobby, his cell phone in his hand. He looks tired
and stressed and my chest aches for him. I hang back and hide
behind a potted plant as I eavesdrop on his conversation.

"A few days ago, it was go bigger, go taller... Now your
father is wondering if the designs are too elaborate," he says,

running a hand through his hair. "I don't want to cut corners because of these tight deadlines."

"I'm sure if you tell Daddy, he'll agree with you." I hear Sonia's voice on speakerphone. "Not easily. And after a long, drawn-out battle of bloodshed and tears. But you're strong-willed. You can handle my father."

Maybe unlike Sonia, who struggles to stand up to him? Perhaps she's hoping having her father engaged in battle with Liam will keep his focus off her while she chases this dream he may not approve of.

Liam sighs. "Yeah, I know. I'll figure this out."

"Hey, Hun-Hun, I have to go," Sonia says, her tone changing quickly—reflecting a mild sense of urgency and a hint of secrecy.

I hold my breath and wait. Will she tell him where she is? Does he already know?

"Just heading into a yoga class."

Nope.

"Get some extra zen for me. Love you," Liam says and disconnects the call.

As he walks toward me, I step out from behind the plant with a wide, friendly smile and he nearly collides with me, his attention still on his cell phone.

"Whoa, sorry—" He places his hands on my arms to steady me when I tip slightly off balance, then surprise registers on his face. "Hails? What are you doing here?"

"I was meeting with a client nearby and thought I'd see if you wanted to grab brunch," I say.

Liam checks his watch. "Wish I could, but I'm just heading into another meeting with the head contractor on the build," he says as his cell phone chimes again. He frowns as he looks at it.

"Things going okay?" I ask casually.

"Creative differences."

"Why don't you hire someone else?" I shrug as though the solution is simple.

"William hired them. His call."

"He also hired *you* to take charge," I say gently, but with intent.

Liam frowns as he glances up from the phone. "You think I'm pussying out?"

Yes. "It's just not like you—not standing up for what you think is the best decision."

Liam nods and sighs again. "You're right. It isn't. Normally, I'd have no hesitancy to speak my mind. Give my point of view and argue my case. With William, it's different because he's Sonia's father. Pissing off the boss means pissing off my future father-in-law, which in turn will piss off my future wife and I'll be cut off again. Not that there's been much time for sex these days," he rambles in frustration mostly to himself.

I wince at the TMI. I'm over him, but I still prefer not to think of him having sex with someone else. I sense he could use a laugh, though, so I say, "If you're not getting laid anyway, maybe it doesn't matter a whole hell of a lot if you piss them all off?"

It works. The tense aura around him eases slightly as he grins. "Again, you're right." He sighs, then stands a little taller. "William put me in charge of this build and I need a crew who is on the same page."

I beam proudly. "There's the Liam I love... I mean, in the totally platonic sense of the word." And I truly mean it. The more time I've spent in the midst of his love life, the clearer it's become that I no longer want to be the object of it.

He grabs me unexpectedly and hugs me and even the familiar scent of his cologne does nothing for me. And when his grip tightens slightly and the embrace lasts a beat too long, I don't linger, soaking it up, I gently ease away.

"Thanks, Hails. This was just the wake up I needed," he says.

"Of course. Anytime. Won't even charge you." I pause then, because I have to know the extent of his obliviousness, "And I'm sure after the first resort, the others will be easier."

Liam shakes my head. "Honestly, I think I'm one and done."

Yep. Still being kept in the dark.

Liam's phone chimes with another message. "I have to get back, but great seeing you."

"You too. And don't worry about a thing—the engagement party plans are right on track."

His face and mind are blank.

"*Your* engagement party," I say with a laugh.

"Engagement party! Right. That's this weekend. I've been too busy to give it a second thought. Great. Thank you…for everything." He waves distractedly as he heads back toward the boardroom and I stand there even more convinced that I'm doing the right thing.

Cracks are already forming in the relationship that have nothing to do with my efforts. Well, not completely.

Communication, trust, and honesty are the pillars of a solid relationship and it seems as though Liam and Sonia are struggling with all three.

As I walk to my convertible a moment later, my cell phone chimes with new email messages—RSVPs to the engagement party. I sigh. A lot of people are going to be disappointed when this wedding gets called off, but for now they're in excited, oblivious bliss.

As I reach the car, my phone rings with a FaceTime call from "Sonia." I quickly turn to block any obvious signs that I'm at her family's resort. Those palm trees in the distance look like every other palm tree in California, right?

I hit Accept and the call connects.

"Well?" I inject as much enthusiasm in my voice as possible. I may not be supporting one of her life choices, so I'll try to balance the universe—and my own karma—by genuinely supporting the acting career. I'll destroy her love life but help make her a star.

Sounds like a fair compromise. She might even thank me...

"He offered me representation!" Sonia says, buzzing with excitement. Her cheeks are blushed and her eyes sparkle— she tried that new highlight and contour technique from AirbrushQueen45—and her complexion is flawless. Definitely brought her A appearance to the meeting with Jay and by the sounds of it, her A game.

"That's wonderful!" I say and I mean it. If he saw potential in her beyond her movie star looks, Jay will benefit her career. Once he commits to a client, he's all in.

"Promise me you didn't have any pull over that," Sonia says.

I shake my head honestly. "I just set up the meeting."

"Okay..." Sonia says, but her excitement fades a little.

"What's wrong?"

Sonia sighs. "I lied to Liam. I didn't tell him about the meeting. I said I was going to yoga." She looks genuinely guilty.

I still can't believe Liam bought that. Did he even see her? No one wears that much makeup to work out. *She* may not be forthcoming, but *he* needs to start paying more attention. It's one thing to not notice his bride-to-be camera ready for a sweaty stretching class, but to not realize what William Banks is scheming with three hotel builds?

Liam's a smart guy. Why is he not seeing what's in front of him? Too stressed and blinded by love? Or are the Bankses really that shady and manipulative?

"You're going to have to tell him now," I say gently but firmly. If this marriage has a chance of succeeding—which it doesn't—Sonia can't keep this to herself much longer. And if their individual dreams mean they drift further apart, then that was always going to happen. I'm just helping them get there sooner, before more money and time is spent on these wedding plans.

More importantly, before my own life gets complicated.

Working with Warren the night before—however briefly—had been unnerving. He'd smelled like sex on a stick when he'd shown up all manly and sweaty after football practice. Thank God the smell of fried food helped mask it or I would have jumped him.

And then the flirty banter in my office...where had that come from? We're no strangers to making fun of one another in sarcastic, biting ways, but the teasing of last night's exchange had been different.

Not to mention the sexually charged finger suck at the bakery...

My sexual dry spell is obviously affecting my hormones if I'm thinking about Warren Mitchell as anything more than an ungrateful pain in my ass.

"I will tell him soon. Definitely," Sonia says on the screen, snapping me back to *her* love life.

"You shouldn't put it off, and you two are a team, right? He should support you in this." Or not, if it's not meant to be...

"Thanks, Hailey. You really are the best." Sonia smiles gratefully.

"Happy to help." And I genuinely am happy...though I'm not helping in quite the way she thinks.

NINE

HAILEY'S DAILY RULE FOR SUCCESS:
If your dreams fail to become reality, create
a new reality, don't abandon your dreams.

LAST NIGHT, I DREAMED THAT SONIA TOLD LIAM all about her passion for acting. The two discussed it. He was honest about his dreams in New York. They hugged. Parted ways. And I got to eat the desserts for the engagement party all alone while celebrating another future saved.

The light of day brought a different reality.

Chickened out. Couldn't tell him.

The text from Sonia meant it was full speed ahead with planning the engagement party. I've been spending so much time on this and not nearly enough on my own career. Sleuthing, organizing, implementing mental warfare, and coming up with ways to break up an engagement without anyone finding out is taking all my energy and focus.

Warren's already waiting outside Brooks's Bar when I pull up. He really is staying close. Which I should hate, especially after the other day, but being around him has less of a nails-on-chalkboard effect now than it did before. Which is dangerous for so many reasons. I'm not supposed to like him or get to know him, and I'm certainly not supposed to be attracted to him, but the sight of him has my heart picking up speed—just a tad.

I'd like to dismiss it as fear of getting caught, but I know it's because he looks gorgeous in a pair of faded jeans and a white T-shirt, runners on his feet and an old, worn baseball hat on his head. There's something sexy about a guy in a baseball hat that I can't explain. It should look amateurish. It goes against all the polished principles I live by, but it's a weakness of mine.

As is the perfect five o'clock stubble along his jawline, which I notice as I climb out of the car and approach.

"Morning," he says, pushing off from the wall he's leaning against.

"It's two p.m."

"Early for us bed huggers," he says with a grin as he opens the bar door and gestures for me to enter.

As I duck under his arm, I get a distinct whiff of cologne. Someone showered today—impressive. And the scent is actually really nice. I'd expected him to wear Axe body spray like he did in high school, but this is a richer, more manly smell—earth toney and slightly wild.

A smartass comment right now would take the edge off the mild attraction, but my mind is blank and I'm afraid I'll accidentally compliment him instead, so I keep my mouth shut.

He follows me inside and we approach the owner, Darren Brooks, who's standing with his back to us. He's jamming to something, but it's definitely not what's playing inside the club—loud hip-hop. Darren stacks glasses behind the bar.

He's dressed in a tight black T-shirt with the bar logo on the back—one I helped him choose—and jeans, likely held up by his signature horseshoe belt buckle.

At least he lost the cowboy hat.

We stop at the bar and I call out. "Brooks!"

He can't hear me. Earbuds in his ears.

I lean across the bar and, in the mirror behind it, catch Warren checking out my ass. I want to be offended or call him out, but instead, I flex my ass cheeks tighter.

I tap Darren on the shoulder and he jumps as he swings around.

I send him a sheepish look as his hand flies to his chest and he pulls one earbud out. "Hailey, Jesus. Kill a guy why don't you."

"Sorry," I say, picking up the dangling earbud and holding it to my ear. "Whatcha' listening to?" As if I need to ask. Darren is a huge country music fan and amateur performer. When he first came to me, he wanted to open a country saloon with open mic nights and a mechanical bull, featuring wet T-shirt contests and BBQ tailgates in the parking lot.

Unfortunately, the location he'd already signed a lease on was in the middle of Silverlake...not exactly Nashville or even the slightest bit Southern-ish.

Convincing him that a hip-hop club would be more suitable to the trendy location had taken some major convincing, with focus group studies and a real breakdown of economics in the area, but eventually, he conceded that it was the better play.

Now he wears ear pods to block out what he calls "chaotic noise with repetitive beats and uninspired lyrics."

As I expected, twangy country music fills my head when I hold the earbud near my ear. The song, about a guy who lost his girl and is now keeping a whiskey label in business, sounds like a dozen others on the radio, but I'd never offend his "religion" by voicing my opinion.

I smile as I hand the earbud back. "Still not a convert, huh?"

"The day I enjoy this—" he gestures around, indicating the music "—put a bullet in me," he says with a deep Southern twang that the customers love. At least the ladies. The clientele may not be on board with country music but they love a country boy.

I laugh and introduce Warren. "Darren, this is Warren Mitchell…" Though I'm not sure why I thought an introduction would be at all necessary. Darren's staring at Warren as though a god has entered the building. "Football fan?"

"Hell yeah," he says, extending a hand to Warren.

Warren shakes it. "Nice to meet you. Nice place," he says scanning the bar.

It's more than nice. With its purple velvet interior and dark mahogany wood accents, expensive crystal chandeliers and modern artwork, Brooks's Bar is elegant, sleek, upscale, and trendy. It's reservation only on weekends and packed every night of the week. Bottle service costs these Gen Z kids their rent money, but this is the place to be seen on the coast. The clientele are the youngest, hottest up-and-coming musicians, actors, and models in LA. And the staff rival the patrons for most eye-catching.

The marketing and promotion on this place when it first opened nearly bankrupted Darren, and at first I was a little nervous…but it worked like a charm. The grand opening had A-listers flocking to the purple velvet rope—which had a lot to do with my calling in my previous clients—but the following week, Darren didn't need any staging to give the appearance of exclusive. The place was a hit.

Just like I'd seen in my glimpse.

"Thanks," Darren says. "It's not exactly my aesthetic, but it draws a crowd."

I hear the hint of disappointment in his voice and have to remind myself that Darren owns his own yacht. Sympathy for what he "gave up" only goes so far when he's living a lush life.

"Drink?" he asks us.

I glance at Warren, but he shakes his head. "We're good. We were just wondering if we could book DJ Scale for an event this weekend?"

He looks uncertain. "He's one of the bigger draws—which night?"

"Actually, it's an afternoon thing. Early evening at the latest. He'll be back in the booth by seven." I'd never consider asking if I thought it would interfere with the club. I'll call in favors from one client to the next, but not at the risk of their business.

Darren nods. "In that case, he's yours."

"Great." I pull out my wallet, but Darren looks almost offended, as he shakes his head.

"Put that thing away, dollface. You know your money's no good here."

I love my clients.

Next to me, even Warren looks suitably impressed.

"You are amazing," I tell Darren, leaning over the bar again to kiss his check.

And okay, maybe to give Warren another chance to check out my ass.

Which he does.

At least I know this attraction is going both ways.

I reach into my purse for my cell phone and quickly text the details of the event to Darren.

His phone chimes on the bar and he nods, seeing the text. "I'll make sure he's there."

"Thank you."

Darren hesitates then turns to Warren. "There is one way you could show your gratitude," he says.

Warren laughs, reaches for a napkin and signs it for him.

"Thanks, man," Darren says, hanging it on the wall of fame behind him, where photos and autographs of famous people are on display. "It's a shame you're not playing anymore."

My gut tightens and I expect the comment to have a negative impact on the chill vibe currently radiating between Warren and me, but he doesn't seem fazed as he shrugs. "Even the best rodeo stars have to hang up their spurs sometime."

"True that," Darren says. "Don't be a stranger—you both have VIP access anytime."

I wave as we head toward the door, and once outside in the heat and sun, Warren says, "That guy seems appreciative."

"He did all the work, I just helped him target the right clientele."

"He listened to your advice even though he obviously wanted a country music bar?" Warren asks as we head back toward our vehicles.

"He did."

"You must be quite persuasive," he says.

"I am," I say turning toward him.

Our gazes meet and hold for a sexually charged moment too long. My body heats up and it has nothing to do with the midday sun beating down on the pavement. Warren's light blue eyes hold a depth I haven't seen in them before. The five o'clock stubble along his strong, square jawline is like some sort of beacon and I have to force my hand to remain at my side.

I bet his stubble would tickle against my neck…

I look away and clear my throat. "Well, another thing checked off the to-do list."

"Yep." He shoves his hands into his pockets and looks reluctant to get in his Jeep and drive away.

An odd lingering silence drifts in the stifling air.

"My place to go over the playlist?" I suggest on impulse.

He nods. Very quickly. As though he was also trying to come up with a way to keep this day going. "Meet you there," he says and my heart does an involuntary flutter that it has no business doing.

Window down, music blaring, I follow Hailey's convertible as we drive along the coast to her place. With the top down, her hair blows in the breeze and she drives ten over the speed limit, as though she's in a hurry to get there.

I don't know what the hell I'm doing wanting to spend more time with her, but booking the DJ was a lot quicker than I thought...or hoped?. Her suggestion to work on the playlist was the excuse I hadn't been able to come up with.

And it definitely seemed like an excuse.

She's been wanting to plan all of this alone, so asking for help on something like a playlist feels as though she wanted to spend more time with me, as well.

This is a bad idea. Neither of us should be playing this weird game of attraction. We've never gotten along. We don't even like one another most days.

I do like her ass though. The image of her sexy curves in cut-off denim shorts—tight ass and shapely hips—will be etched in my brain for a while.

And I know that second lean over the bar was for my benefit. I caught her catching me in the mirror the first time, so what exactly is she playing at?

The Hailey from a few weeks ago would have slapped me or delivered a lengthy lecture for checking her out...this Hailey was inviting the attention.

Then, standing near our vehicles, the look on her face was pure desire. We'd both been reluctant to part ways, and a smart man would have made up an excuse for this afternoon.

I'm readily a fool.

Hailey's blond hair blows in all directions and she raises her sunglasses up over the strands to hold them back. It looks silky soft and I'd like to feel it against my skin. See it splayed out against a pillowcase.

She hits the brakes last minute at a set of lights and I hurry to do the same.

Shit. That was close.

My cell phone chimes in the console and, glancing down, I see a text from "Kelly" on the screen. I pick it up and a quick read reveals she's interested in meeting up, which with Kelly always translates into a booty call anytime of day. She's a teacher. Supersmart, superfun, supersexy and we have a good time together. No strings attached fun.

This invite is my out.

My body is definitely in the mood. My mind tells me it's a good idea.

I glance up and my gaze meets Hailey's in her rearview mirror. The same hint of desire from the parking lot reflects in her eyes.

My mouth goes dry and my hands sweat against the steering wheel.

Blow her off and go hang with Kelly? That would be the logical, safest thing to do before things get more complicated...

I reply to the text quickly:

Sorry Kelly, tied up right now.

Obviously logical and safest aren't doing shit to convince me to avoid the mess that is Hailey Harris.

A jug of fresh-squeezed lemonade collects condensation as the heat of the day reaches its peak. Warren suggested we sit outside and I agreed, but now sweat pools on regions of my body I hadn't known sweat could pool.

I still can't believe he agreed to this. I expected him to bail once we got in our vehicles.

"So, playlist." Best to get to it and avoid making a fool of myself by suggesting other options for this afternoon. I reach for my cell phone and scroll through my music. "I'm thinking classical remakes of love songs." I hit Play on a sloweddown version of Taylor Swift's "Blank Space."

Warren pretends to drift off, snore, and fall off his chair.

I stop the music and shoot him a look. "Okay, well, what do you propose?" Of course it's just a formality. He's not getting to decide on the music.

He moves closer and takes my cell phone. His arm brushes against mine and I expect him to move away, but he doesn't.

My gaze lingers on his forearm as I keep my arm next to his on the table. We're both sweaty and contact makes our skin slick, but neither of us seems bothered.

At least not in a bad way.

What is he doing? What's with checking me out and this intentional breaking of the touch barrier?

And now that his cologne is mixed with a mild hint of sweat, holding my breath is probably the only way I'm going to make it through this afternoon without insisting he leave his T-shirt behind when he goes.

On my phone, he opens a music site and a second later, a loud hard rock song plays. He closes his eyes, bites his bottom lip and starts to air drum to the beat.

All actions that should totally kill any attraction to him and yet...

But the music sucks so I cover my ears. "This is just noise."

If my plan is to ruin the romantic vibe at the engagement party, this might be a good way to do it.

No. I have to let this relationship implode without looking like I'm intentionally sabotaging it.

Subtle tactics. Under the radar.

I take the phone back and scroll through another playlist. I settle on a 2000s boy band remix and instantly the sound of my teen years fills the backyard.

"Absolutely not," Warren says, but the next second, he's on his feet, doing the routine from the video. Hand on his hip, he body rolls, then spins and drops to one knee on the pool deck, spins around, then jumps back to his feet.

I'm in utter shock, impressed that he 1) knows the moves, 2) remembers them after all this time and 3) isn't afraid to arm me with this knowledge for future blackmail purposes.

In fact…

I grab my phone and start to record as he continues the routine and even starts to sing along. He knows the lyrics. And his voice is not half bad. His speaking voice—a deep alto—has me surprised he can pull off the tone of this pre-pubescent boy band.

I laugh from behind the phone camera, but then he walks toward me and gently pushes the phone down, so I put it on the table. He reaches for my hands, but I shove them under my legs on the chair, already slick with sweat.

Undeterred, he bends and grips my hips instead, pulling me up off the chair and onto my feet. As I stand, my body is only an inch from his and there's a sizzling fraction of a second before he takes a step back and nods for me to join him.

"Come on, you know you know these moves."

I do, in fact, know these moves. I performed this dance with a group of friends in the junior year talent show. We came in third place. But dancing in front of Warren…

What the hell?

He's making a fool out of himself, I may as well.

I fall into rhythm beside him and we continue to execute

the entire routine flawlessly. My singing is better than his, obvs, but I can't claim victor on the moves.

Then as he reaches for his T-shirt and pulls it off, as the lead singer does in the music video, I nearly stumble and break my face. His arm flies out to prevent my fall, then he's all up on me, sweat glistening on his tanned, muscular chest and his come hither hands as his hips lead the way, inching closer to mine. His eyes burn into mine in a tantalizingly sexy, flirty way as he sings lyrics that used to set my teenage hormones aflutter.

Now other parts of me are fluttering.

Holy sweet fuck.

Warren Mitchell missed his calling as a member of a boy band.

I stop dancing and move away quickly, before my actions are out of my control.

He laughs as he rejoins me at the table but leaves the shirt off, draping it over the back of the chair.

I eye his muscular body and suddenly, working on this playlist together feels like the worst idea I've ever had. I can barely think straight with him sitting across from me, and allowing this attraction to Warren to grow stronger or turn into something else is a really terrible idea.

We need to get through this and he needs to leave ASAP.

"I have an idea. If we keep playing the songs and disagreeing, we'll be here all day. Why don't you make a list of songs and I'll make a list of songs. We each have three veto's and then the mixed list will be set along with whatever else the DJ plays?"

He shrugs. "Not a bad idea, Hailst..." He stops short of saying the nickname.

And shockingly, I'm a bit disappointed.

Which is ridiculous. Must be the testosterone oozing from

him having some sort of ill effects on my brain, messing with my own body chemistry.

I tear a page out of the notebook and hand it to him with a pen. We both get to writing.

Only suddenly my mind is blank. Or shooting off in a million different directions. I can't think of a single goddamn song to write down—the boy band song permanently lodged in my mind.

Warren's having no trouble. Head down, he's writing up a playlist storm and humming the most awful song from the eighties!

I reach across the table and steal Warren's list of song choices, then jump up and run away. I have no idea where I'm going or how to escape the backyard, but this playlist can't happen.

Warren jumps up and chases after me, catches me effortlessly less than halfway across the yard. "Give me back my list," he says behind me, his arms around my waist, as he lifts me off the ground.

"No," I say, struggling to break free.

He holds me with one arm as he tickles my waist and ribcage with the other. I kick and flail as I laugh but stuff the paper in my pocket. "All these songs suck!"

"You haven't even looked at it yet," he says.

"I don't have to. You have sucky taste. You suck!" I say, but I'm giggling so hard that I can't make the words sound even half serious.

Truth is, he doesn't suck. Not nearly as much as I thought he did. Or nearly as much as I want him to.

He's actually...fun.

"Okay, that's it," he says.

Next thing I know, his hands are under my knees and back as he carries me across the yard and straight toward the pool.

Oh shit.

My body seems to fly into the air for an excruciatingly

long moment, though not long enough that I remember to hold my breath before I hit the water. I take in a mouthful of chlorine in my shock at Warren's actions and the chill water on my scorching, sweaty skin.

As I surface, Warren's laughing on the pool deck.

"I can't believe you did that."

"Shouldn't have messed with my playlist," he says, but then a second later, jeans on, he jumps in with me, creating a tidal wave that nearly drowns me again.

I shriek but the sound gets trapped somewhere in my chest as he resurfaces and runs his hands through his wet hair, slicking it away from his face.

Jesus, he's even hotter wet.

And speaking of wet...

He splashes me, breaking the spell his water droplet–covered torso had me under.

I lunge at him, grip the top of his head and push down, submerging him below the surface. He grips my waist and yanks me down below with him. His arm is still around my waist as we stare at one another under the water, little bubbles of air floating up between us. His gaze is amused, filled with a hint of disbelief that I'm capable of giving as much as I'm taking—as though my fiery, challenging nature is a turn-on for him.

And out of nowhere, a song from *The Little Mermaid* movie starts to play in my mind.

Kiss the girl...

What? No. I don't want him to kiss me. That would be ridiculous...

Out of breath, we resurface. Warren still has his arm around my waist and the temptation to straddle him like a new inflatable—a hard, sexy floatie—is overwhelming. Water droplets form on his face and drip from his five o'clock shadow. His gaze is on me and I know this unexpected fun has the same unsettling impact on him. Blue eyes blaze into mine then flitter to my mouth with a look of unconcealed temptation.

My cell phone rings on the pool deck, breaking the silence and the tense moment.

Thank God?

I twist out of his arms, swim to the ladder and hurry toward my cell as quickly as wet denim will allow. I pick it up and see "Coach Baxter" on the call display and hold my breath.

Please, please, please be calling with good news.

I take a deep, calming breath—not an easy task with my heart still pounding and my body still twitching with desire for Warren—then answer, "Hailey…" Remembering Warren's comment about my influencer voice, I clear my throat and start again in my normal voice. "Hailey Harris."

"Hailey, hi! Coach Baxter from the San Diego Mavens."

"Yes, hi, Coach Baxter. Great to hear from you," I say, aware of Warren's gaze on me, listening as he treads water in the pool.

"Got your email request for a meeting…"

I only sent it a month ago, but whatever. I'm happy he's calling now.

"Like to set something up," he says.

I breathe in silent relief, then compose myself. "Great decision. Let's talk some dates." I take the call inside, away from eavesdropping ears, and drip all over my hardwood floor as I head into my office.

A moment later, I re-emerge triumphantly.

Warren is out of the pool but still shirtless, tanning on a lounger.

My mouth goes dry at the sight of the six-pack and tanned, broad sexy shoulders. Turns out the rest of his physique is just as impressive as the forearms. The upper half anyway. I'd need to see the rest for myself before passing judgment.

He hears the patio door close and opens one eye to look at me, catches my stare. "Good news?"

"I have a meeting with the Mavens coach. It's a start." Nothing guaranteed, but at least someone from the sports world is finally getting back to me.

Warren opens the other eye and studies me for a sec. "Why sports clients?" he asks with genuine interest. "From what I remember, you were never very athletic."

I obviously can't tell him the truth. Even having this discussion is likely to kill the lighthearted mood. We're getting along for once and I hate to ruin that with a reminder that the last non-client athlete I tried to advise was him. "Want to be versed in all industries," I say simply.

"You truly think you can help professional athletes?"

"I do."

I hesitate then feel as though I need to prove it to him. Or more likely, reassure myself that I'm capable. Oddly enough, if I can convince Warren, I think I'll feel more confident. I sigh. "Come with me."

He gets up and forgets his shirt as he follows me inside.

Our wet clothes drip onto the floor as I lead the way to my home gym. "I'm hoping this area will help me convince athletes that I know what I'm talking about."

Warren enters and lets out a low whistle as he scans the equipment.

"It's good, right?"

He nods. "It's a great training facility..."

"But?"

"Athletes already have those. They aren't going to sign with you to work out here."

"I know, I just thought if I looked athletic, it might instill confidence."

His gaze washes over me slowly. "Those arms are not going to convince anyone that you're sporty."

I glance at my arms and make a superhero pose, flexing. There's a muscle there somewhere. If I squint really hard... Okay, so he's got a point. "Well, teach me how to use this stuff."

He looks tempted for a second, but then shakes his head. "You're missing my point. It's not being a weightlifter that will get them to sign on for your coaching. It's knowing the industry," he says.

"I'm...researching," I say.

"That's a start. But you need to get out there. Play the sport. Feel the ball..."

I'd like to feel certain balls.

"You need to experience the games for yourself. The aching muscles afterward and the rush of scoring a goal or touchdown or basket," he says.

He's making sense.

"How am I supposed to do that?"

He takes a breath and then lets it out slowly. "Give me back my playlist and I'll help you."

My heart races at the thought. More time together. Another excuse to see one another? Get physical and sweaty together? I want to hate the idea. But there are a bajillion reasons I want to say yes.

Focus on the one that makes sense—this could help your career.

I reach into the pocket of my shorts and pull out his soaked playlist. I bite my lip as I hold it up. "You may need to write a new one."

A full day of sports with Hailey Harris.

Spending time with her willingly, doing something other than engagement party planning. I need to have my head examined.

I drop my bag of sports gear onto the field and open it.

Inside is a football, baseball and gloves, tennis rackets, and a basketball. The key sports she's trying to break into.

I don't know why I want to help her out, but I sensed a genuineness in her yesterday and the offer just slipped out.

But I'm determined to keep things—meaning my thoughts and my hard-ons—in check today. Unlike yesterday in the water where the temptation to kiss her was so strong, I know I would have risked the punch in the face if her cell phone hadn't rung.

I thought that interrupted kiss cliché shit only happened in TV movies.

Probably for the best, though, as it would have been a huge mistake. We've finally reached a point where we don't want to murder one another and may be able to pull off the engagement party without disappointing Liam and Sonia.

Best to keep this stalemate we've silently agreed to as platonic as possible.

Which would be easier if she wasn't so damn hot.

Striding across the field in tight athletic short shorts and a bra top, her blond hair in a swishing ponytail and bright pink runners on her feet, she looks like SportsPro Barbie. I choose to believe she's wearing this particular outfit because of the hundred-degree heat and not because she's hoping to elicit another near kiss out of me. That is absolutely not going to be happening.

"Hi!" she says, sounding excited and happy to see me, which is a first, and it throws me completely off guard.

"Hey," I mumble. "Ready to get started?"

She bounces excitedly and her breasts are a major source of distraction. "What's first?"

She needs to calm the fuck down before I get excited.

I reach into the bag and take out a football. Something that requires us to be as far apart as physically possible. I toss the ball back and forth in my hands as I nod for her to head across the field. "Let's see if you can throw a spiral."

She nods as she backs away. She holds her arms out, ready to catch the ball.

Oh God, she's adorable.

Which is arguably worse than being sexy. Sexy hits me in the groin area, whereas this cuteness radiating from her warms something in my core.

I don't like it.

I throw the ball at about ten percent my usual speed and she catches it. "I caught it!"

Her excitement rivals mine over winning my first pro championship. "Okay, throw it back."

She positions her hands correctly on the threads and I'm grateful I don't have to teach her that. Distance is my friend today. She raises her arm and throws.

The ball is wonky and wobbly, but it makes it to me. "Shit. Sorry!" she says.

"All good. Just try guiding the ball with your pinky finger. Stabilize it and try to direct its trajectory."

That's it. Coach mode. Think of her as one of your players. You can do this. I toss the ball back and she tries again. And it's better. And each one after that is better.

Twenty minutes later, she's not half bad. She's only throwing the ball about eight feet, but it's not wobbly anymore.

"Ready for the next sport?" I ask, putting the football away.

She nods, approaching.

Nope. Stay over there.

She stops next to me and touches my shoulder as I reach into the bag for the baseball and gloves. "Thank you. For doing this. You're a good coach," she says with such sincerity, it has that unwelcome warmness coursing through me again.

I stand and hand her a glove. "Get back over there."

She grins. "Yes, Coach," she says as she jogs slowly back across the field.

And damn, if I don't love the sound of her calling me that. I'm in trouble.

TEN

HAILEY'S DAILY RULE FOR SUCCESS:
Risky ventures have the biggest reward—
but only if you succeed.

THE MALIBU GOLF COURSE SPANS TWO HUN-
dred acres of lush greenery with a view of the ocean in the distance. Palm trees line the exterior and an impressive clubhouse and resort offer a slice of golf paradise on the coast. The expensive membership guarantees the greens are well maintained, and carts and golf caddies are provided, ensuring you don't need to do anything more than swing back and let it fly, all while enjoying a club-exclusive cocktail.

But that's not the course Mr. Jensen and I frequent every Sunday.

His favorite is about a mile away. Coastal Greens is a smaller, quieter golf club with fewer frills, open to the general public. The dress code is less formal, and if you don't carry your own clubs while walking from one hole to the next, they don't get there. Drinking's allowed on the green and gate attendants look the other way in regard to contraband alcohol. It's a place for golf lovers who prefer the game to taking selfies.

I crack open a beer under the sweltering 9:00 a.m. heat and extend the can to Mr. J. He clinks his condensation-soaked can to mine and we take a swig of beer that's gone warm already. Not exactly refreshing, but nostalgia flows through me at the taste of his favorite cheap beer.

I had my first cold one at seventeen out here on this golf course with Mr. J. He'd always wanted Liam to golf with him, a father/son bonding experience, but it wasn't my buddy's sport, so I agreed to learn how to play. If Mr. J felt disappointed by me filling in for Liam on those weekly outings, he never showed it. Back then, I was desperate for any real guidance that wasn't selfishly motivated and I could always count on Mr. J to give it to me straight.

As far as fathers go, Liam had no idea how good he had it, but I certainly didn't take the man's advice or time for granted.

Out here on this golf course, I learned so many valuable lessons about life, hard work, and respecting women. His pickup line suggestions were obviously not to be taken seriously, but the memories made on this course over the years have stuck with me.

"Seeing much of Liam while he's home?" the older man asks now, setting up his drive.

"Yeah… We've been hanging out." I know he's refusing to come to the engagement party, so I don't want to bring it up, but I sense we're headed there. The disagreement with his son has to be weighing on his mind and just like years ago when he and Liam would be at odds, it does put me in a rather tight predicament. I've always been diplomatic and refused to take sides in whatever argument they had going, but co-hosting the engagement party will definitely be seen as having chosen a side in this one.

But in my defense I agreed before I knew he wasn't sup-portive of the relationship. Hard to say if I would have stepped into this role had I known. My respect for him is deep-rooted but so is my loyalty to my best friend.

He swings back, hits the ball and it sails through the air. "You've met Sonia?"

"Great shot," I say when it lands on the green, then nod slowly. "Yeah, she seems like a nice person." I place my ball on the tee and rotate my shoulders before getting into position.

"I'm sure she is," he says.

I take my swing, but the slight tension in the air makes it a lousy one. The ball only goes several yards and lands way back from the green. Won't be hitting par on this one, but today there's more on Mr. J's mind than golf and I want to be a sounding board the way he's always been for me.

I turn toward him. "Heard you and Marsha aren't able to make it to the party." I noticed Hailey added them to the email invite list despite their insistence that they have no in-terest attending.

It was worth a shot.

Mr. J nods as we pick up our club bags and head off across the green. "First thing me and the old battle-axe have agreed on in years."

That's actually a term of affection he used for Marsha when they were blissfully in love, so it's not said with any malice. I believe he still loves his ex-wife. He's never remarried and I know he still wears his wedding ring when no one is around because there's a very obvious tan line on his ring finger from days working in the sun.

I know the divorce hit him and Liam hard—making them both a little gun-shy about matrimony and lifelong commit-ment—but if Liam has moved beyond that emotional hang-up, I'm curious why Mr. J is so against his son getting married. Does he just not want him to get hurt or is there more to it?

"Can I ask why?"

He shrugs. "It's the wrong decision and we refuse to support wrong decisions. Simple as that."

"But why do you think it's wrong?" Sonia has zero flaws as far as I can tell and Liam seems stressed, but with an aggressive resort build schedule, that's par for the course. Otherwise, he seems to be happy and in love. If he was going to marry someone, it could definitely be worse.

"Because he should be with Hailey."

I stumble over the uneven turf. "Hailey? Really?" My heart pounds slightly as the memory of yesterday's sports training resurfaces. We'd successfully managed to keep it casual and platonic, unlike that day in the pool. It was as if we both knew we were wading into dangerous waters and needed to pull back a little. We didn't argue, which was also good because arguing with her has the same effect on my attraction to her as flirting with her does.

Safe neutrality is the only way to keep things PG.

But I can't deny that even when I'm not around her, I'm thinking about her more than I want to these days. And that's never happened to me before with a woman. Out of sight, out of mind was a concept that I was very familiar with, but it's different with Hailey and it's messing with me.

Mr. J nods confidently as we reach his ball. "That girl was perfect for him."

"Hailey? Really?"

"You sound like a broken record, son," Mr. J says, lining up his next shot. "Hailey challenges him and doesn't put up with any bullshit, but she's as loyal and committed to that boy as it comes."

Something in my gut stirs and I pray it's the lukewarm beer not sitting right. Hailey not being supportive of the union seemed like a way to get Liam back for herself, but is Mr. J right? Does she have Liam's best interests at heart? Either way if Liam is single again, it frees him up for another shot with Hailey.

I wipe beads of sweat from my forehead with the back of my arm. "But they decided they weren't right for one another years ago."

Or at least Liam did…

"Because he moved to New York. But when he came back, I thought…" He shrugs. "That's why I sent him to fix her pool."

"Playing cupid?" I say wryly.

"Hoping they'd reconnect. I thought maybe time and distance would have given them both a better perspective and if they saw one another again—now as mature, successful people—they'd see that a second chance might be in the cards." He pauses as he grips the putter in his hands and bends slightly at the knees. "Didn't bank on that Banks girl insisting on tagging along for the ride."

"You want the two of them to get back together?" Maybe it's just his own soft spot for Hailey making him feel this way. I know he was as much of a father figure to her back then as he's always been to me, so maybe he just misses that connection.

Why is this revelation bothering me so much?

He hits the ball and it sails into the cup. He turns to me with a grin. "I know you're not a Hailey fan…"

I wasn't. I still shouldn't be…but she has been growing on me in the last few days. She's different than I thought she was and I'm forced to re-evaluate everything I believed about her. She's actually funny and I always knew she was smart, but getting to know her through the eyes of some of her clients has been enlightening.

And after much, much internet searching, I did find the articles Sonia had mentioned about Hailey's other clients—the ones she doesn't publicize—which makes her that much more endearing.

She's a good person and I like being around her, which has blown my fucking mind, but here I am—in a situation-ship with Hailey Harris that I never in my wildest dreams thought was possible.

And shouldn't be.

Letting my guard down, getting to know her and starting to feel things for her I can't quite label yet is even more clearly a bad idea if Mr. J thinks she should be with Liam. Hell, until now, I hadn't even given much thought to the history between the three of us. I've been too busy resisting and denying my attraction to Hailey to really work out what it means.

"But that girl is truly special," Mr. J says, cutting into my thoughts. "And I think Liam should open his damn eyes and finally see it."

Unfortunately, *I'm* starting to see it, but Mr. J has raised a good point. Even if I could wrap my mind around the fact that I'm attracted to Hailey. And even if in some wild stretch of fate, she might actually be attracted to me. Even if the stars aligned and we could somehow move forward—past our tumultuous history—and open up to the idea of being together and not just right now in a half truce until this wedding happens…

How could I possibly go for my best friend's ex?

I'm still plagued with the thought that night at my weekly poker game. A tradition that has become almost sacred as it's my only real tie to my former life. Sunday nights when my football buddies and I sit around the poker table in my basement, with beer and snacks on hand, trash-talking one another, I forget that my career is over and that these athletes have gone on to accomplish all the things I'd set out to do myself.

Luckily, their skills on the field don't translate to the poker table.

"Royal flush," I say as I put down my hand and drag in a stack of poker chips. Even distracted, I'm still stealing their hard-earned league money.

"Motherfucker," Damien Jones—quarterback for the San Diego Rogues—says as he tosses his cards onto the table. "This is bullshit."

He says that every week. He's the worst player of us all but thinks he's hot shit, so he'll never fold. Good thing the guy's bankroll can support his lack of poker face.

I take a swig of beer, emptying the bottle, then reach into the cooler next to me for a new one.

My cell phone chimes on the table and I see a text from Hailey that reads:

Eight forty-five my place tomorrow morning for party setup. Don't be late.

I grin. Her bossiness is starting to grow on me.

Damien nods toward the phone. "Looks like someone's gotta booty call lined up for after we leave."

The other guys laugh and rib me for my playboy ways. It's a reputation I'm okay with upholding among my happily married bros. They'd never believe I was actually feeling *actual* feelings for someone anyway, and I'm not sure I believe it just yet. After my conversation with Mr. J, I'm not sure I can allow those feelings to continue.

As if I have any control over the matter. If I did, I wouldn't have caught them in the first place.

Damien deals out the next hand and I clear my throat. "Hey, what do you guys think of the whole bro code thing?" Maybe it doesn't apply in adulthood.

"Bros before hoes?" Jeremy Dexton—a linebacker for the Santa Monica Heat—asks, collecting his cards and peering over the outsized, gold-trimmed dark Gucci sunglasses he borrows from his wife.

"No, more like dating someone's ex."

Jeremy shakes his head. "That's like dating a dude's sister. You don't."

I nod. That's what I thought...

"No exceptions?"

Damien sends me a curious look. "Which one of our exes are you trying to hook up with?"

I scoff. Before marrying his beautiful, amazingly patient wife, Alexis, Damien had the worst taste in women. This guy was like a magnet for gold diggers. "It's not like that. I was just curious."

Jeremy sends me a look. "There are enough women in this city that you don't need to fuck up a friendship to get laid."

Loud and clear.

But what if it wasn't just about getting laid? Did that change the rules?

It's after midnight when I complete my pitch document to Coach Baxter. I took Warren's advice—though I'll take that secret to the grave—and did my research. Baseball plays, stats, etc... I couldn't coach a team, *yet*, but I was able to identify key areas in a player's career where they could use some guidance.

I'd always thought that researching and truly understanding the industries was a waste of time. My glimpses reveal most of what I need to know—which team to sign with, which to avoid, future injuries... But maybe I could develop my business a different way. Still use my ability, but rely on it a little less.

I scan the presentation a final time, then hit Send. I yawn, stand and stretch.

"Ouch, ouch, ouch." My entire body is sore from the sports

training with Warren yesterday. I can barely lift my arms and I was tempted to slide down the banister this morning to avoid tackling the stairs.

Three hours learning some sports basics had been tough, but Warren was an incredible coach—patient, informative, and sincere in wanting to help me.

But there had been a distance I could feel.

Obviously, the day before in my pool had unsettled him as it had me. So, it had been a relief that he was focusing on the task at hand and keeping any ridiculous flirting at bay.

A big relief.

I do not need this thing with Warren escalating to something it doesn't need to be. Shouldn't be. It's not like we could actually date. We're totally wrong for one another, we have history that forbids it, and with my gift preventing me from fully opening up to another person, any relationship with him would be doomed from the start. My glimpse into Warren's career-ending injury would always be the elephant in the room and how could a long-lasting relationship survive that underlying tension?

As I leave my office, my phone chimes with a message from him. I look at it and read:

I'll be there bright and early.

The idea of seeing him shouldn't be making me this excited, but the butterflies in my stomach tell me that despite all common sense, there is a definite attraction.

One that could be a huge distraction if I let it.

Operation Breakup has taken a back seat in recent days... but I need to stay focused.

Stopping this wedding all comes down to tomorrow.

ELEVEN

THE NEXT DAY, A CREW SETS UP A TEMPORARY
stage in my backyard as we decorate for the party. Across the
yard, Warren stands on a ladder, hanging a string of white
lights. He glances toward me and if I didn't know better, I'd
swear there was attraction in his gaze. Things seem to have
shifted over the last week working to pull this off.

I head his way and pause next to the ladder. He's of course
ignored my instructions to let the lights drape several inches,
but they look better his way. "Looking good."

"Why, thank you," he says with a wink that sets my heart
racing.

Eyes on the prize, Hailey.

"I meant the lights," I say awkwardly.

"I know," he says with a grin.

How did the grin that used to grate on my last nerve suddenly become a highlight of my day?

My cell phone rings and I reach into my shorts pocket. A glance at the caller ID reveals "Coach Baxter."

That was quick. Good sign or bad sign to have a decision this early?

"I have to get this," I say distractedly, my gaze still on the ringing phone.

"Take your time. It's not like you're helping anyway," Warren jokes, and I have no time to focus on whether or not we are flirting.

Nervously, I move away and answer the call with enthusiasm in my voice. "Hey, Coach Baxter. Wasn't expecting to hear from you so soon." Immediately assume the upper hand by letting the opposite party know they've shown their cards.

"Didn't want to leave you waiting after the impressive pitch we received last night," he says and it's impossible to tell from the tone if they're in or out...but he did say impressive so my hopes rise.

"Thank you. I appreciate that." If only all coaches were as responsive as Coach Baxter.

"So, I reviewed it, and Kylie and I discussed it this morning. We thought you had some great ideas, and your viewpoints on her career trajectory were really outside the box. Playing up her weaknesses and moving her into positions the opposition won't expect was quite ingenious."

My confidence grows. "I do think that strategy is a good one for her." After watching countless hours of footage, I noticed Kylie wasn't being utilized to her full potential in the second baseman position. "Sure, it's a little unorthodox, but we can't always do what the competition is doing if we want to get ahead."

A long pause on the other end, then, "Yeah, well, Spencer Stanley feels differently. He feels playing to her strengths is the better approach," Coach Baxter says, and my spirits take a nosedive.

They've been chatting with Spencer too. That shouldn't surprise me, but I thought maybe I'd hit on a team he hadn't. I was hoping Spencer wasn't targeting female athletes…

I swallow hard and take a slow breath before answering. "Spencer Stanley, right. He's really great. I'm sure he has a lot to offer Kylie, as well." The fastest way to discredit yourself is by discrediting someone else. "But I think his approach is a little more old-school."

"It's tried and true."

Shit.

I wait.

"We've decided to go with him."

I force a breath. "Of course. Whatever you feel is best."

"I did enjoy your pitch, Hailey, and appreciate you taking the time."

"Absolutely. Take care and good luck to Kylie." I disconnect the call. "Fuck," I mutter. How is Spencer doing it? He's not thinking outside the box or offering anything new to his potential clients.

People like safe. They like to hear advice that's in-line with their own thinking. Maybe I need to switch my approach… But the idea of compromising my own creativity to gain clients doesn't appeal to me. If I'm trying to rely on my strengths—other than my gift—then I need to be true to who I am, what makes me different.

Unfortunately, the imposter syndrome resurfaces—could I actually pull this off without using my glimpses?

Warren descends the ladder and approaches. "Everything okay?"

"Just lost another potential athlete client to Spencer Stanley."

Warren nods sympathetically.

"What? No snide comment?"

Warren hesitates, looking severely conflicted as he strug- gles with something for a beat. "Hey, why don't you come to poker night at my place next week," he says.

"Are you trying to make me feel better? Because stealing my money in a poker game when I just said my expansion plans aren't going so shit hot is a weird way of doing it."

He shakes his head. "I'm inviting you because there will be six professional football players held captive, with money on the line, forced to listen to what you have to say."

My mouth gapes. Okay, that does make me feel a little bet- ter. Who the hell knew Warren Mitchell was capable of lift- ing my mood? I mean, physically, I'm sure he's capable of all kinds of therapy... Focus, Hailey. "Seriously?"

"Can you play?"

"Not really."

"Even better. Sunday night at eight or seven fifty if you'd rather," he says with a wink.

I'm still in shock and slightly suspicious of the offer, but I nod. "Yeah, okay. I'm in."

"Great."

Not only is it a nice gesture, but it's a future opportunity to hang out together.

The gate buzzer sounds from inside the house, interrupt- ing the energy vibrating between us. "Must be the desserts," I say. I head toward the gate, then cast a glance at Warren over my shoulder. He's still staring at me, and where his expres- sion used to radiate attraction now there's a different look—a softer look—affection?

Yep. The earth definitely shifted with that tremor.

Hailey looks mortified as she stares into dessert boxes with the Frost God logo sitting on her kitchen counter. "What the hell are those?"

I fail to hide a grin as I peer over her shoulder. "In my expert opinion, Kama Sutra poses." And very well done by the looks of them. Yates is truly an artist.

Hailey shoots me a look, then grabs her cell phone and dials Yates. She puts the call on speaker as the pastry chef answers on half a ring. "I know! I messed up!" he says.

Hailey's shoulders sag in relief. "Thank the Frost God, you realize there was a mix-up. When can we expect the driver back with our order?"

"No, like I really messed up. Your order was delivered this morning to some sex toy sales party," Yates says. "They ate them but left me a three star review because the designs weren't risqué enough—which made me realize the mix-up."

"They're gone?" Hailey asks, panicked again.

"You can keep the Kama Sutra designs. Free of charge," Yates says graciously.

Hailey's white-knuckled grip on the edge of the counter says she's fighting for patience. "I'm not sure those will work for our guests. Do you have anything in the display case that we can get in a hurry?"

"Not enough to accommodate your numbers. There was a rave last night at the club down the street...late-night munch-ies are good for business. I'm so sorry, Hailey." Yates's voice is truly remorseful.

Hailey takes a calming breath. "Okay. It's okay. We will figure it out." She disconnects the call and I'm impressed by her composure.

"We're stuck with these?"

"Yep." She bites her bottom lip as she stares at the erotic desserts, molded in various shapes.

The old me would gloat about the fact that she had to have decadent, expensive desserts and the whole thing backfired. I would remind her that my suggestion of hot dogs and burg-ers on the grill would have been problem-free. But instead, I just want to help her solve this mess.

I open several drawers until I find what I'm looking for, then take out some baking utensils. I roll up my sleeves and get to work.

"What are you doing?" Hailey asks, moving closer.

"Making them look less X-rated," I say, cutting off edges and smoothing out the frosting to blur the images. Sorry, Yates!

Hailey moves even closer and admires my handiwork. She tilts her head from side to side. "Holy shit, that might actually work." She picks up a cut-off piece and pops it into her mouth.

I reach for one and do the same. "Still tastes fantastic."

"So good," she says, reaching for another piece.

We continue to eat the discards as I work and then the next thing I know...

In a psychedelic haze, dressed only in our underwear, Hailey and I lie on floaties in her pool and stare up at the clouds. I'm wearing Hailey's oversized, diamond-encrusted sunglasses. I point to the sky as various shapes emerge in a brightly colored effervescence. I'm completely oblivious to how I even got here and somewhere deep in my subconscious I'm freaked out, but too high to care.

"That cloud looks like a unicorn," I say.

"Do you hear the palm trees singing?" Hailey says. "It's magical."

"What if we're all just in a mason jar?"

"And the stars are the airholes."

Wow. Mind blown.

I fight through the mild confusion as I watch her listen to the melody of the palm trees. I blink several times and shake my head to clear the fog. "We can't serve those desserts."

Hailey still looks slightly dazed, but she too seems to be coming around. "Hot dogs on the grill, it is," she says as she paddles her way to the edge of the pool.

She climbs out and the sight of her in her pale pink underwear and matching bra has my mouth watering. I'm completely lucid now.

She checks the time on her cell phone and gasps. "How is it after noon already? How long were we floating in there?" She scrambles to put her shorts and tank top back on over the damp underwear. Wetness seeps through the shirt and her nipples press against the fabric.

Lingering effects of the hallucinogen kick in and the nipples start glowing and rotating like a spiral. I blink it off and try to focus on her voice. She's panicking about something...

"The...tables...should...have...arrived...by...nowwww." Her voice sounds like it's been filtered through a slow-motion special effect.

Tables. Right.

She calls the rental company and I watch her expression change as she listens, then disconnects. "Is no one in this city competent?"

"No tables?" I'm still too high to be fazed by it.

"They double-booked." Hailey paces, rubs her temples, tries to sober up to deal with the latest crisis. But then she pauses, lured into a deep conversation about aliens with a potted cactus.

I have to pull it together.

I climb out of the pool and bend at the knees to look into her face. "Don't sweat it. I have a few at my place."

Hailey looks at me like I've just discovered a way to maintain world peace. "When did you become Mr. Save the Day?"

I'll admit coming to the rescue—*her* rescue—has an odd effect on me. Probably because she's so self-sufficient and composed all the time. Watching her stressed and unraveling and knowing I can help is empowering.

"What can I say—America's Hero," I say with a wink.

"Okay, hotshot, let's go."

★ ★ ★

Twenty minutes later, Warren pulls his Jeep in front of a modest two-story house in a nice neighborhood. He drove, as apparently having only one percent body fat helped him metabolize the cannabis quicker, and I'm still sporadically hearing inanimate objects. What the hell was in those desserts?

I frown and say, "I thought you lived in that bungalow on 8th Street?"

Warren laughs. "You thought I still lived in the house near campus I shared with six other dudes?"

"Um, yeah."

He shakes his head as we open the doors and climb out.

Inside, the house is even more of a shocker. It's a neat, nicely decorated home. Football-themed items throughout but not tacky. I'm impressed by the matching decor and modern color scheme, sleek appliances, and even a few house plants that look to be thriving. "This place is really not bad."

Warren's earlier easygoing demeanor has changed. He's back to slightly tense and broody, as though having me in his personal space puts him on edge. "Glad it meets your approval," he says. "Don't touch anything."

I send him a look. So much for my knight in shining armor. Or rather, diamond-encrusted sunglasses. Looking at him now, I can't even recognize him as the guy who was envisioning unicorn-shaped clouds and taking about existential crises.

"Tables are downstairs," he says.

I nod but then notice a certificate from California State University on a table near the door, next to a frame that he's yet to put it in. I pick it up and read the fancy script that says... "You have a diploma in sports psychology?" Shocked would be an understatement.

Annoyed, Warren takes it from me. "I told you not to touch anything," he grumbles.

"When did you get time to do this?"

He shrugs. "Maybe some days I get up before noon."

Okay, so maybe I've misjudged him.

"Come on," he says leading the way down the hall to a flight of stairs.

I follow close behind, still trying to process the idea of him studying to become a sports therapist. Not that I doubt he's capable of that, but because it's impressive in ways I wasn't expecting and now I'm questioning everything I know about him and wanting to learn more.

I've known him most of my life, but the relationship has always been superficial. We've never really had deep, meaningful conversations. He was Liam's best friend—a fun, easygoing third wheel with a solitary focus on football. We lost touch after the breakup, until that day at the airport. Working together to plan this party has been a mix of tearing one another's throats out and flirting until it's not safe, then reining it in.

But now I find myself wanting to actually know him. Know why he chose online studies, why he coaches on a local level instead of accepting offers from big colleges he must be receiving... Why he's still single.

But getting to know him would be dangerous and being completely vulnerable with him is impossible, hence the standstill that is the story of my life.

I follow him down a flight of stairs into...

Ah, the man cave.

Downstairs is more of what I was expecting. Large, comfy-looking sofas and chairs. A flat-screen TV the size of a small movie theatre screen. A poker table in the corner near a bar with a stocked liquor shelf and beer fridge.

I pause, seeing his sports accomplishments on display along one wall. Football championship trophies and medals from junior high to his professional days. Top athlete awards and VIP trophies. He was an all-state champ and held the top stats for three years as a quarterback. Photos show him in uniform with various teams, from the ones with Liam in high school to professional teams. I peruse them all in real amazement. He has had one hell of an impressive career.

A wave of guilt washes over me that I had a hand in putting an end to it...but it was going to end either way, even if I'd let him board the plane that day. I refuse to regret my actions.

Warren looks uncomfortable as he grips one of the tables stacked against a wall.

I continue looking at the items. His championship rings sparkle behind the glass. "Great career," I say.

"Yeah. Wanna help?"

I pull my gaze away and join him. I take a deep breath and clear my throat. "I am really sorry about what happened that day in the airport." I'm not sure I've ever truly apologized and he looks surprised to hear it now.

He sighs, looks like he wants to move on, but says, "You never did explain what that prank was about."

How do I explain any better than I tried to that day? "I was afraid you were going to get hurt," I say slowly. "I have a gut instinct about these things. It was probably the wrong way to go about it and I didn't mean to ruin your career."

Warren places his hands on his hips, his gaze drifting to the display case of accomplishments. "I could have tried again. It's not all on you," he says after a long pause.

"Why didn't you?" I ask gently. I'm desperate to know, but afraid to spook him back into silent withdrawal with too many questions.

"I don't know. I'd reached a level of success and got complacent." He shrugs. "I thought I could take some time off and they'd welcome me back when I was ready." He pauses and runs a hand through his hair. "You were right—there's nothing worse than taking your foot off the gas and then watching others achieve your dream."

Hearing the words *you were right* coming out of Warren Mitchell's mouth should have me bragging to high heavens. But I feel for him. A rare beat of connection passes between us at his vulnerability. I'm surprised and kinda touched that he shared something personal.

But I sense this is all I'm going to get for now. So, I grab the other end of the table and we lift. "Full disclosure—I don't get up at four forty-five a.m. I mean, I do, to post the live motivational video, but then I go back to bed."

Warren grins and there he is, the casual, fun-loving guy from my backyard. The one I'm getting to know better. The one who—dare I say it, against all common sense and better judgment—I'm starting to…like.

"Can't believe you're trusting me with such a deep, dark secret," he says with a wink.

Correction: starting to like…a lot.

Hours later, the engagement party is in full swing. Guests arrive, mingle, drink champagne. At the grill, dressed in jeans, collared shirt, and an apron that reads What's Up Dog?, Warren serves hot dogs and hamburgers. Surprisingly, the guests aren't complaining. They seem to be enjoying the "laid-back, casual with classy accents" vibe we've been forced to go with.

Across the yard, Sonia and Liam look happy, in love, having a great time, surrounded by Sonia's family and friends. I can't help but wonder how Liam feels about his family not being here. Not supporting this. I'd been hoping that his parents would pull through in the final seconds, even though I know ultimately this is for the best. I'd like to talk to him about it, but Sonia's been glued to his hip since they arrived.

Champagne glass in hand, I watch them from across the yard and a feeling of conflict washes over me. I can feel my resolve weakening.

They look so happy…

"Beautiful party, dear."

I jump, spilling my champagne at the sound of Amelia's voice next to me. "Amelia! Hi! What...um...are you doing here?" She dressed for the occasion in a beautiful pale blue sundress, her hair coifed in a bun and a glamourous amount of makeup.

"Heard the party and thought it was one of your events."

"Oh, right." She has an open invitation to those. "Actually, it's an engagement party for a...friend."

She looks disappointed. "Oh, sorry to intrude..."

"No intrusion at all!" Sonia's voice is full of excitement as she and Liam approach us. "You're Amelia Cranshaw! I've watched all your movies."

Amelia turns to her with a beaming smile. "Thank you, dear."

Sonia continues to gush and Amelia continues to eat up the attention and praise and this shouldn't bother me, but an odd sensation washes over me—something like protective jealousy.

Amelia's my friend—back off, Sonia!

"Are you an actress as well?" Amelia asks Sonia.

My heart stops and it feels as though the yard around us has gone completely silent as the question lingers in the air.

I glance back and forth between Sonia and Liam, holding my breath. Will Sonia be honest? Is this how her secret will come out?

"Sonia? An actress?" Liam scoffs like the suggestion is absurd before she can answer.

Sonia's expression changes to one of annoyance as she turns toward Liam. "Why is that so far-fetched?"

Liam looks slightly taken aback. "'Cause acting was just a phase for you...it's not actually your thing—thank God." He turns quickly to Amelia. "No offense to your profession."

"None taken, dear. You're not exactly my audience," she says, putting Liam firmly in his place. Then to Sonia, "You could be one if it was actually your thing."

Sonia smiles at her gratefully and Amelia shoots me a look that suggests this couple is doomed before she walks away…

…giving me the confidence to proceed with my plan.

I motion for DJ Scale to cut the remix of an upbeat Whitney Houston song, then clink my glass for everyone's attention.

Sonia's family and friends turn their attention toward me and I smile brightly. "I hope everyone is having a good time. I want to take a moment to personally offer my congrats to the beautiful couple." I raise my glass and smile at Liam and Sonia. It feels deceitful and I can acknowledge that I'm not a very nice person right now, but I'm doing this for their own good. Especially if that tense interlude a moment ago is any indication. "And… I have a fun surprise planned. If I could get you two to sit right up here." I've already positioned two lawn chairs back-to-back in preparation.

Sonia and Liam look slightly nervous as they approach and sit.

I turn toward the BBQ and motion Warren to come closer.

He shakes his head. Doesn't want the spotlight, but I cross the yard toward him and drag him forward. He removes the apron and gives a shy wave to the guests.

"The best man, everyone!" I announce to the crowd. A good man who's being dragged into my scheme. I push guilt aside—he insisted on being a part of all of this.

The guests cheer for him and I hand him a piece of paper. He glances at it. "What's this?"

"Your game questions," I say casually, as though I mentioned this plan of mine to him before. I pick up writing pads and markers hidden under the dessert table (dessert turning out to be fresh-cut fruit we picked up on the way back from Warren's, the erotic baked goods safely disposed of in the dumpster at the end of the block) and turn to the guests. "We are going to play Couple Compatibility!"

The crowd gathers closer as I hand Sonia and Liam the writing pads and markers. "Rules are simple. Warren and I will ask a series of questions and Sonia and Liam will answer, without looking at the other's answer. Points for matching answers."

Warren looks slightly uneasy and the couple don't seem overly confident either. If they are truly compatible, they have nothing to worry about. Part of me hopes they can prove me wrong.

"Ready?" I ask.

Nods in response.

"First question—Where is the perfect place to spend Christmas?" I ask.

The two write, then hold up their answers. Sonia has written "Banks Resort in the Alps." Liam has written "Family cottage on the coast of Florida." They compare answers and Sonia laughs, but it's definitely not a happy sound.

"It's tradition to go skiing for Christmas. I told you about it," she says to Liam, a forced-looking smile on her face as she eyes the crowd.

Liam smiles at her. "Yeah, no the Alps it is. Totally forgot. It's tradition," he says.

A tradition he's going to hate. Liam doesn't enjoy winter sports or being cold for that matter. His move to New York was solely for career advancement. Besides, his own family tradition of Christmas on the beach means a lot to him. Even after the divorce, his parents would get together at the cottage in Florida and put aside their differences long enough to enjoy the holidays as a family for Liam's sake. They always put him first.

Which only solidifies how much they must be against this marriage if they're standing in solidarity on its boycott.

I gesture for Warren to ask the next question and he reluctantly does. "Where will you be headed for a honeymoon?"

They write and reveal. Sonia wrote "Italy." Liam wrote "No time for a honeymoon." Sonia frowns when she twists in her chair to read his response. "No time?"

"We're breaking ground on the resort right after the wedding," he says and I notice his gaze meets Mr. Banks's across the yard. The older man nods his approval, but Sonia doesn't look happy.

"Maybe you can take a honeymoon once all the resorts are built," I interject and both Sonia and Mr. Banks flinch at the plurality I used. Fantastic, so Liam still doesn't know.

It fuels my commitment to the cause. Better to keep the momentum moving. "Next question—How many kids do you want?"

They write and reveal. Liam—"4." Sonia—"1 (maybe)."

Liam frowns. "I thought we both liked the idea of a big family?"

"We do, but liking the idea is one thing. Four kids is a lot of work," she says.

"I was an only child. I don't want that for my kid," Liam says.

Sonia forces an awkward, embarrassed-looking smile as she glances around the yard. "Can we talk about this later?" she mutters to Liam.

He shrugs but doesn't look pleased.

Warren's up with his next question, but he shakes his head and tucks the paper away instead. "I think it's time for more dancing. DJ Scale, play 'Warren's Playlist,'" he calls across the yard.

From the stage, DJ Scale gives Warren a thumbs-up.

I shoot Warren an annoyed look as the music resumes—now nineties rock—and Sonia and Liam head to a quiet corner of the yard to chat...or argue by the looks of the expressions and hand gestures. I watch from a distance, until I feel Warren's hand on my arm, gruffly pulling me aside.

"What was that?" he asks.

I wave a dismissive hand. "It's a popular wedding game. It was just for fun."

Warren eyes me with a look of disappointment. "Fun for who?" He shakes his head and walks away.

I sigh, not thrilled with myself, but certain I'm doing the right thing...for Liam. It was just a few simple questions about important life choices and they disagreed about each one. Best to learn that now, rather than later, right?

The party continues, but the overall mood has shifted. I try to catch Warren's gaze as he resumes his post at the grill, but he avoids me for the rest of the evening.

With Operation Breakup moving a step in the right direction, Warren's attitude should be the least of my worries, but unfortunately, his opinion of me suddenly matters. A lot.

Hours later, the backyard is empty. I stand on a ladder, taking down the lights, while Hailey steadies it for me. I descend and tuck them into a box as she looks at me hesitantly. In a rare occurrence, she's been quiet since the event ended.

"About the game..." she starts.

"I was thinking about it and while it may not have been the most appropriate way to bring it to light, you do have a point. Liam and Sonia haven't been together long and maybe they are rushing things a little." I'll give her that much at least.

Hailey releases a stressed-sounding but appreciative thank-you.

At first, I thought Hailey was just being Hailey, but the more I think about it, the union does feel a little rushed and I know that Liam is making a lot of sacrifices. Some are expected in a relationship. Compromise, and all that, but I can recognize Hailey's point that they feel heavily one-sided—in Sonia's favor. Maybe the game was the only way to get Liam to open his eyes or truly hear the concerns of the people who care about him.

I've been in full support up until now, and my support of whatever he ultimately decides will be unequivocal, but maybe I too need to admit that I'm worried about him and these decisions.

I shove my hands into my pockets and rock back and forth on my heels. "Are you still coming to poker night on Sunday?"

"Am I still invited?"

"Yes."

"Then yes."

My gaze meets Hailey's and not for the first time today a beat of unexpected connection and attraction passes between us—chemistry sizzling below the surface.

And as long as it stays there, we don't have a problem.

TWELVE

HAILEY'S DAILY RULE FOR SUCCESS:
If you're not an expert at something, admit it
and be humble enough to learn.

MUSIC PLAYS OVER THE SOUNDS OF LAUGHTER
and good-natured banter in Warren's man cave. I'm sitting at
his poker table with six athletes, as promised. I'm losing mis-
erably, but I'm having a great time.

More than anything, I'm happy to see Warren again. I'd
hoped that a few days apart would help diminish my attraction to him. But apparently there's some truth to the saying
absence makes the heart grow fonder.

At least on my end.

It's been hard to read him this evening. He's casual and
confident and winning, so naturally he's in a great mood. His
connection with his buddies is obvious and that speaks vol-
umes to who he is—a lot of professional athletes have trouble staying connected once careers end. But he's keeping a

slight distance from me, and his gaze—when it does drift my way—is void of any real intensity.

Had I imagined the connection between us last week?

The last game ends after midnight and everyone gets ready to leave, but Warren sends me a look.

I'm up. Time for my pitch!

I clear my throat and stand. "Hey, before you all leave, I was wondering if I could have just a few minutes of your time."

The players look slightly uneasy—they obviously know what's coming—but Warren says, "Dudes, you took all her money, it's the least you can do."

I send him a grateful smile and he winks at me.

That wink has gone from irritating to cute to completely catching me off guard, and I almost sag in relief at the briefest hint that I hadn't imagined our connection. Not that anything can come of it.

I force a more professional demeanor as I smile around the table. "Who'd like to go first? Maybe we can head into the spare room?" Five minutes with each of them is all I need to glimpse into their individual futures and formulate a pitch that resonates...

Uninterested expressions stare back at me.

A phone chimes and Alan—a kicker for the San Francisco Dolphins—stands. "The wife. Gotta split. Sorry, Hailey. Great to meet you though."

"Oh, um..."

With a fist bump to Warren, he's gone.

Shit. Lost one already.

I glance at Warren and he sends me a look that says "this is as good as it gets."

I repress a sigh as I sit back down. Team pitch it is, then. But how the hell am I going to touch their lifelines this way?

I'd wanted to start getting clients on my own merit and hard work, now's my chance to try.

I clear my throat and start my spiel. "As all of you know, I am a life coach and I'm building my roster of sports clients."

"Who do you coach already?" Jeremy asks.

Should have expected that one. No one wants to be the first to jump on an empty bandwagon. "Well…no one, but I have feelers out there."

Lack of interest all around. I'm crashing and burning. This is the first time I've had to rely on anything but my gift.

Think, Hailey, think! How do I impress these guys? After research, I know more about football and the leagues, but my mind is going blank in this pressure cooker of a moment. I've never had to think on my feet like this before.

My phone vibrates, tucked under my leg on my chair, and I ignore it.

Then Warren kicks me under the table. I shoot him a look and he sends a nod toward the phone. I glance down at it and discreetly open the text from him that reads: Jeremy wants to make a move to Dallas.

My eyes widen. He's tipping me off?

I glance back up and direct my attention to Jeremy. "Hey, Jeremy, are you happy with San Diego?"

He shrugs and nods—not going to give me anything—but I sense it's a lie.

"But could you be happier somewhere else? Maybe a dream team you've aspired to?"

He looks at me like, "How'd you know?" and I push on.

"Loyalty is admirable, but how loyal do you think the team is to you? If you start to slack off next year or get a minor injury—" I nod to the brace on his right elbow "—do you think they'll keep playing you? Put in any effort to get you in top shape?"

He hesitates and folds his arms across his chest. "There's always a rookie to replace me, I get it."

"Then maybe you should explore the options. Go out there

and get what you want before a rookie steals that opportunity, as well."

I've hit my mark. I can see Warren smile from the corner of my eye and I relax a little.

"Moving teams is a delicate thing..." Jeremy says and his large biceps twitch. It's his tell—I noticed it before he folded at each hand of poker.

"So, let's meet and I'll help you strategize. If in the end you don't want to take the risk, no harm done."

He hesitates and I glance at the brace, see a potential opening to touch him. "How about this? Let's arm wrestle and if you win, this discussion is over. If I win, you meet me for a drink."

He relaxes and grins as he eyes me. "You think you could take me?"

No, but I need to touch him to put together a more solidly convincing pitch. I'm surviving—barely—on Warren's tip, but it's not enough. I'll get there, but right now, I need my old standby to seal this one and convince the others to hear me out. "Maybe against your left arm. Worth a shot," I say with an innocent shrug.

A second later, we're seated across from one another as the other men watch with amusement. Eyes locked in silent intimidation, we reach out and join hands.

Our lifelines connect and my visionary powers are activated.

Jeremy sits in the Dallas general manager's office. On the desk in front of him is the best contract of his career. He signs it and the manager hands him his new jersey with the number 17 on the back. He stares at the number with a look of pride.

When I blink back, I've lost the arm wrestle. Obviously. But I have exactly what I need.

"Sorry, Hailey—didn't think I'd let you win, did you?"

Jeremy asks with a "maybe next time" smile as he releases my hand and stands.

"Wouldn't dream of it," I say. I pause as he collects his wallet and car keys from the table. "But, uh, hey Jeremy, it's too bad you don't get to wear your number out there on the field."

He pauses. "What do you mean?"

"Number 17—it's the one you want to wear, right?"

He looks slightly freaked out that I could possibly know that.

"Just sayin' negotiations with another team might allow you to do that."

From the corner of my eye, I see Warren's wide grin and I know I've nailed it. Player numbers are sacred and Jeremy's been wearing one that doesn't sing to his heart for ten years.

I wait.

Jeremy shakes his head as though he can't believe he's agreeing to it. "One drink."

I contain my excitement as I nod professionally. "One drink."

The rest of the players are suitably impressed and I'm able to gain lukewarm commitments from them as they leave. I'll take it. Far better than I'd expected. And it only cost me four hundred dollars in lost poker money. Bargain.

Once everyone is gone, Warren approaches, carrying a large garbage bag. He tosses recyclables into it as he asks, "How did you know about the number thing?"

"I remember seeing it online somewhere that he used to wear that number in high school," I say as I start to help him clean up. It's not a lie. I did my research on these guys and the glimpse just sparked my memory.

"Well, it worked," Warren says.

I stop and give him a warm look. "Thank you," I say with more sincerity than I've ever felt in my life. My gift has guided me to a lucrative, successful career, but I've never had help from another person before. No mentor, no support system… It feels nice.

Warren stops and turns toward me. "No problem," he says gruffly.

We are standing toe-to-toe and looking deep into one another's eyes.

A moment of tension simmers between us and the next we're reaching for one another. Warren grabs my face and his mouth crushes mine with a passionate desperation.

I wrap my arms around his neck and jump, wrapping my legs around his waist. He grabs me and supports my weight with his hands under my ass as he deepens the kiss. My hands tangle in his hair as all the tension and buildup over the last few weeks comes pouring out in the impulsive yet inevitable kiss.

Warren lowers me to the poker table, scattering chips everywhere, and leans over me as we continue to make out. Hands and lips frantic as we kiss as though we can't get enough of one another.

Maybe he's been missing me too this past week.

His hands clutching my waist and his mouth searching mine certainly indicate that this has been a long time coming for him.

My body sparks to life and I raise my hips to connect with his as I slip my tongue between his lips and force his head even closer. I don't want the kiss to end and I can't get close enough to him, can't get deep enough into this embrace.

Warren's hands hold me tight to him, then one drifts to the edge of my tank top. His fingers slip beneath the fabric and goose bumps surface on my skin as he gently tickles along my waistline just below my belly button. His hand slides higher, dragging the fabric upward as he trails along my ribcage.

I can't breathe and all I feel is longing as I pray for his hand to move higher...

But it doesn't.

Fuck, his restraint and respectfulness is even hotter than if he'd ravaged me like a selfish caveman.

He pulls back reluctantly and his gaze burns into mine.

His silent question is met with an enthusiastic, resounding head nod.

Yeah, I fucking want this.

Warren picks me up, and my mouth presses against his again as he blindly, clumsily carries me up the stairs and into his room. We crash against the wall and door frame and I'll probably find bruises in the morning, but I feel nothing but pleasure in the heat of the moment.

We break away from one another, panting for air, as we enter the room and I barely take in the surroundings as he tosses me onto the bed. There could be football-themed bedsheets and I wouldn't care.

He climbs onto the bed next to me as I sit up and lift my hands above my head and nod at his questioning look. His fingers tickle my skin as he lifts the edge of my shirt over my stomach, slowly up over my ribcage, over my breasts and then up over my head.

Static catches my hair and I shake the strands around my shoulders.

His gaze takes in my lacy bra and breasts swelling over the top. The look of appreciation and desire steals my breath.

Warren Mitchell is a player. Making women feel desirable is his thing.

Yet, he's looking at me as if he's never seen breasts before and it's absolutely intoxicating.

Well, if the sight of my bra is blowing his mind...

I reach around and unclasp the bra. I slowly slide it down over one arm, then the other, then let it fall away from my body.

Warren's desire burns in his gaze as I take his hands and place them on my breasts. He moans and the pleasure running through me at his touch is far from expected. I've been touched before…not recently and my body count doesn't exactly make me an expert at intimacy, but I know his touch affects me more than any other ever has.

He massages gently as he moves closer and lowers his head to my neck. He kisses tenderly along my flesh and my entire body reacts. Goose bumps cover every inch of my skin as I cling to his broad shoulders, my fingers digging into him. His five o'clock stubble tickles my skin from my ear to the hollow of my collar bone and I want to feel that sensation on every inch of my body.

"Hailstorm…" he mutters against my skin.

The sound of my nickname on his lips isn't taunting or teasing and for the first time, I don't tell him to stop calling me that.

In fact, I don't want to stop anything he's doing.

I reach for his jeans and unbutton them. Then I push the fabric down over his hips and ass. He stands next to the bed to allow the fabric to fall to the floor; he steps out of them and crawls onto the bed on top of me. He reaches for my jeans and slowly unbuttons them. He lowers his head to my stomach and places several tantalizing kisses below my belly button as he unzips the denim, then roughly yanks it down. I raise my hips to allow him to continue dragging the fabric down my body, then toss it to the floor.

His Adam's apple bobs as he takes in the matching lace thong underwear. My body is vibrating with excitement and anticipation as my legs part.

In his underwear, he falls between my legs and his hands trail the length of my inner thighs. His fingers reach my groin and linger before his hand slips into the front of my underwear.

I arch my back at his touch, feeling myself grow wet.

His gaze burns into mine as he touches the soft spot between my legs and the look reflecting in his eyes has me more on edge than his touch. His finger slides along my clit and folds and I'm already aching and craving him.

I reach down and stroke him through his underwear. He's hard already and I can't believe it's me having this effect on him.

A few weeks ago, we were enemies.

Now lovers?

Seems ridiculously ironic.

He seems to be thinking the same as his expression holds a hint of questioning—like how the hell did we end up here?

I don't want to overthink it and I don't want his overactive mind putting on the rational brakes, so I pull his face down toward mine as I wrap my legs around his waist.

His fingers plunge inside my body as his mouth lands on mine. Hard, demanding, and sensual, he kisses me until I'm breathless and clinging to him for air.

With one hand he removes my underwear.

I'm lying there fully naked, fully exposed but feeling confident and sexy and probably the most unexpectedly…

Safe.

Warren pulls away and removes his underwear. He reaches into a bedside drawer for a condom. He tears it open with his teeth, then slides it on over his long, thick erection.

I take in his sexy, muscular body and I'm filled with anticipation like I've never experienced for a man before. He's physically perfect and slightly intimidating—a man in full.

He returns to the bed and picks me up effortlessly, placing me over him as he lies on his back. He's giving me full control over this. Full power. It's sexy as hell.

Beneath the burning lust, the questioning look is back in his eyes and I'm more than happy to put his mind at ease.

I want this. I want him.

I stare down at him as I grab the headboard with one hand

and, with my other hand pressed against his chest, I lift my body over him and allow him to enter me. He releases a slow breath as though trying to pace the intensity of the sensations.

I ride him slowly, seductively. Up and down, feeling the length of his cock slide all the way in and almost all the way out. I stare down at him and he stares up at me with all the desire any woman could want.

The feelings radiating through me are more than just physical pleasure, which is terrifying and yet makes this feel...right.

This is just physical for him. Protect your heart, Hailey.

Warren grips my hips and takes back some control as he lifts and lowers me over his body. His hard cock plunges deeper and deeper with each stroke.

I'm so close to the edge.

His gaze is locked with mine as he reaches up. I think he's going to fondle my breasts, but instead his hands cup my face and he gazes at me with affection and lust as his orgasm topples over. He moans and his body jerks as the sensations come over him, but he gently strokes my jawline with his thumb as he plunges into my body.

The dichotomy of the rough and gentle. Desperate yet patient. Demanding yet loving is too much.

The first ripple of pleasure sweeps through me...the sensations of an orgasm like I've never experienced before.

I moan in pleasure as my body erupts and trembles. I fall forward and Warren immediately reaches up and wraps his arms around my waist, drawing me against his chest, plunging himself deeper, increasing the erotic sensation within my body.

The tender contradiction tops the list of unexpected actions in this time and space and my heart fills with an emotion that's almost like...

But it can't be.

His breath is warm on the side of my face as he whispers into my ear. "Hailstorm."

I hear the word repeated over and over, but it sounds faraway as I ride out the best orgasm of my life.

He rolls our bodies and pulls me in close, tucking me against his chest, as my heart rate struggles to settle. He kisses my forehead, my cheeks, my nose...

Kisses before sex are foreplay, but kisses like this after sex are the most intoxicatingly dangerous thing in the world.

Might even make a woman fall in love if she's not careful.

Hailey Harris is in my bed.

Not only in my bed, but tucked in close to every curve of my body, leg strewn over mine, head resting on my chest... she's holding my fucking hand. Well, the back of it anyway.

I have no idea how this happened. I have no idea what I'm going to do about it. I've never let a woman stay the night. This is new territory to me. Right now, all I can do is lie here as still as fucking possible and make sure she doesn't wake up and beat the shit out of me for somehow having manipulated this into happening. I have zero delusions that she planned this or will be thrilled about it in the morning.

How I'm feeling is a mystery. Physically, I feel incredible. Best orgasm of my life—not that I'd inflate Hailey's ego with that knowledge. If she ever asks, I'll give it a six. But emotionally, I'm numb. Like that feeling I had after my first professional touchdown or after my first championship win... The kind of numb where your body is in protection mode because the emotions are too much. Self-preservation kicks in to prevent a high with an inevitable crash that could be devastating.

Hailey moans in her sleep and moves even closer. Her body's like a furnace and I run hot, so sweat starts to pool on my lower back, but I don't care. I like the feel of her pressed against me and I wish I could mean that in a sexual way, but it's an odd protective thing…like I think she feels safe enough to be asleep next to me.

Given our history, I didn't think either of us would ever willingly be unconscious and vulnerable next to one another…but oddly enough the temptation to give her a permanent marker mustache is only mildly amusing.

I still chuckle at the image though and she stirs.

I tense and go completely still.

Don't wake up, don't wake up…

I haven't processed all this yet and I'm certainly not ready to talk about it or run for my life.

Her eyes flutter open and she looks sleepily up at me.

I hold my breath and count down the seconds until she loses her ever-loving mind.

Instead, she smiles sleepily as her eyes close again and she snuggles back in.

"A sleepover at Warren Mitchell's house—who would have thought?" she mumbles and something deep in my core tells me I'm a goner.

Who the fuck would have thought?

THIRTEEN

HAILEY'S DAILY RULE FOR SUCCESS:
When life throws an unexpected curveball,
catch it and learn to play the game.

I FEEL THE WARMTH OF EARLY MORNING SUN-
light on my cheeks as it streams in through open blinds. Its effects are slightly blinding as my eyes flutter open.

Sunlight? Did I forget to shut the blackout blinds last night?

Instantly, I'm wide awake. My eyes fly open as I sit up and take in my surroundings.

It wasn't a dream. I'm naked. In Warren Mitchell's bed.

I pull the sheets—not football-themed, and actually soft as silk four hundred thread count—up around myself as I scan the room.

Clothes are strewn on the floor. Warren's and mine. Tangled in a heap of abandon. Much like our actions the night before.

The clock on the bedside table reads: 9:45 a.m. Shit, I missed posting my Monday motivational message to my followers.

I reluctantly turn...

Warren sleeps soundly, one arm draped across his exposed stomach, the other raised above his head on the pillow. Bedsheets are low on his torso, revealing the incredible six-pack and obliques I familiarized myself with intimately the night before. One leg drapes over the side of the bed and his face is pure peaceful slumber.

As if having a woman stay the night is not an issue for him. A common occurrence. It probably is and I can't define my feelings in this moment, but they're a combination of panic and slight disappointment in myself that I slipped into this forbidden territory.

Warren is Liam's best friend. Reason number one why this shouldn't have happened.

I'm trying to sabotage his best friend's wedding. Reason number two.

And now that I've opened myself to Warren, as much as I can at least, I may never recover. Reason number three—the one that has my heart racing the most.

My phone chimes and I roll over to look for it. It's not there.

Right. Not my bedside table. Not my bedroom.

Pulling the sheet with me, I get up slowly and quietly. I don't want to wake him. Maybe I can slip out without him noticing and then avoid him for the rest of my life.

My phone chimes again.

"Shh…" I say as I reach for my jeans on the floor and take my cell phone out of the pocket. The battery is low as I read the string of texts from Sonia:

West Coast Luxury just announced three new resorts in California in the next eighteen months!

So?

Which means we're bumping up our own construction schedule!

Poor Liam…

So, change of plans…

She's typing…

Wedding is this weekend!

What the actual fuck?

In the bed, Warren stirs. He rolls to his side and opens one eye, as though he's afraid to look. He sees me and his expression is conflicted. I mean, I'm feeling the same way, but seeing it on his face makes my gut twist and my heart sink.

Maybe if he'd awoken with a look of bliss and no regrets, I'd feel better.

But there's no time to focus on this now. We have a disaster.

"This isn't good," I say, pacing the room.

Warren gets up, completely naked—sexy abs and other… things on display. I eye him with an overwhelming lust. The sex had been incredible. Maybe we could have another go, since we've already fucked things up anyway…

Focus on the disaster, Hailey!

I avert my eyes as Warren opens a dresser drawer and reaches for underwear. "You weren't complaining last night," he grumbles.

"Not us, you idiot. I mean, that's probably not great either…but this!" I show him the text from Sonia and his face takes on a suitable look of panic.

"This weekend? How the hell are they planning to pull that off?"

His cell phone chimes with a text—the sound coming from

somewhere in the pile of sex blankets. He searches for it, finds it, and I read over his shoulder a text from Liam.

Best man duties start now.

Both of our phones chime simultaneously.

"A ping location for a tuxedo rental shop," Warren says, sounding about as thrilled as someone who's been promised a root canal.

My message is a ping location to a bridal shop with a caption from Sonia that reads:

Meet you there in an hour.

Great, looks like they're calling in the troops—us—to pull a wedding off in a week. Less than a week.

Clutching the bedsheet to my body, I search the room for my clothes. Jeans, sweater, bra... I look around.

Warren reaches under the bed and finds my thong. He holds it up with a sheepish look. "Looking for this?"

I snatch it from him and put it on quickly. I turn away and let the blanket drop as I continue getting dressed. I can feel his gaze on me as I hear him putting on his own clothes.

Should I say something? What? Last night was fun? Last night was the best night of my life? Last night can't happen again?

He clears his throat and I turn slowly in anticipation.

Which of the three will *he* choose?

Our gazes lock and hold.

"Last night was..."

My breath sucks in, in the long silence that follows. He waits as though he wants me to finish the sentence.

I can't. I won't.

"We should go," I say instead, breaking our gaze.

"Yeah," he says sounding relieved.

And I guess I know which way that sentence would have ended.

Inside a posh, lavish wedding shop on Rodeo Drive an hour later, I comb through a rack of dresses as I sip champagne. It's the first thing I've consumed today, so it's making me light-headed and slightly enamored by the wedding attire. After the breakup with Liam I never really gave much thought to marriage. If I hadn't been able to be completely vulnerable with Liam—the one person I'd gone ninety-nine percent of the way with—it was obvious I'd never be able to go all in. So, I put everything into my career, planning to find fulfillment there.

And I certainly never thought much about weddings, but surrounded by all the tulle and lace and intricate beadwork, my mind floods with surrealist fantasies I don't usually entertain.

Sonia is in the dressing room with a dozen different gowns. I can hear her struggling with the fabric and then a series of "no," "nope," "no fucking way" as she gets increasingly annoyed with the choices.

Buying off rack wasn't in her plans. A famous fashion designer in Paris was creating a one-of-a-kind gown for her, but there's no time for that now.

I sip my champagne in front of a three-way mirror and notice I'm a hot mess. More mess than hot. Being summoned across town means I haven't been home yet. Dressed in yesterday's clothes and unshowered after my night with Warren, my hair is slightly wavy from sweat and there are traces of mascara under my eyes. I quickly wipe them away and run my hands through my hair, then secure it into a high messy bun with the hair elastic I keep on hand for emergencies.

Thank God Sonia's been too obsessed with this dress-finding mission to notice my disheveled appearance because I have "one-night stand" written all over me.

I sniff my arm and sure enough, the scent of Warren's cologne lingers on my flesh. I breathe it in again and memories of our night of impulsive passion flood my mind.

It had been unexpected...or rather overdue, but still wrong. His reaction this morning hadn't given me any reason to believe otherwise. Which was good. If he actually wanted more from this thing between us, it would be harder for me to resist. Which I have to. However disappointing.

Sonia finally exits the dressing room, wearing a breathtaking simple silk A-line gown that hugs her figure perfectly. She looks incredible and someday when she's about to marry the *right* man, I hope she gets a chance to wear a dress this perfect.

But right now, I need to focus on making sure *that* day isn't this Saturday.

"You look beautiful," I say honestly. I need to ease into this conversation.

"It's not too much? I mean, we're only having a small wedding now," she says with deep disappointment in her tone as she studies herself critically in the mirror.

I see my in and I take it. "Are you sure you want to do that? Why not wait a while so you can have the wedding of your dreams?"

Sonia seems to think about it as she stares at her reflection.

Maybe this will be easier than I thought.

But I'm not that lucky. "No, I want to do this now. The resort construction schedule is going to be nonstop this fall into early winter and possibly into next year."

They're determined to go through with this rushed wedding based on the Banks Resort build schedule. That, in itself, should be a big red flag.

"This dress is gorgeous and you look stunning. I just want

to make sure you don't regret not getting to wear that Pierre Cargot design you had your heart set on." Appealing to her desire to impress is the only ammunition I have right now.

She pouts. "That's the biggest disappointment in all of this, but I have him designing a beautiful gown for the first resort grand opening instead."

"Perfect. Problem solved," I say and drown the contents of my champagne glass.

Her face suddenly lights up and she swings around to face me. "Hey! I forgot to tell you—I landed a role in a thriller! It's just a small part, but it's a start."

It doesn't escape my notice that Sonia is more excited about the role than her upcoming wedding.

But this is the aspect of her life that I can be genuinely excited about, and I don't want to be a downer in this big moment. "That's fantastic!" I say.

"Because of you. Thank you for everything—sincerely."

I nod and hesitate, but she's cued up the perfect opportunity. "What did Liam say?"

Sonia avoids my eyes in the mirror as she smooths the fabric of the dress over her hips. "I still haven't told him. I will," she says quickly. "After the wedding. We just have so much going on right now."

Excuses.

Sonia knows Liam won't be happy about the life, career, and future she's trying to build in California when he hopes to move back to New York eventually. I want to point out that starting their marriage with a secret like this will set the wrong tone for their future, but I need to approach this carefully. I simply nod, smile supportively, then sip the champagne.

Liam needs to find out soon. The clock is ticking.

"Okay. I think this is the one," Sonia says. "Your turn."

My eyes widen. "What?"

"Your maid of honor dress," she says, climbing down from the platform in front of the three-way mirror and heading toward a rack of dresses.

I follow her. "We're still doing that?"

She sends me a look. "Of course. The plans for our wedding party are the same. I've told my cousins to stop by for their fittings this week. I picked a simple, classic, short—" she lowers her voice "—kinda ugly design that won't show me up."

"Wonderful," I mutter.

"Oh, but not for you! I want you to choose whatever you like. My treat," she says as she continues to peruse the selection.

That's nice of her, but I feel even more guilty letting her pay for a dress I'm hoping to not wear.

"This one is perfect!" she says, taking one from the rack a moment later and holding it out for me to see.

It is perfect. We've only known one another a short time, but Sonia has nailed it. The pale blue, sweetheart neckline, tank-style, floor-length dress she's holding is exactly my style...

"Try it on," she says, not waiting for a reply as she practically forces me into a change room with the dress and shuts the door.

With no other choice, I try it on and the thing looks even better than it did on the hanger. It fits perfectly and accents all my best features. Wedding attire is magical—it makes everyone look and feel like a princess.

But in this scenario, I'm the wicked queen...

I stare at my reflection—the breathtaking gown and the otherwise sexed-up appearance. I touch the soft, delicate fabric and smooth it over my hips.

What would Warren think if he saw me in this?

No.

The wedding can't happen, even if I desperately want to wear this dress to tempt Warren Mitchell into another ill-timed, impulsive, second-night stand.

Inside a formal wear shop, a sales rep fits Liam and me for our tuxedos as we stand on platforms in front of mirrors. Finding a jacket that fit me was a bit of a challenge, so I look ridiculous in the tight forty-six tall coat. The guy tries to tell me it's the style to wear a suit this tight these days.

Maybe for hip, stylish, twenty-year-olds, but I know he's got nothing else in stock.

Liam's cell chimes constantly with texts and emails as another rep tries to mark his pants for hemming.

He looks stressed, tired, and more than a little preoccupied. Which is why I'm not going to bring up my hookup with Hailey. He doesn't need that right now and it's not like it's ever going to happen again. Best to keep it to myself...at least until after the wedding.

Though this wedding is obviously the least of his worries, so why is he feeling this pressure to rush it?

I'm reluctantly starting to agree with Hailey, which is something I'd never in a million years dreamed of happening. And it's not because of the sex last night or my growing attraction to her.

I see now that she has a point. Sonia and Liam are good together, but are they the best option for one another? How could they know after only six months? I like Sonia a lot, but I feel like my best friend may be getting bullied into this marriage...among other things.

Liam types furiously on his cell phone as he yawns. He sways slightly off balance and the poor tailor is forced to steady him. "Sorry," Liam says to the guy, shaking off his exhaustion.

"This new timeline is putting the pressure on, huh?" I ask.

"I haven't slept more than a few hours in three weeks."

"Why not wait on the wedding then?" I don't understand the mad rush. They're together anyway. What will rings and a marriage certificate change?

"I suggested that, but Sonia wants to do this now."

"What do you want?" Doubt anyone's asked him that. Does Sonia know the immense pressure she's putting on him? Does she care? Suddenly, I'm envisioning a life of stress and one-sided compromises for my buddy.

"Does it matter? Happy wife, happy life, right?" Liam says with a wry laugh.

"I don't know about that." My mother had every reason to be happy—money, prestige, etcetera. But she still found a way to drive my father up the wall. Not that he was a saint either.

"I just need to get these resorts underway... Once the actual construction begins, then we can re-evaluate things."

"Go back to New York?" I'd hate to see him go, but I can tell it's where he wants to be. Hailey was right when she said California was not his dream.

Man, I keep saying that phrase far too much. Maybe seeing her naked and holding her while she slept really has impacted how I feel about all of this, but I don't think so. More likely, I was team Sonia in the beginning to irritate Hailey.

Liam shrugs. "Maybe," he says, but it's much more hopeful sounding than the one word implies.

"Does Sonia know about this re-evaluating?" I ask and study his expression in the mirror.

"Yeah." He pauses. "I mean, we discussed it," Liam says, but he avoids my gaze.

Which means Liam voiced his wishes and Sonia continues to ignore them. If my friend goes ahead with this wedding, his days in New York are over. His days of following his own passion and life goals are in his rearview. The Bankses will continue to expand and make plans they'll expect him to carry through—family commitment and all that.

Unfortunately, I have to say it again, Hailey's right. This wedding is a mistake.

FOURTEEN

HAILEY'S DAILY RULE FOR SUCCESS:
As deadlines approach, ensure your push to
the finish line leaves no room for failure.

FIVE DAYS LATER, THE FOUR OF US ARE SEATED
in a booth at Malibu Moon as Sonia crosses items off the
wedding to-do list. Things are coming together easily and
almost…effortlessly. The bride-to-be looks remarkably relaxed and at ease today.

While I'm panicking.

I haven't even had time to think about whatever's going
on with Warren. I mean, I've thought about it. A lot. But
with Sonia demanding my full attention—on flower selection, cake design, music playlist, big day hair, and makeup re-
hearsals—and my own attempts to convince her to postpone
the wedding while pretending to go along with it, I haven't
been able to dedicate any brain power to figuring out what
exactly to do about Warren.

If there is anything to do about Warren.

Across from me, seated next to Liam, he's barely acknowledged me today. I haven't heard from or seen him since the morning after… Obviously, he's chalked it up to a one-night stand and moved on.

Good. That's good.

But he looks so good…dressed in a tight black T-shirt and board shorts. His arms folded on the table, those impressive biceps on full display. He got a haircut yesterday and it looks amazing—obviously in preparation for the wedding. I remember running my hands through his hair and discovering it's much softer than it looks…

Snap out of it, Hailey!

I blink and avert my eyes from the man I'm suddenly obsessing over.

I've got two days! I need to think of something and fast.

Most of the wedding planning is done, so there are few opportunities left to highlight the flaws in this plan. The bridesmaids have secured their ugly attire. The groomsmen's tuxedos are ordered. Sonia picked out the song for her walk down the aisle when she was seven years old, so that's covered.

Think, Hailey, think!

What else could sabotage this wedding?

My eyes light up. "What about stags and stagettes?" Not that I'm sadistic enough to encourage a night of debauchery or anything, but a reminder of their single life might trigger some doubt…

Next to me, Sonia shakes her head. "I don't think we need those." She glances at Liam, who is practically falling asleep at the table. "I doubt this guy can stay awake long enough for a lap dance," she says with a small laugh.

Poor Liam.

I really feel for him. The pressure he's under with the resort deadlines is taking its toll. Dark circles under his eyes and newly formed stress wrinkles on his forehead have me seriously worried about him.

And even more determined. This will be his life if he goes through with this. At least for a while until it all comes crashing down.

"Oh, come on, one last night of freedom," I say persuasively. I glance at Warren for backup on this.

Warren nods, surprising me. "I agree with Hailey."

"You do?" Obviously not with the same intentions.

He nods again, his gaze landing on mine for a beat before he turns back to the couple. "You two are already sacrificing a lot of the things you wanted for the wedding. Sonia, you and Hailey go out and have fun. Liam and I will go out too…and no strippers. Just a basketball game tonight. I have courtside seats."

Even exhausted, Liam can't argue against that temptation. He glances at Sonia. "I'm sure you could use a night out before the big day."

Sonia hesitates, but then turns to me with a smile. "Okay… sure. Why not? But just the two of us and not too late."

Perfect.

"I'll have you home by midnight," I say. Hopefully with a whole new mindset and a cancelation to-do list.

After the sun sets, we hit the town.

Inside Brooks's Bar, the usual hip-hop plays and beautiful people dance and drink. Sonia and I sit in a posh booth in the VIP section of the club—courtesy of a last-minute text to Darren who hooked me up. I pop a bottle of expensive champagne (on the house) and pour two glasses. I hand one to Sonia and extend mine in toast. "To true love and new opportunities!"

We clink glasses and my mind reels.

I got her out. Now what?

I guess I was hoping that when I arrived at the resort to pick her up, she'd miraculously tell me the wedding was off. But she looked happier and more relaxed than she has in days.

Sonia takes in the club and I try to figure out what to say. This is likely my last chance to talk her out of this, without actually talking her out of this.

Manipulating people is a lot trickier than it seems.

Are you sure you want to get married when your career is on the rise? Think of all the movie stars you could bang if you were single?

Probably not.

Married women are likely to age quicker than their single counterparts?

Not Sonia. She'll look radiant forever.

I've got nothing.

"This place is so great," she says, leaning closer to yell above the music. "I take it you know the owner if you were able to secure this VIP experience on short notice?"

I nod as I sip the champagne. "He was a client of mine."

Sonia looks at me in awe. "Did you always know this was what you wanted to do with your life?"

I laugh. "Honestly, growing up I was the most lost teenager ever." The truth slips out unfiltered and slightly unexpected, but I don't get the usual uneasiness I typically do when I overshare.

"That can't be true."

I stare at the liquid in my glass and an unfamiliar sense of wanting to open up to someone overwhelms me, so for the first time in my life, I go with it. "It is. I went to the same high school as Liam and Warren, but I didn't exactly belong. I lived outside the district and my mom worked hard to pay my tuition. She always said our family suffered from a curse and she wanted me to be the one to break the cycle of poverty."

Sonia's expression is thankfully not one of sympathy, but one of respect. "You did it. She must be proud."

"I hope she would be."

She touches my hand gently. "Sorry. I know what that loss feels like."

She lost her mother in a car accident four years ago so this is something we have in common. This unexpected friendship has me severely conflicted and I'm disappointed that it can't actually be something.

"Then, how did...this transformation...happen?" she asks, gesturing to indicate who I am now.

"In high school, I discovered I had..." I pause. Can't be *that* completely vulnerable. "...a knack for helping others reach a goal or potential. Providing support, being that one person that believed in whatever they wanted to achieve or offering advice from an outside perspective."

She smiles. "I'm envisioning a Lucy 'help booth.'"

I laugh. "If only I'd been smart enough to charge for my services back then. Anyway, it just seemed like a natural fit and then the popularity of life coaching made it possible to pursue it as a career."

"But how do you always know how to help people?" She crosses her long legs and settles in with genuine interest. "I mean, I can barely figure out my own life."

"It's easier from the outside looking in I guess." I take a sip of my drink.

"Well, I for one am eternally grateful for your guidance and...friendship?" She looks hopeful.

"And friendship," I say. For now anyway...

Disappointment creeps into my chest. I hadn't even thought of how this whole thing would impact my life. I hadn't believed it would. But first this connection with Warren...now Sonia. Losing both of them at the end of all of this will be tougher than I'd imagined.

Ripple effects. Collateral damage.

A song comes on and Sonia's face lights up. She jumps up

and grabs my arm, spilling my champagne as she drags me to my feet. "I love this song."

"Oh, I'm not a dancer," I protest as I try to resist being pulled toward the dance floor.

She refuses to listen and a second later, I'm surrounded by sweaty bodies moving to the hip-hop beat with nothing left to do but try not to look completely awkward.

Sonia's body moves to the rhythm and I just try to match her.

"There you go, girl," she says as she moves closer and we dance together. Male gazes on us suggest we're causing a bit of a stir, or at least Sonia is, but I find I'm actually having a good time.

There's nothing I can do about the wedding right now, so I give in and have fun. For as long as it lasts...

As the song ends and we fall back into the VIP booth, she pours another round of champagne and hands me the glass. "So...what about your love life?"

I nearly choke on the liquid as I shake my head quickly. "Nonexistent." It's true. The thing with Warren was just a one-time thing. It can't and won't happen again.

"I find that hard to believe. You're beautiful and smart and successful. You must have guys sliding into your DMs all the time."

If I do, I don't notice as I never check my social media DMs precisely for that reason. I shrug. "Relationships aren't a priority. I'm focused on my career," I say simply and honestly. And no one has ever set my heart racing the way Warren does...

Something in Sonia's expression changes slightly. "You think it has to be one or the other?"

She's asking my advice and my gut twists. She's teed it up. Here's the perfect opportunity to put doubt in her mind about getting married while trying to launch her new acting career.

I hesitate.

Come on, Hailey! This is perfect!

My heart and mind are in conflict for a long, torturous beat as I stare at her.

She waits.

I smile and shake my head. "No. I think you could absolutely have it all."

Sonia smiles in relief as she continues to relax and enjoy her champagne, and I realize in that moment that I've chosen to fail my mission.

Operation Breakup is over.

The loud, packed stadium is alive with hometown fans. Jerseys and foam fingers as far as the eye can see. On the court, the home team is on fire and the score is tied with five minutes left in the fourth quarter. Liam and I sit courtside, drinking beer and eating hot dogs as we watch the nail-biting game.

The face-off...their ball... Sanchez dribbles his way down the court, expertly dodging the defense on our team...

I get to my feet.

Block the shot...come on...

He dodges, jumps...and it's blocked by Olivier.

Liam jumps to his feet, spilling his beer, and we high-five one another, chest bump, fist-bump, and celebrate with everyone around us. The crowd goes wild in the stands as the team celebrates on the court. The vibe all around us is electric and for the first time since he's been back, Liam and I are actually enjoying a night out like old times.

As play resumes, we sit back in our seats. My phone chimes with a text, but I ignore it. It's not Hailey. I've assigned her a particular ringtone—the boy band song—and she's honestly the only person I'd be interested in hearing from right now.

I haven't at all since the morning-after scene and usually I'd be breathing a sigh of relief, but I'm not. Instead I'm constantly checking my phone to see if the volume's turned up, resisting the urge to reach out to her about some mundane thing and replaying that final conversation in my mind.

I should have handled things differently. Honestly. But I panicked in the light of day and well, she didn't exactly make it easy for me to say that the night before hadn't meant nothing.

Her lack of communication and the cold shoulder vibe she gave me at Malibu Moon earlier today said she's not wanting a repeat of that night or a discussion about it. But damn, if she didn't look hot in a white tube top and cutoffs...almost as though she were tormenting me.

Somehow Hailey Harris has found a new way to drive me up the wall.

The phone chimes again and Liam sends me a look. "You need to check that?"

"Nope," I say, my eyes locked on the action on the court. I take a swig of beer.

Four minutes left on the clock.

"You hooking up with anyone these days?" he asks casually as he watches the game.

I nearly choke on my drink and sweat pools on my lower back. He can't possibly know. I know Hailey wouldn't tell him... Maybe she told Sonia? Am I being set up here?

Shit.

"Um...no one special." The lie punches me in the gut. Hailey's become surprisingly special to me, but it's the safest answer I can give. If he is testing me, it's my way of reassuring him that the hookup with his ex meant nothing and won't be happening again.

Because of her lack of interest...

"Hey, I uh, wanted to say how cool it is that you and Hailey have put aside your differences for Sonia and I. Means a lot."

I nod, feeling guilty as shit. "She's not so bad." She's fucking incredible actually.

Liam sends me a shocked look. "Did you just say she's not so bad?"

I shrug.

He shakes his head and returns his attention to the court. "Never thought I'd see the day." His tone is slightly off—as though he's not thrilled that Hailey and I are no longer trying to kill one another. My gut tightens, but it must just be my own guilt deflecting.

Liam's cell rings and he immediately takes it out of his pocket. I glance at the caller ID and see "William." I check my watch. It's after ten p.m. "Ignore it. You're off the clock," I say.

Two minutes left in the game and our team has the ball.

Liam looks tempted to follow my advice but then sighs, gets up and moves to take the call, away from the noise.

Is he fucking serious? There's less than two minutes left.

I stare at him moving past the fans seated courtside, pissing everyone off as they try to watch the game.

My friend's in over his head and it's not going to get any better. As opposed as I was initially to whatever scheme Hailey was hatching to try to mess with this wedding, I hope she's succeeding tonight in these final seconds.

The crowd erupts around me and the horn blasts indicating the final buzzer.

I turn back toward the court in time to see that I missed the game-winning basket.

Damn it.

Half an hour later, after dropping an apologetic but distracted Liam back at the hotel, I stare at the fountain near the resort's front entrance, sparkling with neon lights. Impressive, but not what he wants for his career.

As I drive along the streets, my thoughts switch from Liam to Hailey. I wonder how her night out with Sonia is going and resist the urge to crash their evening by driving to Brooks's Bar and joining them. They're definitely having more fun than Liam and I did. It's not even 11:00 p.m. and I'm headed home, as Liam declined drinks, saying he had work to do.

I still haven't read the text messages on my phone—four have come in now—and I know I could be naked with any one of the senders in about eight minutes if I felt so inclined, but I can't get Hailey out of my mind and I don't think casual sex with someone else is going to help this problem. All I'll be thinking about is her and that wouldn't be fair.

I pass a convenience store on my right and my eyes narrow as I see a group of teens hanging out near the back.

Marcus.

I sigh as I slow the Jeep and peer out the window.

He's with his crew and I see empty beer bottles on the ground next to them. They play fight and act rowdy...typical teenager behavior.

Then I see Marcus pull a pipe and small bag out of his pocket. Drugs.

Shit.

I swerve quickly, cutting off traffic on the outside lane as I pull the Jeep to the side of the road. Horns sound and a driver flips me off as they pass. I wave an apology as I climb out. I leave the Jeep running and the door open as I approach the teens.

They turn my way and a couple back away. One calls out, "Hey, Mitchell! What's up, bro?"

I ignore him as I approach Marcus. He looks guilty as shit when he sees me. Then defiance appears on his face. He puffs up slightly, but the edge I feel from him is all show for his friends.

"A word," I say.

"I'm uh, hanging with my friends right now, Coach."

I fight for patience. "We could do this here in front of them. Your call."

"Ooooh. Marcus is in trouble," a voice among the group taunts.

"This dude your daddy?" another teen says.

Marcus shoots his friends a look. "Shut the fuck up."

"Marcus? We doing this here or...?"

He sighs and walks off toward the Jeep. I follow him and my mind races a million miles an hour as I try to recall all the stuff I learned in the sports psychology course about dealing with teenage athletes.

They're hormonal, their frontal lobe hasn't quite developed yet resulting in poor decision making and oh, yeah, they hate to be told what to do.

Fantastic.

"I saw the drugs," I say evenly. Not accusing, just stating a fact.

He shrugs. "They're not mine."

"If they're not yours, don't have them on you. Simple."

He shoves his hands into the pocket of his hoodie and glares at me. "Look, I told you, I'm not using. Why are you riding my ass?"

"Why am I...?" Is this kid for real? Calm breath in and out. The evening with Liam already has me in a shitty mood. I need to cool it. Not take it out on him. Still... "You know, you're right. Why am I riding your ass when you're clearly intent on sabotaging your football career?" Okay, so maybe not exactly cool and calm, but the kid's killing me.

"What career, man?" he asks. "Chances of getting scouted are a million to one." He stares at the ground.

I bend at the knees and move closer to look him in the eyes. "For others—absolutely. Not for you."

Marcus scoffs.

Damn, this kid's refusal to believe in himself is destroying me. I'm desperate to take a softer, more encouraging approach with Marcus—the complete opposite of the intimidating, ultimatum-filled way my father coached my career—but I've been trying that, and I haven't gotten through to him.

I step closer and touch his shoulder.

He shrugs me off. His buddies are watching.

I shove my hands into my pockets. "Destroy the drugs."

His head snaps up. "What?"

"You heard me."

"Coach, this is…"

"I don't want to hear it." My voice is stern and steady, but inside I'm a mess. Marcus isn't going to understand how serious I am about all of this, how serious I want him to be, until he's faced with a choice. "I've been clear about the rules of being on the team."

"I told you I'm not using," he says in frustration. "I'll take a piss test."

I fold my arms and stare at him. "This isn't up for debate. Carrying drugs will land your ass in jail if you're busted and it's only a matter of time until the influence of these jerkoffs you hang out with gets to you."

"This is bullshit," he says.

"Drugs or the team. The choice is yours." My stomach's a mess and my mouth is a desert.

Marcus stares at me defiantly. I've never seen a teen so angry, but I know it's fear and pressure he's under. I want to give him a hug and tell him his life can be better than all of this. But I need to just stand here and hope he makes the right choice for his future.

Fuck this is hard.

"Marcus, let's roll!" one of his friends calls out.

He glances at them and then back to me. He looks conflicted and my heart breaks for the kid because I know in my gut which choice he's going to make.

He hesitates, then moves around me. "Gotta go."

"Marcus…" He knows what this means.

"Tell the team I said good luck with the championships."
Fuck.

He walks away, rejoins his friends, and they take off. And there's not a damn thing I can do but feel like I failed him in some way. I slam a hand onto the hood of the Jeep as I climb back in and drive off.

"As promised, before midnight," I say as Liam opens the resort room door.

"Best. Night. Eva!" Sonia's slurring reveals she's even more far gone than originally assessed. I've kept her from drifting into incoming traffic on the short walk from the club.

"Wow, okay, party girl...you're a mess. Let's get you to bed," Liam says, taking over as we step inside the room. He wraps an arm around Sonia's waist and she immediately turns into him, draping her arms around his neck, and starts to kiss him. Awkward, gropey, and uncoordinated movements as she slobbers all over his face, I assume trying to find his lips.

I look away to give them privacy, this time not out of any sense of jealousy. Strange how a few weeks ago, this sight may have sent me into a tub of ice cream, but now there's no attraction for my ex. Just a real hope that these two can figure out a way to prevent what I'd seen in my glimpse. Liam disentangles from Sonia's attempt to molest him in front of the audience she's obviously forgotten about. "Come on." He starts to lead the way to the bedroom and glances over his shoulder at me. "Just give me a sec."

I nod and wave to Sonia, who blows me a kiss in return.

Inside the bedroom, I see him help Sonia to the bed and she collapses onto it. He takes off her heels, lifts her minidress over her hips, and forces her to sit up as he removes the dress.

She reaches for him as he pulls back the bedsheets and he dodges her attempt to draw him down on top of her.

"In you go."

She pouts as she climbs in. "You never want me anymore."

The sad tone in her voice tugs at my heartstrings.

Liam lifts the bedsheets up over her and leans to kiss her forehead. He stares into her eyes as he says, "I do want you. Bad. But you need sleep. Big day, day after tomorrow."

Liam kisses her cheek, then quietly leaves the room, closing the door behind him. He rejoins me in the seating area. "Thanks for looking out for her."

Speaking of... I open my purse and hand him a bottle of Gatorade and a pack of painkillers. "She's probably going to need this in the morning."

He laughs as he takes them. "Best maid of honor ever."

I shift slightly under his gaze and glance down, before saying, "Well...good night."

"You don't have to go. Have a drink with me?" he says quickly, surprising me.

I don't think it's a great idea. I need to distance myself, allow the wedding to happen and get my own life and career back on track. I've been neglecting so much the past few weeks in my narrow-minded obsession with Operation Breakup. But something in his voice makes me cave. I sense he could use an ear right now and my ultimate goal from the start was looking out for him. The least I can do after trying to sabotage his relationship is be there for him as a friend.

"One drink."

Moments later, we sit on the balcony, glasses of wine in hand. I stare out at the magnificent view of the ocean and lights of the city that stretch out in front of us. "These resorts are incredible. I can see why you accepted the job."

He takes a sip of wine before answering. "That was more for Sonia."

I nod. "I was surprised when you came back. You always talked about designing skyscrapers... Luxury resorts weren't your thing."

"I do miss the city," he says.

"But we do all kinds of things for love, right? Sacrifices. Compromises and all that." Maybe if he can truly embrace this opportunity with the Bankses, it might relieve some of the strain it's having on the relationship. Maybe the outcome could be different.

"Exactly. Yeah. Of course. And I mean it's not forever. The goal is to move back to New York eventually."

Maybe that was his goal...

"What?" Liam asks.

"What what?"

"That silence meant something."

"No it didn't."

Shit. Too quick.

"It absolutely did."

Damn it. The problem with a shared past is that he knows my tells.

I hesitate. What can I say? It's not my place to reveal anything and I realize this "it's none of my business" stance is coming a bit late, but now I'm not worried anything I say or do will mess things up. Never expected this sudden change of heart, but here we are. "I just know Sonia's happy here, that's all."

Liam nods. "Near her family, the ocean, and in the warm weather, I know."

Silence lingers in the air around us.

"Hey, why don't you show me these dance moves of yours?" I say suddenly, surprising him. I need another glimpse. Before I'm completely done meddling, I just want to see if maybe the future has changed. If recent events have made things better or worse. As much as I don't want to interfere, the idea of both of them hurting a year from now still weighs on me.

"What? Now? No." Liam shakes his head adamantly, but I've already put my wineglass down and reached for his.

"Come on. It's my duty as maid of honor to make sure the bride isn't humiliated on her big day," I say taking his glass and setting it aside.

Liam laughs, shakes his head, but I stand and pull him to his feet. "Fine. But I'm still a little rusty."

Our hands meet as he wraps an arm around me. Our life-lines connect and...

A violent bright light and loud blast hits me, knocking me off balance—interspersed with flashes of a glimpse into Liam's future.

Barstool...empty whiskey glasses...

Blinding light piercing through my senses.

Liam, miserable and spiraling, with his cell phone in his hand... staring at an unanswered call.

Loud, ear-shattering screech...

One last blurry image that rocks me to my core.

I pull back quickly, away from him, stumbling off balance as my equilibrium is knocked off course from the effect of the glimpse.

Liam reaches out to steady me, his expression intense as it searches mine. My heart pounds and the mood around us has shifted.

"It's been really great seeing you again, Hails," Liam says, his voice deep and gruff, revealing far more than the actual words do.

Panic fills my chest.

How long was I in there? And what the hell was happening out here? What does *he* think is happening? "Liam..." What? What do I say? Dancing was a bad idea. Very bad idea.

Inside the bedroom, we hear Sonia make a beeline for the toilet, followed by the sound of vomiting. I pull away from him abruptly and I've never been so grateful for the sound of retching. "Maid of honor duty calls," I say, heading toward

Sonia, struggling with my balance from the lingering after-math of a glimpse that now, somehow, involves me.

Shit, shit, shit.

This complete shitstorm I've created is like a tornado of shit spiraling around me.

I'd needed another glimpse.

The only reason I insisted Liam show me his dance skills was for an excuse to connect our lifelines. It wasn't because I wanted to dance with him or have him hold me or look at me the way he did.

Shit.

And what I saw was... Oh shit, shit, shit.

The lingering blinding light and loud blasting effects of having seen myself in Liam's future have me feeling dizzy and nauseated as I walk away from the resort toward the taxi stand.

I'm the reason Liam is heartbroken a year from now.

When our lifelines connected, I'd expected to see Sonia's number on his call display like in the previous glimpse...

Instead, it was mine.

I'd wanted to prevent Liam from making the mistake of a lifetime, but I may have led him into a different one.

I've fucked with fate one too many times.

Thank God Operation Breakup is officially over.

FIFTEEN

HAILEY'S DAILY RULE FOR SUCCESS:
Letting things play out as they will sometimes
leads to unexpected joy.

WITHOUT MARCUS ON THE FIELD, IT'S LIKE THE rest of the team have forgotten how to play. I always knew he was my strongest player, but I didn't realize just how much he carried the team and held everyone together.

Frustrated, I stand at the edge of the football field and fight for patience as play after play gets fumbled.

"Take five!" I yell.

Scouts are coming in two weeks. This year's championship trophy was well within our grasp, and now the whole season is at risk. The others looked up to Marcus. They had confidence in the team because they had confidence in him and his leadership qualities. I'm not sure how to get the team back on track and my own disappointment over cutting Marcus is definitely affecting my ability to coach.

I take a swig of Gatorade from my bottle and rotate my shoulders.

Head in the game. Focus on the kids out on the field.

Easier said than done as I see Hailey crossing the field toward me. She's dressed in a beautiful pale pink sundress that shows off her tan. Remembering her lack of tan lines makes me instantly hard. Her hair is curled and loose around her shoulders and it blows in the light summer breeze. Time stills and the *Notting Hill* soundtrack seems to play as she walks toward me. All I can see is her.

She stops next to me with a slightly nervous expression. "Thought you might need this," she says, extending the tuxedo. In my dazed state, I hadn't even noticed she was carrying it.

"Thanks. Totally forgot about picking it up." The wedding is tomorrow and it appears to be going ahead.

"Thought you might," she says and there's a long awkward beat between us.

Guess we said all we needed to.

I clear my throat. "Tomorrow's the big day."

"Yep."

Man, this is awkward. Tomorrow will be torture. As maid of honor and best man, we're going to be glued at the hip for wedding photos, the walk down the aisle, the wedding party dance... Damn, holding her in my arms again knowing she's totally not into me might kill me.

Maybe I should say something. Put her mind at ease that we're cool, even though I'm totally not. It was just an impulsive...mind-blowing, life-changing, night.

"About the other night..."

Hailey's scanning the field. She frowns and interrupts. "Hey, where's Marcus?"

Okay...so maybe she is cool with not talking about it.

I sigh and lower my voice so the others won't hear. I told

them Marcus had other things going on and needed to take a step back from the team, but I'm sure they could read between the lines. "He was using."

Hailey swings toward me in panicked desperation. "You kicked him off the team?"

"Rules are rules. He was warned." What's *she* so upset about? I'm the one who lost my star player and Marcus is the one who is throwing his entire future away.

How did this become about Hailey Harris? Thought we'd moved beyond that.

"Scouts are coming. This could be his future. He needs this," she says.

I frown. What the hell is her deal? "You don't even know him." She's right. He does need this. But I can't let him play when he's not focused enough on the goal to stay the course and see it through. Fame and fortune will destroy him if he's already giving in to drugs and alcohol as outlets. I hate that he's choosing this path over the one that could change his life, but there's nothing I can do that I haven't already tried.

But Hailey's not giving up. "Warren, please. Trust me. Just give him another chance," she pleads. "Think about what you'd give for another shot."

I don't know why she's so bloody invested in this kid, but she's getting to me. If there was a way, I'd take it. I sigh, place my hands on my hips and stare off at the team for a long moment before turning back to her.

"Look, the rules are simple. Marcus knew them. How will it look to the rest of the team if I let him come back—no questions or punishment?" I need to set the example.

"Make sure there are conditions, but don't write him off just yet."

"What is it to you?" I ask.

She dances from one foot to the other and her genuine concern hits me in the feels. "I just...know what it's like to come from a place of having nothing and wanting a better life and not knowing exactly how to get there. I had my mom...although our time was cut short. Marcus has you." She pauses. "He needs you even if he doesn't realize it yet."

Gut punched.

"I'll think about it," I say and she nods.

Our gazes meet and hold for a long torturous beat as I try to read her mind. The last few weeks have been an emotional roller coaster.

I clear my throat and try again, "So, the thing the other night..."

She looks intrigued about what I'm starting to say, but her cell phone chimes, interrupting the moment. She glances at it, then holds it up. "Sonia. We're headed to the spa."

Right. "Well, have fun relaxing."

She hesitates. "You were saying something..."

I was, but does it really matter? There are far too many reasons why Hailey Harris and I shouldn't be together. I should chalk it up to an experience and learn to move on. After the wedding, there won't be any real opportunity to see her again anyway... I shake my head. "It was nothing."

"Okay," she says and I detect a hint of disappointment in her tone...or maybe it's relief. She walks away and I watch her go. Her passion over the Marcus situation is making me that much more attracted to her, and my own insecurities are ensuring there's not a damn thing I'm going to do about it.

Soft, tranquil piano music plays as Sonia and I lie on massage tables in a dimly lit treatment room. The scent of lemongrass fills my senses and masseuses massage us with hot stones and reflexology techniques. After the painfully awkward meeting with Warren, where I completely chickened out of the conversation about our night together and how we were going to deal with our bridal party duties tomorrow, I'm desperately trying to relax, but Sonia wants to talk.

"I told Liam about the role," she says, her voice slightly muffled with her face down in the hole of the massage table next to me.

A new tension creeps through my body at the mention of Liam. Last night on the deck was weird and my glimpse still has me freaked out and suffering an off balance equilibrium. Now, instead of trying to stop the wedding at all costs, I'm desperate to make sure it happens. Wild turn of events, but here we are. Supporting this new focus, I was hoping Sonia would continue keeping her secret for now, but I had been the one encouraging her to come clean all along. "And?"

"He wasn't exactly thrilled about it. We had a huge fight."

Uh-oh. "He wasn't supportive?"

"The whole Hollywood scene isn't his thing. He likes his privacy and he thinks that's not possible with me involved in acting."

A series of hot stones are placed along my spine and for a second, I'm too blissfully in peace to focus on the conversation.

But Sonia's words are eerily familiar.

"He had a similar issue with my career choice." Maybe Liam needs to be different, more open. Less judgmental about other people's dreams and life goals and more supportive. Sure, right now he's the one making a few sacrifices, but ultimately he's still doing what he loves—designing and building.

"Really?"

"That was one of the main reasons things ended. I had to put my personal life—or a version of it—on display and he wasn't comfortable being part of that." Liam allowed my career choice to come between us and I realize now just how close I'd come to sacrificing it for him... I'm happy now that I didn't.

"Maybe I shouldn't take the part," Sonia says.

"I don't think giving up your own dreams is the right choice. If you do you'll only end up resenting him. Maybe explain it to him..." The masseuse hits a hot spot on my lower back and I moan. "Oh, that feels good."

"He's given up his plans to be here, work for my father. Maybe that was the wrong thing to expect."

"He loves you. He wouldn't have made that decision if it wasn't what he wanted to do," I say. All along I'd been trying to protect Liam, but what about Sonia? She deserves to follow her dreams, as well. Liam is still doing the job he loves, with the woman he loves... Maybe he's the one who needs to compromise—the way he agreed to already—for their relationship.

Maybe the future I saw is on him. Maybe his own inability to support a partner is what leads him there. And I need to take a back seat and watch things unfold, no longer try to prevent it. "And I think he just needs time to come to terms with your acting career, but the minute he sees you on that screen, he'll realize it's exactly where you belong."

"Thanks, Hailey. You've been amazing."

Guilt overpowers my relaxation. I haven't always been. "Of course."

Sonia stops talking and enjoys her massage, but now I can't.

My mind reels as my newfound friendship with Sonia has me wondering where we go from here. Six-month contracts—no more—has always been my motto, my safety net to prevent things from going sideways or people from getting too close. But I don't want to say goodbye to Sonia...

Outside the spa an hour later, Sonia looks refreshed and vibrant as we walk toward the car. I feel less heavy and weighted down, as well. Letting go of Operation Breakup is freeing. I'm still worried about Liam getting hurt, but I'm also worried about Sonia. I still don't think this union is the best thing for either of them, but my plans to sabotage it are done.

"That was just what I needed," Sonia says but her phone chimes with a new email and when she checks it, panic crosses her features.

"What's wrong?"

"It's the wedding favors. They didn't ship until this morning. Expected delivery is in four days," she says. Sonia dials the company number as she paces the parking lot.

I listen to her plead and explain nicely, calmly...then go full-on demanding Bridezilla. "Do you know who I am? Do you know who my father is?" Her tone is shrill and cutting.

Throughout the stress of this entire thing, I've never seen her this way. It's slightly terrifying and makes me glad I've just decided to truly be a friend to her—no more lying or manipulating. I would not want to be on Sonia Banks's bad side.

I intercept and take the phone away. "Let me," I say to Sonia. Then into the phone, "Hi, there...sorry about my friend. She's a little stressed."

"She's an asshole," the female voice on the other end says.

"Well, she was promised a delivery date."

"Subject to change. Says so right on the order."

I fight for patience. "I understand they can't get here today but is there any way they can be delivered by noon tomorrow?" The wedding is at 1:00 p.m. I can receive them at the hotel and get them set up myself. "We'll pay a surcharge... whatever it takes."

"You rich people think money solves everything." The woman scoffs.

"Doesn't it? I mean, I'm sure there are other deliveries you can move around."

"The problem isn't our schedule," the woman says tightly. "It's a big crater in the highway caused by that tremor a few weeks ago. Trucks over a certain weight can't cross until the necessary repairs are made, so they're forced to take an alternate, longer route."

That damn tremor strikes again. Thought we were over its effects.

Yet the minute I shift my thinking about this wedding and my relationship with Sonia...another of its ripples pops up. A shiver dances down my spine despite the sweltering heat. Is fate trying to tell me something? Is ignoring my glimpse the right thing to do?

"Okay, I understand. Thank you." I disconnect the call and hand Sonia her cell phone. "There's nothing they can do."

Sonia presses a hand to her chest as she continues to pace the parking lot. "What are we going to do? We can't have a wedding without favors. What will guests think?"

Personally, I don't think anyone would care. What the hell does anyone do with them anyway? I once found a crumpled origami favor with two mints inside in the bottom of an old purse who knows how long after the wedding.

But Sonia cares.

I stop her and calmly look into her eyes. "Hey, don't stress. Don't undo all the relaxation from today. I'll take care of it."

"What do you mean?"

"I'll make favors." How hard could it be?

Sonia looks doubtful. "Fifty? The wedding is tomorrow."

"Trust me," I say and for the first time, I mean it.

Sitting at my kitchen table at 1:00 a.m., I open a notes app on my cell phone and type in "Best Man Speech." Then I stare at the blinking icon. Other than keeping the rings safe and helping to seat guests tomorrow, this is my only duty, but it's a heavy one.

Public speaking's not my forte and love...

I scoff.

Maybe it's more than that. A few weeks ago, I could have

thrown together some cheesy shit with a few compliments to Sonia—how she makes Liam a better man—yada, yada, yada and a fun, embarrassing anecdote about Liam and be done with it. But now it's hard to write a speech in support of a union that I don't think is the right choice.

It's none of my business, so I just need to cobble together a few heartfelt well-wishes and try not to mess it up.

My cell phone vibrates in my hand and I jump. Then my heart races even faster when I see a text from Hailey that says:

Need your help asap. Get over here.

Three dots...typing, then, Please.

She had me at Need your help.

An hour later, I'm sitting on Hailey's living room floor, making emergency replacement favors for the wedding.

Pale pastel ribbons, tulle, little mesh bags, expensive chocolates, and the tiniest bottles of champagne I've ever seen are laid out all over the floor. My assembled gift bags aren't so pretty, but the prime objective is to get them done.

Hailey sits cross-legged across from me, working at warp speed. She's dressed in baggy jeans and a sweatshirt, her hair piled high on her head and glasses on. I didn't even know she wore glasses, but she looks incredible in them. The whole casual look suits her. Every look suits her.

I'm overdressed in comparison. As soon as the text came in, I showered in record time, doused myself in too much cologne, and then put on khaki pants and a button-down shirt. I hadn't known I'd be sitting on her floor putting chocolates into little bags.

I don't know what I thought I'd be doing. Or what I'd hoped to be doing. She needed me and I was here. So far conversation has been brief—a quick tutorial and then we've been working in silence.

I clear my throat and rack my mind for something to say. "I can't believe you're doing this."

"Liam and Sonia deserve a nice wedding," she says as she ties off a mesh bag with a bow.

I used to think so, but the more time I'm spending with Liam and seeing just how stressed he is, how much he's giving up, I'm not so sure this is the best decision for him. Of course, I'd never say that.

I'd been hoping Hailey would.

"Since when do you support this union?" I ask, reaching for another little champagne bottle and cramming it inside the bag with two chocolates.

She notices and shakes her head. "One white chocolate, one milk chocolate."

I glance at the bag and see two white chocolates. I switch one out and wait for her to answer my question.

She sighs when I continue to stare at her expectantly. "Look, I can admit when I'm wrong. And besides, they're grown adults—they can make their own life choices."

"But isn't your entire career based on helping people make decisions?"

"For their *careers*. I've decided love lives are none of my business."

What about her love life? Where's that at?

We continue to work in silence, but now all I can think about is whether or not she's seeing anyone. Or if there is anyone special in her life… Work seems to be her priority, but oh shit, what if she's bringing a date to the wedding? My invite includes one, but I'd never bring a woman to a wedding—sets up a lot of…expectations and whimsical thoughts.

I clear my throat. "So, um… Are you bringing a plus one?"

She pauses. "Hadn't even really thought about it."

Do I look happy about that?

She studies me. "You?"

"I don't think so." The answer is definitely no, but I'm keeping it open in case she does decide to bring someone and I have to send out an emergency date request text to one of the women on my contact list.

"I'm sure you'll be able to work your way through the bridesmaids by midnight," Hailey says.

Ouch. That gut punch hit harder than it should have.

A few weeks ago, she'd probably be right in the assumption. And maybe I haven't had a come to Jesus moment based on one night of passionate sex with her, but I do feel different... or at least I think I want to be in my approach to relationships.

In my silence, she glances at me. She must see the impact of her words as her expression softens. "Sorry, that was mean."

I shrug. Can't fault her for the truth. After all she's experienced my love 'em and leave 'em approach for herself. Or at least she thinks she has. "My reputation may have warranted the comment."

Our gazes meet and hold and Hailey looks away first. She finishes the final favor and suppresses a yawn. "That's the last of them."

I check my watch as I get to my feet—painfully as the muscles in my legs have seized up from sitting cross-legged. It's almost 3:00 a.m. "I guess I'll see you in...six hours." The wedding prep starts at 9:00 a.m. with the ceremony scheduled for one.

Hailey nods as she walks me to the door. "See you in six hours," she says.

I open the door and go to leave. Then stop, close it again, and turn back to her. "Hey, about the other night..."

We need to address it. I need to address it.

But Hailey waves a dismissive hand. "Don't sweat it. It's not like it meant anything, right?"

Right there, that disappointing sinking feeling in my gut, confirms I was hoping it did. "No?"

Hailey hesitates, but then she shakes her head. "'Course not. And after tomorrow, once Sonia and Liam say 'I do,' I can go back to being nothing more than the woman who ruined your career."

As much as I'd love that, she's become so much more. She's gotten under my skin in a different way. I'm not sure how I feel about it, but not having her around will definitely leave a void. We've been spending so much time together, I'm not sure what I'll do once that ends. But if she's not feeling the same connection...

"Great, yeah," I say awkwardly. "Just wanted to make sure we were both on the same page."

"Absolutely."

She sounds so sure that there's no room for any glimmer of hope on my end. I nod, leave the house, then glance back as I walk away hoping maybe it was all bravado, maybe she's had a change of heart, but she simply closes the door and turns out the interior lights.

Resisting the urge to knock on the door and call bullshit for fear that I'm the one who's full of shit for thinking I have the capability for any kind of follow-through, I climb into my Jeep and drive away.

As I travel down the quiet highway toward home moments later, I see the billboard ad for the life coaching event in two weeks. I stare at the photo of Hailey, illuminated by the street lights, lost in those mesmerizing blue eyes and captivating smile and my gut tightens.

"You cannot be falling for Hailstorm."

SIXTEEN

HAILEY'S DAILY RULE FOR SUCCESS:
It's the final moments of preparation that
mean the most.

LIAM AND SONIA COULDN'T HAVE ASKED FOR A more perfect day for a wedding. Staff finish setting up for the ceremony, positioning chairs in front of the flower arches in the courtyard of the Banks Resort, and soft music plays over the speakers as I scan the preparations from the bridal suite balcony. Dressed in my maid of honor dress, hair and makeup done, I just want this day over with. The last few weeks have been…enlightening. I realized that I need to let this happen so the future I saw for Liam doesn't become a reality. So I'm not the one who destroys his happiness.

I don't have feelings for him anymore and that has never been so clear as it is now, when my feelings for Warren are hitting like a brick to the forehead. He's nothing like I expected and so much more than I'd allowed myself to believe.

Reaching out to him the night before to help with the favors had been a last-ditch attempt to see if maybe the spark between us was something...or could be... But he'd obviously come from a date, and he confirmed that the night between us didn't mean anything.

But then so did I.

After this wedding, we will go back to...what?

I haven't seen him today, but I know he's in the groom suite getting ready with Liam and the other groomsmen. My heart races thinking about seeing him in a tuxedo amid all the love and gooey emotions. I hope he's not a distraction to my main mission—get the vows locked in.

My cell phone chimes and I glance at the selfie of Sonia—looking completely perfect in her wedding dress—with a message that reads:

Photos are done. We're ready to go. I'm getting fucking married!

Yep. Better get fucking married so I can stop sweating and fighting the mild anxiety attack that something will go wrong.

The bridal party is here. The venue is ready. Guests are arriving. Party favors have been placed on the tables. In an hour, I can relax.

I leave the room and knock once at the groom suite next door, before using the key card to enter.

Warren's the only one inside. He paces, his cell phone in his hand. Dressed in his tuxedo pants, white dress shirt, sleeves rolled and buttons undone, he's the most gorgeous, aggravatingly undressed man I've ever seen. I want to scold him for the lack of polish when it's so close to go time, but I'm drooling over the sight of his forearms and chest. Polished is overrated. His dark hair is gelled in a predictably messy look and he obviously forgot the memo to shave, but damn if that lingering stubble isn't the most tempting thing I've ever seen.

He stops when he sees me enter and his gaze sweeps from my face to my strappy stilettos, all the way back. When his heated, lust-filled expression meets mine again, my cheeks flush with heat. So much for the other night not meaning anything.

We are both so full of shit.

"You almost ready?" It sounds anything but the casual, un-fazed tone I was aiming for.

"Yeah," he says though he looks anything but. The confi-dent-bordering-on-egotistical guy I know is nowhere in sight. He looks panicked, slightly green, and sweaty.

"What's wrong?" My heart stops. "Oh my God, did you lose the rings?"

He shoots me a look. "Don't get your hopes up." He reaches into his pocket and produces the wedding bands.

I breathe a genuine sigh of relief. I'd told Sonia they were safer with me, but she insisted we let Warren perform his best man duties. "I told you, I'm not trying to stop this wedding."

Warren's barely listening as he scans his phone again and looks frustrated.

"Seriously, what is it?"

"This best man speech."

My eyes widen. "You actually wrote one? Not just gonna wing it?"

"This is a big deal."

"*I* know that. I just didn't think *you* did."

Warren sighs and grabs his jacket. He slides into it and again I admire how handsome he looks. His tall, muscular frame fills out the jacket and his broad chest and shoulders remind me of how safe I'd felt wrapped in his arms.

"Let's go," he says, heading toward the door.

"Wait. Let's hear it."

"Don't trust me?"

Such a loaded question. With a best man speech or with my heart? The jury's still out on both. "If you're worried about it, it might be good to rehearse in front of an audience."

Warren hesitates then reaches for his cell phone. He opens the speech, takes a deep breath, pauses. "What if it's bad?"

"Better for me to hear it than the bride and groom. Go."

Warren shoots me a look at my bossiness, but clears his throat and starts to read. "Love is fucked up."

My eyes widen, but I wholeheartedly agree with the statement, so I allow him to continue. I need to hear where this is going.

"It has a way of completely turning a person's world upside down, messing up well-laid plans and making its victim reconsider everything they ever thought they knew." He glances up at me then continues. "It has a way of sneaking up, knocking you off guard and tearing through your soul. But it also has a way of healing, of opening a person's eyes to a different future they'd never dared to imagine—one full of unexpected passion in moments of love and in moments of pain. We can live without everything else. But what's a life without love? To the beautiful couple..."

My mouth is agape when he glances up.

"Well?"

"You wrote that?"

He looks worried again. "Is it too much? Too sappy?"

"No! It's...um good. Really good actually." Has me rethinking my Aristotle quotes.

Warren studies me, unconvinced. "You're not just saying that to be nice?"

"When am I ever nice...to you?"

We stare at one another, share a moment. Chemistry sizzles between us along with a lot of unsaid words. But now's not the time...

"You look amazing, by the way," he says, his voice deep and gruff.

Or maybe it is…

I swallow hard as his gaze takes me in. "Are you just saying that to be nice?"

"When am I ever nice…to you?"

We move closer together, our eyes locked on one another. There's a moment when he looks at me and his expression changes. I've started to live for that moment.

Warren reaches for me and I immediately step into his arms. We kiss. Soft, uncertain, hesitant at first, then more passionate. I cling to his suit jacket as he backs me up against a wall and kisses me senseless.

His hands grip my waist, fingers digging into the silky fabric of the dress as his mouth searches mine for answers neither of us are willing to verbalize. Challenging me to either back away or go all in.

I know what I want to do, but I still don't know if this is just a physical thing for Warren. I don't want to be just another conquest to him and I'm not even sure I'm capable of going all in, so keeping the guardrail around my heart is safe…

Yet, my body sinks into him and every inch of our bodies connects as I wrap my arms around his neck and deepen the kiss.

He reaches up and grips my wrists, placing them above my head on the wall as he breaks away to kiss my neck, my chest, my collar bone and down over the swell of my breasts through the fabric of the dress.

I moan as my entire body trembles with a desire for Warren that I've never felt for anyone before.

He reluctantly pulls away far too soon, leaving me far too unsatisfied. He hesitates a beat, before saying, "I've been thinking…what if I don't want to go back to thinking of you as just the woman who ruined my career?"

His burning gaze has my heart pounding even faster than his kisses.

I open my mouth to answer, with no idea what's about to come out, but Warren's cell phone chimes in his pocket. He looks annoyed at the interrupted moment as he reaches for it and takes a step back. He reads a text and tucks it away. "Sonia. Says we're needed in the courtyard."

Disappointed, I nod as we move away from one another. I straighten my dress and a quick glance in the mirror reveals my lipstick has disappeared. I glance at Warren's lips and see traces of it there. I step forward and reach up to wipe it from his mouth. Our gazes are locked on one another—his last question, still unanswered, lingering in the tension-filled air.

He reaches for my hand, holds it for a beat, then slowly releases it. "I'll go get the groom," he says huskily.

I nod again. Somehow, I've lost my voice. More so, I've lost my sense of reason. Warren wants to continue this...whatever this is... It's what I want too, but can I go all in with him?

He heads toward the door and opens it.

I search my mind for something to say...but I've got nothing.

He pauses, sends me a final questioning look before leaving the suite.

As the door closes behind him, air escapes my lungs and, in that moment, I know exactly what I want.

But he's gone.

The sex with Hailey was fantastic, but that kiss was on a whole other level. I've never been so attracted to a woman before. She drives me fucking wild in all ways. Being with her doesn't make sense, but I've let go of trying to reason these feelings I have for her. They are what they are.

Unfortunately, her lack of response moments before has me

regretting voicing how I feel. Maybe I've read things wrong.
Maybe it is just a physical thing for her.

I turn the corner and see Liam pacing the hallway. I take
a deep breath and force thoughts of my crash and burn from
my mind as I approach him. Need to focus on my buddy and
getting him married. Then this whole thing will be over...

"It's go time." I clap my hands and nod in the direction of
the courtyard, forcing enthusiasm into my voice. Whether
this marriage succeeds or not, I'll be there for Liam. Right
now he needs me to stand next to him at the altar and that's
what I'm prepared to do.

But Liam shakes his head. "I'm not ready."

"You forget something in the groom suite?"

"No. I mean I'm not ready to get married."

I walk toward him calmly, but inside I'm freaking out. I'm
not exactly cut out for this. I literally just decided I wanted to
give dating a try...real dating with one woman in particular.

"Take a breath," I tell Liam.

"We've only been together seven months. This is too soon."

You think? I should just agree and help him escape, but I
know that's not what he wants or expects from me right now.
This is simply a cry for help. He wants to be talked off the
ledge. I think fast. "You love her, right?"

"I think so."

Not the most encouraging answer. Is convincing him the
right thing to do? Shit, where's Hailstorm when I need her.
The realization that she's the only one I want to rescue me
from this situation is so telling, I nearly black out. I blink.
Focus on Liam. I need him to relax.

"Not exactly vow material, man," I say teasingly, hoping
to break his intensity.

"I haven't even written my vows."

"What? Liam! The ceremony is about to start." Sweat pools

on my lower back and I tug at the neck of my dress shirt. This is a five-star, luxury resort—where the hell is the ventilation?

Liam nods. "This is what I'm talking about. Last night, I'm sitting there trying to write how I feel about Sonia and I couldn't quite put it into words. And the more I tried to talk about compatibility, the more I realized we're not compatible. And then I tried talking about future goals, and all I could think about was that game at the engagement party..."

"That was just a game."

"But what if Hailey's right? What if I'm giving up my dreams and I end up regretting it? Resenting Sonia?"

I sigh. "Hailey's not right and she admits she was skeptical about the relationship at first, but now even *she's* convinced you two are perfect together." Overstating a little, but I can hear the music playing in the courtyard and time's running out.

Unfortunately Liam looks disappointed. "She is?"

Why the hell is he concerned about Hailey? "Yes."

He seems pensive for a moment, then he seems to calm. "Okay, I just need another minute. Go on out. I'll be there in a few."

I hesitate but check my watch. I'm supposed to be seating guests. I tap him on the shoulder. "You got this," I tell him, then pray he actually does as I head down the hallway.

As I turn the corner, I see Hailey walking toward me. "Where's Liam? The ceremony is about to start," she says.

"He said he'll be out in a minute." Is there time to kiss her again? Does she want that? Our conversation was cut short so I have no idea where I stand with her...and it is torture.

"Is he okay?" she asks.

Right. Focus on getting Liam down the aisle, then figure out where things stand with Hailey. "Fine. Cold feet, that's all."

Apparently, that's not fine. "Cold feet?!"

I know I should be concerned about Liam, but all I can feel right now is relief that she's freaked out not relieved or hopeful.

"Maybe you should talk to him."

She hesitates, checks the time on her cell phone. "Okay... go on out there. Try to delay a few minutes."

"I'm on it," I say.

Hailey heads off to find Liam and I stare after her a moment, an odd foreboding in the pit of my stomach, before heading into the courtyard to try to delay a wedding.

I find Liam outside on the upper balcony overlooking the courtyard. He's leaning on the rail, staring at the guests waiting below. "Hey, you," I say softly, afraid to spook him.

Liam turns and looks relieved to see me. "Everything looks beautiful," he says in an almost trancelike tone. Then his gaze sweeps over me and a look of sincere attraction appears on his face. "So do you."

Uh-oh. That expression is targeted at the wrong woman.

A month ago, I'd have relished the compliment. Started planning my own wedding with him based on the way he was looking at me. The way he *used* to look at me. Now I'm freaked out by it. This can't go sideways.

"Thank you," I say politely, but more importantly, "So does your bride-to-be."

Liam looks conflicted. "How do I know I'm not making a huge mistake, Hails?"

He most likely is, but if he's made it this far, I know a big part of him wants this. He's nervous, he's uncertain, but he wouldn't be here right now if he didn't love Sonia, and whether that love lasts a week or a lifetime, he should continue giving it a chance. I walk toward him. "I guess you don't, but that's what love is, right? Taking a leap of faith, not knowing the outcome, but trusting in the connection you two have."

Liam stares at me. "You and I had a connection once."

"But that was a long time ago."

"Was it? I mean, the other night…"

I shift uncomfortably. "That shouldn't have happened. Nothing happened, really. Just a bit of nostalgia popping up… like a regurgitation of past feelings." I can't possibly make it sound less appealing that.

Unfortunately, Liam reaches for my waist and draws me closer. "Maybe it was the intervention I needed to see that this is a mistake. There's still something between us."

I press my hands against his chest. "I was manipulating you."

He holds tight. "I don't think that's all it was."

"Believe me, it was." I take a deep breath. Time to fess up. As much as I possibly can. I open my mouth…

But suddenly, Liam's is pressed against it, preventing me from voicing any argument. I gape in surprise and he takes it as an opening—literally—to shove his tongue into mine.

I expect the "kiss" to have impact, despite the ill-timed nature and the fact that I've gotten over these feelings for him. But it doesn't. No lingering sentiments of first love coming back to tug at heartstrings. No memories of fiery passionate kisses from our youth to cloud the mind. No sense of longing or fulfillment…

Just guilt and a slight repulsion.

Liam's actually a really bad kisser.

Not the point. Pull it together, Hailey!

I try to push him away, but his grip on me tightens and my panic only increases when I hear the first gasp from a guest below, which ultimately leads to chaos and me running for my life.

SEVENTEEN

HAILEY'S DAILY RULE FOR SUCCESS:
When all else fails, try the truth.

THE EMPTY FOOTBALL FIELD IS ILLUMINATED BY floodlights, and a summer breeze rustling the palm trees is the only sound in the quiet, empty neighborhood. Warren, still in his tuxedo shirt and pants, sits in the bleachers, lost in thought as I approach.

"Hi," I say nervously when he doesn't look at me. I've been walking and thinking all evening—unsure what to do or where to go...until my heart led me here.

He continues to stare off across the field, body leaning forward, hands folded, elbows resting on his knees. He looks deep in thought.

"I know what it looked like..."

He turns toward me. I'd expected anger but not the hurt reflecting in his eyes. It's painful to see, but also a slight relief to know that his feelings are genuine enough to be this upset.

"I just can't believe I actually thought you were being hon-

est when you said you weren't trying to stop the wedding."
He shakes his head as though the disappointment is more at
himself than me.

"Warren, I swear to you, I wasn't." I want to assure him
of that, but more importantly, I want to assure him that his
feelings and trust in me are still valid. That I have changed
in these last few weeks and what we had was real. I know I
need to deal with the Liam and Sonia fiasco and I will—with
them—but right now, I want to fix what's going on with
Warren, with us.

Or what could be us.

"Yet you kissed the groom. Moments after you kissed me,
by the way."

"He kissed me!"

Warren scoffs.

"Oh come on, do you really think I would have kissed
you if I was going to make a last second play for Liam?" That
would be ridiculous. He has to realize that.

"Honestly, Hailey, I've given up trying to figure you out."

Hurtful, but fair.

Over the last few weeks, I've felt the same way about myself numerous times. I take a deep breath. "I'm sorry about
everything." Seems like a good place to start. "I'm just as devastated about what happened as everyone else." I wasn't there
to see the aftermath as I was running for my life, but my heart
aches when I think about what Sonia is going through right
now, how conflicted Liam must be, and how their family
and friends are dealing with it…not to mention Liam's career
prospects with the Bankses moving forward and how this all
impacts the new resort chain.

Warren scoffs again. "I doubt that. Sonia's a mess and her
family are really upset."

"You've spoken to Sonia?" I'd expected him to be at *Liam's*
side throughout the chaos.

"Someone had to clean up the mess after you and Liam both bailed."

"In fairness, I was running for my life…"

Warren shoots me an exasperated look.

"Okay, so I messed everything up! That wasn't my intent." That's a lie. I backtrack. "Okay, at first it was, but not *during* the wedding. Today, I promise you, I was fully on board and just trying to make the day happen." For all our sakes.

Warren peers at me. "Why? What changed?"

"Come on, Warren. You know what changed," I say softly. Everything. Over the last few weeks my feelings for him took such a sudden turn that I hadn't had time to catch up, to process, to fully evaluate things…and then the kiss with him today revealed everything I needed to know. My own feelings had been crystal clear. They still are. I'm ready to take a chance on trusting someone…maybe not with the full version of who I am right away, but in time. Something about this connection with Warren feels different than any other I've ever had—it feels safe and makes me believe that I might actually be able to make that ultimate trust fall.

But Warren swallows hard, then shakes his head. "I don't think I do. Anyway, like you said, what happened between us was nothing."

I want to argue that we both know that's not true, but I can feel the guard he's put back up. His fear and hesitancy has him retaliating and while I'm desperate to break through that wall and reassure him that what was happening between us wasn't nothing—not even close—I know anything I say right now will fall on a closed heart and I deserve that.

The only thing I can do is focus on Sonia and Liam. I swallow my own emotions and repress the urge to reveal my feelings for Warren.

"We need to get them back together."

Warren looks incredulous as his head swivels toward me. "You're still interfering? Haven't you learned anything?"

Apparently not. "I want to make things right."

"*Liam* has to make things right."

Still firmly on team Sonia, got it.

"That's the thing. Liam thinks he's meant to be with me." He's been calling and texting for hours. I'm ignoring him. Just like in my glimpse.

For once, I would have loved to have gotten it wrong!

Warren gets to his feet and throws his hands up. "Oh, for fuck's sake Hailey."

"But *I* know we're not meant to be!"

Warren turns toward me. "A month ago, you felt differently. And news flash—their lives aren't up to you. You think just because celebrities and professionals think your advice is gospel, it gives you the right to mess with everyone how you see fit."

Truth hurts, but okay, I can own that. "I know. I do. I just...um..."

"Just what?"

Warren stares at me expectantly and I summon all the courage I've never been able to muster before. I need to tell him. Everything. The whole messy truth that sounds like something out of a speculative fiction movie. The secret I've kept to myself my entire life...

"I have this thing...a gift," I blurt out.

He frowns. "What are you talking about?"

Here we go. Ultimate trust fall. "I can see into the future when my lifeline connects to another person's. Not my own or anyone I'm close to. I've had it since I was a teenager and it's never been wrong. I saw Liam heartbroken and originally it was because of Sonia—if he went through with this marriage—but now I think it's because of me." There. I said it. The truth is out. I'd thought I'd feel lighter if I ever shared this burdensome secret with someone, but only terror seizes me. I've just completely opened myself up to devastation.

"You're saying you're psychic?" he says it slowly and I know he thinks I'm full of shit.

Who wouldn't? It's the reaction I always knew I'd get if I told someone, but somehow it still aches that he doesn't immediately believe me.

I take a deep breath. "That day at the airport, I saw what would have happened if you'd gone to the tryouts. I saw you get hurt. Really hurt," I say. May as well keep going. I'm in this far already. And maybe if I tell him everything, there might be something he can grasp on to as a glimmer of truth.

Instead, Warren stares at me for a long beat, then shakes his head. "I don't believe this."

"I've never told anyone…besides my neighbor, Mrs. Cranshaw, but she thinks I'm a palm reader, so she doesn't count." I shake my head. Getting off track. "It's how I've built my business."

He raises an eyebrow. "You see into your client's future and that's how you advise them?"

I nod and predictably, understandably, Warren stares at me in disbelief. "And you supposedly saw Liam's future? He's with you?"

I hear the condescending tone, but I expected no less. "No. He was unhappy with Sonia and I intervened, thinking she was going to hurt him, but it turns out it's all my fault."

"Why?"

"I don't love him. I don't want a second chance. I can see his future now—I couldn't when we were together—which means I don't feel that way for him anymore." I do want to keep the focus on the broken couple and give Warren time to process, but I can't resist taking an opportunity to try to make him understand how I feel. I take a step forward and reach out to him. "The connection between us…"

Warren pulls away abruptly. "There is no connection."

"Bullshit."

"Not anymore," he corrects with a resolute tone.

Disappointed, I take a deep breath and nod. He doesn't believe me, naturally, and now he'll never want to be with me.

He stares at me with pain and uncertainty reflecting in his eyes as though unsure whether to be mad at me or pity me. Then he moves past me and leaves me alone in the stands.

I watch him walk away across the field to the parking lot. I collapse onto the bleachers, feeling more desperate, vulnerable, and alone than I ever have and I have no one to blame but myself. I've interfered, meddled in ways I never should have. Warren's right, I do think I have a right to mess with people's lives.

And what impact has that truly had?

An hour later, Brooks's Bar is hopping as the bouncer lets me in the velvet rope, past the disgruntled callouts of twentysomethings who've been waiting in line for hours. Loud hip-hop blasts from the speakers, the heavy, repetitive, discotechnic beat echoing in my chest. I almost wince—it's loud and obnoxious. Strobe lighting is almost dizzying as I bump into people on my way to the bar. Strange looks are sent my way and I know I must seem like a walking disaster in my torn maid of honor dress and messy hair and makeup, but after leaving the football field, I came here almost on autopilot.

Darren stands behind the bar, doing flair work for a stagette. Women are seated on stools across from him, captivated and looking interested in more than his bartender skills. He expertly pours a round of pink shots, not spilling a drop from the shaker, and the ladies applaud the performance.

I butt my way through them to get his attention, and Darren smiles when he sees me. "Hey, Hailey, nice dress."

I glance down at it with disdain. "Just came from a wedding."

The bridal party next to me swoon.

"Which didn't actually happen." I can't help it. It slips out.

The one wearing the bride-to-be sash looks freaked out as her entourage send me dirty looks and rush to reassure her that *her* wedding will be perfect.

Darren shoots me a look and says, "Shots on the house ladies," to make up for my blunder.

The women move away from the bar—me—and Darren turns back to me, concerned. "You good?"

"Not really."

"What can I get you?"

A time machine?

I sigh and fight the intensity of the conflict brewing inside of me. "I needed to talk to you."

He finally notices my disheveled state and immediately puffs up and scans the bar for whoever might have messed with me. His Southern, country bad boy nature means he'd tear the person apart and I feel even worse that he's so caring and protective of me.

Have I always put *his* best interests at the forefront?

"It's not like that," I reassure quickly and he deflates.

He tosses the drink shaker into a sink behind him and nods for me to follow him to the end of the bar, away from the speakers.

"What's up?" he yells over the music, pulling out an earplug.

I stare at it in his hand. "I think I made a mistake."

"You've come to the right place then. Lots of that happening as we speak."

"No, I mean in my guidance, my career advice. This club. Your business."

He frowns. "There's a line about a mile long outside and

those stagette women are overpaying for VIP service, even with the free shots."

"I know. The bar is thriving...but..." I nod toward the earbud. "You're miserable."

He laughs good-naturedly. "I wouldn't say that."

"But this wasn't the bar you wanted."

"The bar I wanted would have been shut down in six months and I would have been slinging hay bales on my family farm for the foreseeable future."

"We don't know that," I say. I mean, market research supported what my glimpse into Darren's future had revealed, but that doesn't mean he couldn't have made it work. With hard work and determination, he could have followed his passion and maybe the bar wouldn't have been this hopping and profitable, but he could have succeeded...on his terms.

He leans his elbows on the bar and levels with me, square in the eye. "Hailey, what's this about?"

"I just think I may not have had your best interests in mind."

"Of course, you did."

"I'm just saying I think we could have at least tried your way..."

In fact, maybe it isn't too late. An idea hits and I move away from the bar. I approach the DJ stand and awkwardly climb up onto the platform.

DJ Scale smiles at me and yells into the mic, "Hey, yo! Hailey Harris in da house!"

The crowd cheers (except for the stagette ladies) and I'm mortified. Not exactly the way I like to look when a spotlight is pointed on me. I give a forced smile and wave, then resume my mission. I lean close to him and move one of his headphones to the side to say, "Can you change the music for me?"

"Name your jam."

I whisper my request in his ear and his expression changes to an odd look as he shakes his head. "I don't think…"

"Please. Just try it."

He glances across the bar at Darren, gives him a questioning look, and Darren nods as though to say, "Do what Hailey wants."

The hip-hop vibe comes to a halt with a deafening sound of screeching vinyl. Followed by a long pause as club goers stop dancing and turn toward the DJ booth.

DJ Scale sighs and shrugs as if to say "your funeral" as he starts the track I requested.

A twangy Shania Twain song comes on—"Any Man of Mine"—it was admittedly the only country song I know and only because it was my mom's favorite. She had this line dance from the video she always did while cleaning the house…

Here goes nothing.

I climb down from the DJ stand and make my way nervously to the wooden dance floor. The strobe lighting has stopped and the houselights have come on. The crowd looks annoyed, confused…amused as they move to the edge of the dance floor.

I'm alone in the middle of it and every fiber of my being wants to flee from the bar with whatever part of my pride I have left, but I've got this far and there's no turning back.

I take a deep breath, put my hands on my hips the way my mom did a million times in our kitchen when she was practicing for her weekly line dancing night with her friends—the only time she ever had fun and let her hair down.

I count the beat and close my eyes, trying to summon the image of her.

I see it. Her smiling face, her foot tapping to the country beat. A lump forms in the back of my throat and tears sting the backs of my eyes.

It's been an overwhelmingly emotional day.

One, two, three, four...

I open my eyes and break into the line dance sequence. I'm awkward and slightly off beat, but I keep going.

The crowd don't know what to think.

I force enthusiasm as I gesture for them to join in. "Jump in when you're ready. On the beat."

No one does. But cell phone cameras come out. Naturally.

"This is fun." I kick my heel and swing toward the bar, slightly off balance. "Darren, get out here!" I say, but it sounds more like a desperate plea for help than an invite to dance.

He hears it too as he jumps over the bar and onto the DJ stand a second later. He grabs the mic and forces a laugh. "Just kidding folks," he says as he hands the mic back to DJ Scale, who sends me a sympathetic look as though I've just committed social suicide.

Immediately the song is cut off and the lights go down. Strobe lights and hip-hop music are back a second later. People stare at me as they reluctantly refill the dance floor. I stand there, in the torn maid of honor dress, helpless and depleted.

I'm a complete and utter train wreck.

I feel Darren's hands on my shoulders leading me to the exit in a foggy daze of psychedelic lighting and bad decisions. Embarrassment hasn't set in yet, I'm too numb for that, but I'm sure it's coming. In waves.

We reach the door and Darren turns me gently toward him. He pulls me in for a hug and I sink into him, resting my head against his chest.

I hadn't realized just how much I needed this hug, this comfort, this supportive gesture, but I cling to him and fight the waves of sadness, guilt, despair, and remorse washing over me.

He pulls back and bends at the knees to look at me. "Everything is always worse in the glow of neon light. Get some sleep, dollface."

He gestures to the bouncer and a second later, he walks me to a taxi waiting near the curb.

I climb in and he leans in to kiss my cheek. "I'm happy, Hailey." He closes the door and the taxi driver turns to me. "Where to?"

Darren might be happy, but what about the rest of my clients?

I hesitate, common sense telling me to go home...

"Forty-eight Pine Street," I say instead.

The taxi pulls up in front of a beautiful, big house in a nice neighborhood twenty minutes later. It's dark and quiet, but the lights are on inside Alice's front office. Through the window, I can see her at her laptop.

"I'll just be a second," I tell the driver.

But as soon as I climb out, he tears off almost before I have time to shut the door.

"Hey!" I yell after him. I hadn't even paid him yet. Was I really that obnoxious recounting the events leading up to this tragic moment in time?

I stare at Alice's house for a beat before heading to the front door. I ring the bell and listen for the sound of footsteps approaching from inside. I glance at the maid of honor dress. Maybe I should have headed home and changed first...or come by in the morning—it's after midnight. Not exactly professional to be crashing in on a former client like this, but it just seems poetic...and justified in my current state of heightened emotion.

Ironically, in this moment, I'm everything I try to help my clients avoid.

A moment later, Alice answers, surprised to see me. "Hailey? What are you doing here?"

Say it quick and be done. "I'm here to tell you, you should write that book of your heart. The sci-fi Western romance.

Do it. I was wrong to tell you to follow the market and write something else."

Alice sighs and looks slightly sheepish. "I did write it. And well, it kinda sucks."

"I'm sure it doesn't," I say quickly. I've gotten into her head, made her doubt herself. "You're a brilliant writer, Alice."

"No really, the book sucks," she says matter-of-factly. "I get it now. What you were trying to say all this time."

"I don't always know what I'm talking about."

"You were right, Hailey. The mystery series sells and readers love it. I just re-signed with the publisher for three more books."

That's wonderful for her, but... "Are you happy?"

Alice looks slightly conflicted by the question. She takes a deep breath before saying, "I'm making money doing what I love. I receive countless emails from fans telling me how my books have impacted their lives, which gives me another layer of fulfillment not many people get in their lifetime. My days consist of imagining new towns and characters and letting them live lives I'll never live and say things I'll never get to say... Can anyone really ask for more than that?"

"That does sound nice." I used to think I made an impact on people's lives too and deep down, I know there's truth in that belief, but right now, I'm only seeing the faults in my actions.

Alice must sense my inner turmoil as she sends me a grateful look. "Sometimes, we don't always know what's the best thing for us." Alice steps forward and gives me a hug. There's a finality to it, closure I can feel even before she says the words "But you were right." She takes a step back. "I'm okay on my own now."

Tears rim my eyes as I force a smile and nod, not trusting my voice to speak. This was the moment we were trying to get to, but now that it's here, I know I'll miss Alice.

She closes the door and I wipe a tear away as I scan the quiet, deserted street.

No taxis in sight, I start to walk.

Light reflects on the surface of the pool as I sit on the edge with my feet in the water. I toy with the tattered hem of the maid of honor dress as I stare at my reflection in the water.

My heart feels heavy and despite the reassurance I received from Darren and Alice an hour ago, years of questioning spiral through my mind.

I'm recalling every client, every piece of advice and every life path I've encouraged people to take over the years. The collateral damage of other people's success has always been a panic attack–inducing thought so I never entertained it.

Now I wonder about the people I've coached.

I see their success on the outside, but what has it cost them personally?

I pick up my phone and scroll through my contact list, which consists of all my former clients. Not because I wanted to keep in touch. Six months and I was out. Unless I needed them to help another client. Networking, that's how success in business works.

But it's just a glorified way of using people, calling in favors from those who will feel compelled to assist.

I scroll through the photos from the past few weeks. Sonia and Liam together at my VIP party, at the engagement party… Sonia and me recording her audition tape, dancing at Brooks's Bar, at the day spa in robes and slippers…

Photos of Warren and me…

One of Warren in my sunglasses, lying on the dollar-shaped floatie, has me laugh-sobbing. That day had been the biggest disaster on all counts and yet it was the best chaotic mess I've ever enjoyed. Being with him, being around him, discovering other layers of him was a wild journey I never thought I'd take.

I put the phone down and close my eyes, but I can't erase the image of his face—the cocky grin, the way he stared at me with desire and lust when we were together in his bed, the way his expression held real emotion earlier in the suite before everything went wrong...

The one that hits hardest is the look of hurt on his face tonight as he broke my heart because I'd broken his.

My feelings for him are undeniable. The last few weeks my entire life has been turned on its head and for the briefest of moments, it felt like I could truly have it all. I thought I could take the leap of faith, but I never should have let my guard down. Falling for Warren was the worst thing I could have done, being vulnerable with him has put my entire existence at risk...

At minimum it's shattered my heart.

Tonight, I'm spiraling, and the deafening silence around me is a reminder of just how alone I've created my world to be.

EIGHTEEN

HAILEY'S DAILY RULE FOR SUCCESS:
Sometimes believing is the hardest act of faith.

I'M LOSING MY SHIRT AT POKER SUNDAY NIGHT, but my mind is just not in the game. It hasn't been in any game all week. I'm letting the team down when they need me most because my focus is not on the field, where it should be.

Unfortunately, Hailey Harris is everywhere I look. The video of the wedding disaster has gone viral. Several guests had captured the kiss and the aftermath on their cell phone, posted it and that Stanley Spencer jerkoff—Hailey's biggest professional rival—made it go viral.

And of course once the media sinks their teeth in...everything in a person's past gets dug up and aired. Like the news article on my cell phone now with a headline that reads: "Not the first time Hailey Harris has messed up someone's life. Ask professional football star Warren Mitchell."

Under the headline is a photo of Hailey and me in cuffs being escorted to the airport security office.

Feels like a lifetime ago…

"Hey, Mitchell, you playing or what?" Jeremy asks, tossing a poker chip at me to get my attention.

"Yeah." I scan the flush in my hand. I fold then hesitate before asking, "Hey, those tryouts a couple years ago for the Rangers… What happened to the quarterback? The front-runner?" The guy was drafted first pick, then seemingly vanished. His media rep confirmed he'd walked away from the deal and the sport.

"The one who replaced you when you bailed?" Jeremy asks.

"Yeah."

Uncomfortable looks are exchanged around the table. No one wants to talk and my gut twists.

"Come on, guys…"

My pulse starts to race at the way they all squirm in their seats.

Finally, Jeremy sighs and sits back in his chair. "Freak accident on the field with the linebacker."

Damien shakes his head. "Last we heard, he was learning to walk again."

Jesus. I instantly feel ill…and a chill spreads throughout my entire body.

Saw you get hurt. Really hurt.

There's no way Hailey could have known. "I don't remember hearing anything about it. They must have released some sort of statement."

"They did, but it was around the same time Cliff…" His voice trails.

I had other things going on, and with my brother's death I hadn't been paying attention.

"It was a tragic, unexpected accident. In this line of work, we all know it can happen to any of us at any time," Jeremy says.

It could have happened to *him*. But it didn't. Realization dawns. Maybe Hailey isn't lying.

Marcus needs this opportunity...

Her words echo eerily in my mind. If she was right about me, maybe she's also right about Marcus.

I climb the stairs to the Kent house first thing the next morning with breakfast and coffee from the deli down the street. I knock and scan the neighborhood as I wait. All night I tossed and turned and flip-flopped about this decision, but I know in my gut I have to try one last time. Marcus is a fantastic player and he just needs someone to support him and believe in him. I'm willing to do that, but I need to know he can commit. If he walks away from this today, I'll let it go. I'll have no other choice.

Maureen answers, surprised to see me. "Hey, Coach."

"Hi, Maureen. Marcus home?"

She nods but frowns. "He said he was off the team."

"That's what I came to talk to him about."

She hesitates, closes the door a little more. "I don't know, Coach. He's got a lot going on right now."

"I know. And believe me, I'm going against my own rules by offering him this opportunity to play next week for the scouts, but the thing is, I believe in Marcus. So very much. More than he does. I know he's great. I know he can do this and it absolutely kills me that *he* doesn't. I can't make his decisions for him, I can't make him play his best out there. He needs to want it..."

"I do." Marcus's voice, coming from the hallway behind her, catches our attention and I look past her at the kid.

For the first time, the chip on his shoulder is gone and he looks like a nervous, scared teenage boy trying to figure out his life when the odds seem stacked against him. The false bravado is gone and there's the faint bruising of a black eye healing. Not the last if he continues on his current path.

His mother turns toward him and her tone is cautious.

"Marcus, I thought we decided playing football wasn't the best thing right now."

She's scared and practical. It's hard for her to dream big for Marcus when life has proven to be difficult and unpredictable and not always handing out dreams.

"I know, Ma...but I really do think I have what it takes," he says.

Finally.

"I was just afraid to take a shot and fail, so I quit before I could mess up. But now... I want to do this. I want to go all in." His voice is stronger as he continues.

I know the pressure on him from all sides is huge and I feel for him. Choosing what he wants over what his friends are pressuring him to do takes courage and guts at that age. Doing the right thing seems impossible.

I tried for years to live up to my father's expectations. Cliff did too and it was the toll it took on my brother that made me realize I needed to live my life, *my* way, for me.

So does Marcus.

"I'm sorry, Coach," he says approaching me. "The other night..."

I nod and struggle with my sense of compassion for the kid and needing to be the strong authority on this. He broke the rules and walked away. This ticket back can't be an easy one.

"I get it. I do. But this offer to play is the last shot." If he messes up this chance again, there's nothing else I can do. This career in professional sports is only going to get more challenging. There will always be doubt or temptations or times he wants to quit or take an easy road, but if he can stay the course, remembering his passion and drive and love of the sport, he could truly thrive where so many fall short.

He steps closer and lowers his head. "I'm sorry I let you down."

I reach out and draw him into my chest. I heave a deep sigh as he hugs me. "Just don't let yourself down. That's what matters."

Clutching my coffee cup, I sit at my desk and stare at the viral video with the caption: "Life Coach Steals Groom at Client's Wedding" with the hashtag #CancelHaileyHarris. The video has gotten over a million views and there's no doubt in my mind who helped it trend.

I sigh as I sip the coffee. My follower count on social media is dwindling and subscribers to my app have plummeted. Ignoring my DMs has never been so important. I'm sure instead of the usual dick-pics, it's flooded with hate mail. This video is far-reaching and destroying my career. No one cares to hear the real story behind the kiss and it's hard to defend myself when my actions hadn't been pure in the beginning.

My goal was to break up a wedding and I succeeded.

And now I'm living with the consequences.

I reach for my cell phone and dial several potential clients. No one answers. Not that I expect them to.

I scroll through my messages and see the last one I sent to Sonia has been received but no reply. She has every right not to speak to me again, but I'm deeply and truly sorry and I miss her.

Consequences.

Deep down, I always knew this gift of mine would be a detriment—it was just a matter of time. What I didn't expect was this devastatingly heartbreaking disappointment as I watch everything I've built come crashing down and everyone I care about turning away.

A knock sounds on the door. I didn't hear the gate buzzer and I'm not expecting anyone, so I'm not surprised to see Amelia standing at the door when I open it.

"Hi, dear," she says, holding a pot of tea. "Thought you could use a friend."

The words bring another rush of tears to my eyes as I step back to let her enter.

A moment later, in the kitchen, she places a mug of tea in front of me, then takes a seat at the table. "Drink."

I sip and grimace as a sour taste and unpleasant smell reach me. "What is it?"

"Don't ask. But it will make you feel better."

"Is it laced with something because I don't think there's enough disgusting tea in the world that could make me feel better right now." My professional reputation is in shambles and my personal life—whatever there was of one—is crumbling.

And Warren… I can't erase the disappointed, hurt expression from my mind. I can't stop thinking about him—about the kiss, about our time together. My chest aches and the feeling in the pit of my stomach keeps growing with each passing day of not hearing from him or seeing him.

I miss him the most.

Amelia sits across from me and touches my hand. "So, you made a mistake…"

"It wasn't just giving a client the wrong advice. This mistake was life altering." While bad professional advice would be devastating enough, this had much further reaching impact. "I broke up a couple."

Amelia shakes her head, her gray curls falling across her thin, frail shoulders. "If they were truly happy, you wouldn't have been successful in breaking them up."

Her words of wisdom don't have the soothing effect I know she intended. She may be right, but deciding on a life together should have been Sonia and Liam's sole decision. I never should have interfered.

I slump in the chair. "I'm a fraud." I've always known it,

but now it's just solidified. There's no way I can continue my career this way. Even if it wasn't slowly being sabotaged by that viral video and my questionable actions, I don't feel in my heart that it's the right thing to do anymore.

"It doesn't matter how you're able to help people, the key is that you do," Amelia says as she nudges my teacup closer and urges me to drink.

I take another god-awful sip and realize maybe this is my penance. "But how many people who took my advice are now unhappy? I mean, even if I was right about Sonia hurting Liam, who was I to interfere?"

"Someone who cared about him."

"Or did I just care about myself? Use the situation to ease my own conscience while I went after what I wanted?" Or thought I wanted—which is even worse.

Amelia sends me a thoughtful look. "We've been neighbors for a long time and all I know is, I see a lot of lost souls going into your office and a lot of optimism walking out."

Her words do make me feel a little better, but I can't tame the spiraling thoughts about the lives I've impacted—directly and indirectly—with my actions.

Amelia extends her hand. "You've always been a positive guide for me."

I hesitate as I stare at her lifeline. "I don't think I should do this anymore."

She reaches for my hand and grasps it. Our lifelines connect and my visionary powers are activated.

Inside Amelia's house, her living room is cold, quiet...

I shiver, feeling an unfamiliar eeriness even through time and space...

Amelia's rocking chair is empty and a pile of unread scripts sits on her desk.

Tears burning my eyes, I squeeze Amelia's hand. "You

know, I think it's time you took that trip to see your son," I say gently.

Amelia nods her understanding and doesn't let go of my hand. This time she holds on tighter. "Will you come with me?"

I swallow the lump in my throat. "Of course."

I may not be confident using my gift to help others anymore, but this is one way I can be there for her—when she needs me, when it matters.

My Jeep pulls up to Hailey's front gate the next day. I lean out the window and hit the buzzer. As I wait, I run a nervous hand through my hair. I have no idea what to say to her. Do I believe she has psychic abilities...no? I don't know. Maybe?

If she did somehow know about the accident at tryouts or whether she just had a bad feeling that day in the airport, either way, she saved my life or at least prevented a life-altering injury.

But what do I say to her? Where exactly do we go from here?

Truth of the matter is that she still broke up a wedding, kissed her ex moments after kissing me, and made me question my own sanity...

Despite that, I can't stop thinking about her. I think about her the minute I wake up and she's the last frustrating thought I have before I drift off into a restless sleep. I don't want to date—I've deleted my hookup contact list—or even spend time with the guys. I long to see her, touch her, be near her annoyingly addictive energy. I miss her smile, her laugh, her taunting banter. I miss our bickering and damn, if I don't desperately want to feel again the way I felt when I kissed her.

That still doesn't help me figure out what the hell I'm going to say to her. Or whether she wants to hear it.

She hurt me, she hurt a lot of people...

But I hurt her too.

With my words and actions and rejection the night of the wedding mess, I pushed her away and while it was an act of self-preservation, I'll deserve it if she decides to protect her heart now.

I wait a few more minutes, but she doesn't answer.

I put the Jeep in Reverse and back out of her driveway. Window down, the warm summer breeze blows through the Jeep as I drive away from the beautiful, rich neighborhood. My heart and mind in conflict.

As I hit the highway, the life coaching billboard comes into view and I see that it's defaced with graffiti that reads: #CancelHaileyHarris. She's been given devil horns and there's a broken heart painted on the sign.

I stare at it and sigh.

Somehow I know that her heart was in the right place throughout all of this, even if her actions caused chaos, and she doesn't deserve to lose everything over one mistake.

Wish I'd come to that conclusion a little sooner.

Amelia's son lives in a beautiful bungalow two hours outside Los Angeles. In the passenger seat of my convertible, Amelia looks like Hollywood royalty—her hair wrapped in a bandana and wide-rimmed sunglasses on. She glances nervously at the house.

"Looks like a nice neighborhood," I say to break the thick silence. We barely spoke on the drive over. I wish there were some way I could offer her the reassurance she needs. Family is complicated—I know that better than anyone—but I hope this reunion goes the way she deserves, because I also know how hollow it feels not to have a family.

When she makes no motion to get out, I climb out and open the door for her. "Okay, time to be brave."

Amelia hesitates, her eyes on the house. She looks older

today, a little frailer, and I know the stress of this visit is weighing on her. But I also know that time's running out to make amends and heal, and if she doesn't do this now, while there's still a chance, she'll regret it.

"What if he won't talk to me?"

"He will."

"I put my career before family for a long time, what if I'm too late?"

"You're not."

"You've seen it?" She looks hopeful.

"I don't need to. He's family. Go. I'll wait right here."

Amelia climbs out and slowly walks up the front steps. She stands in front of the door and I see her shoulders rise and fall in a deep breath.

This has taken a lot of courage, and I know what this means to her to be here right now. Mending fences after years of stubbornness and heartache is a huge step to take and I'm proud of her—no matter what happens.

Her son, Aaron, opens the front door, and his face is full of surprise when he sees her standing there.

I hold my breath and press my sweaty palms against the legs of my pants as I watch and wait for his reaction. If my heart is pounding this hard, I can only imagine how Amelia must be feeling.

Aaron finally smiles, happy to see his mother, and I release a huge relieved breath as he ushers her inside. As she steps in, she glances back toward me and the look on her face is happiness and gratitude like nothing I've ever seen before. Even more radiant than she's ever looked on the silver screen.

It steals my breath for a second as emotions threaten to overwhelm.

Leaning against the vehicle, I wave and smile through my tears. I may not always help people, but today I've truly supported a friend when they needed me and I'll take the win.

NINETEEN

ON THE RESORT ROOM BED, A SUITCASE IS PAR-
tially packed with Liam's clothes.

I duck as a shoe comes flying toward me.

An enraged Sonia alternates between filling the suitcase and throwing things my way. Maybe a Zoom chat apology would have been safer. "Please just let me explain," I say, holding my arms up to prevent injury.

"You acted like my friend," she says, balling up a dress shirt and throwing it into the suitcase. "You agreed to be my maid of honor."

"I tried to decline that," I say and duck as the other shoe narrowly misses my head.

Okay, I deserved that one.

"Doesn't matter, I came to say I'm sorry." She deserves that much and so much more, and after witnessing Amelia reconnecting with her family after such a long time, I needed to do this now. I don't expect forgiveness, but I need to be brave enough to face the music and deal with the consequences.

"You're sorry? For breaking up my engagement? For kissing my fiancé? For lying to my entire family? For allowing me to trust you with my career goals?"

"All of that—yes. Deeply, deeply sorry and also I was so wrong. I'm not in love with Liam and he's not in love with me."

"Really? Tell that to fifty wedding guests who saw you two kiss!" Sonia continues to pace the room. Fuming, she continues to toss clothing into Liam's suitcase. She picks up a bottle of champagne, takes a swig from it, then continues.

"Look, I admit, at first I wasn't so sure that the two of you were meant to be..."

At Sonia's look,

"In hindsight, I realize that wasn't up to me to decide."

Sonia hesitates for a beat, then squares her shoulders. "If Liam loved me, he wouldn't have kissed you on our wedding day."

"He was just freaked out. I'd messed with him. Again, so sorry!" I say quickly when she scans the room, looking for something heavy or sharp to throw next.

Sonia scoffs. "Warren was right about you. You're manipulative and untrustworthy..."

I flinch at the secondhand insult from Warren, but Sonia's not done with the attack. "Living in your mansion with your wealthy clients, playing with people's lives for a living, you have no sense of morality—right and wrong."

"I won't deny that my moral compass can get a little skewed. I just want you to know that I am truly sorry and you are—were—the closest thing to a friend that I've had in a long time."

Sonia looks conflicted for a long moment. Her expression is one of hesitancy and hurt and it gives me the slightest glimmer of hope that somehow we can get past this. I miss her. I miss her friendship. We'd really connected despite my efforts not to get too close. She's a fantastic person, and spending time with her, despite the circumstances, had filled a void in my life that I hadn't wanted to acknowledge—the lack of real human connection. I hate that I messed it all up when for the first time, I'd been willing to let my guard down just enough to risk having a friend.

Sonia sighs, looks like she might for a second concede, but then turns away. "Please leave."

"Sonia."

"Get the hell out, Hailey."

The words are spoken softly but resolutely, leaving no room to argue or hope that there's potential of a future friendship.

Deflated and defeated, with no other option and nothing left to say, I leave the room.

Parents, football fans, and scouts fill the stands for the league championship finals. On the sidelines, my entire body is full of nervous sweat for the athletes out on the field. This game could change their lives.

Adrenaline pumps through me as I remember facing this moment years before—a young, hopeful athlete full of dreams, adrenaline, and ambition. The pressure but also the anticipation, hope and drive fueling my actions.

The opposing team's coach looks just as nervous as I am, and I nod in his direction. He holds up a triumphant fist. This game is different than all the others. Right now, while we are competitors in a season championship game, we are also allies, working together to showcase the talent and athletic ability of these kids we care so much about. It won't matter today the final score or which team walks away hoisting the league trophy. Each player is on display. Each toss, each throw, each catch, each touchdown matters.

Everyone here is rooting for the future of this sport.

The game starts and time passes in an almost blur.

On the field, Marcus shines. His focus, determination, skill is all on point. Passes are caught. Touchdowns are scored. The kid is on fire and I'm so pumped up, I'm practically floating as I run along the sidelines watching one amazing moment after another. The teen has stepped up and brought it when it matters. I can feel the confidence and energy radiating from him that only being given a second shot can evoke. The feeling that it's now or never—time to leave it all out on the field. He is the superstar I knew he always was. He believes it now too.

Everyone on this football field does.

The ball is thrown toward him and he runs with speed I've never seen, dodging players on either side, an unstoppable, unbeatable force as he makes his way toward the end zone...

His movements are concise as he plows through the obstacles that stand in his way.

I hold my breath as I watch, then the crowd around me erupts in the stands as Marcus scores the touchdown of his young career.

I hear his mother cheering the loudest and my heart is full that she's been able to see this moment. Truly enjoy the sacrifices that the family has made and see that her son's talent was worth taking this shot on.

I'm overwhelmed with so many emotions and the only thought that pops into my mind out of nowhere is I wish Hailey was here to see this.

I force the sense of longing away as I glance toward the stands and the scout sends me a nod. It's short, brief, but so full of meaning that I finally feel myself relax. Marcus has a bright, amazing future ahead of him.

On the field, the team rushes to their star quarterback and hoists him up onto their shoulders, celebrating the touchdown, the victory, but more importantly the rare moment of being part of something special. As they pass by, Marcus sends me a grateful look from beneath his football helmet as he raises his arms in the air.

I sit in a booth at Malibu Moon and clutch a coffee cup nervously. On my cell phone, I scroll through the social media hashtag #CancelHaileyHarris. My followers have dropped off even more and those who have stayed are deeply disappointed in my actions. Each comment is more disheartening than the previous one.

Money obviously doesn't buy loyalty.

How many other clients has she manipulated to further her own agenda?

I never believed that was her real hair.

Liam enters the café and looks apprehensive as he approaches the booth. With his hands shoved into his shorts pockets and a reluctant gait, he's not looking forward to this face-to-face any more than I am. I put the phone away and my brain is scrambled on what to say. We haven't spoken since the kiss and the cooldown period hasn't done much to calm my frantic thoughts and conflicted heart. How do I break it to him that I'm not into him, not wanting to rekindle our relationship, that I was just trying to stop him from making a huge mistake?

I can't tell him the truth. I learned that lesson from my confession to Warren. I don't need this secret circulating. If social media was trying to kill my reputation for a kiss, having a secret superpower would have me trending in ways I never want to happen.

But I invited him here this morning to clear the air, so I have to say something...

He sits across from me and we both speak at the same time.

"I'm not in love with you!"

We both stop, stare at one another, and simultaneously slowly relax.

He sits back against the plush seat of the booth and gestures for me to speak first.

I've basically said what I need to, but I should probably elaborate. I take a deep breath. Best to start with an apology. "I'm sorry I meddled in your relationship."

He nods slowly. "Appreciate that, but I'm the one who freaked out and kissed my ex-girlfriend at my wedding."

"So, we're both to blame."

Liam shoots me a look.

"Like 60/40 in your favor," I say.

Liam sighs as he leans forward and folds his hands on the table. "Sonia refuses to talk to me. The front desk at the resort has literally banned me from entering. She won't answer my calls or texts." He looks tired and truly wrecked and my guilt only increases. I thought apologizing and clearing the air would help ease how shitty I feel about all of this, but seeing him this upset makes it worse. He deserved to be happy. Deserves to be happy...

If only...

Nope. No more meddling.

"She wasn't thrilled to see me either," I say. Even if I wanted to keep messing with their relationship, Sonia's not having anything to do with me.

Liam looks surprised. "You saw her? How? Your photo is up at the front desk of all Banks Resorts."

Right, the "do not admit this unhinged person" sign. So-

cial media caught wind of that too and now *that*'s a trending meme. I'm all over the internet these days and not at all
in a good way.

"A hotel staff member was a previous client...he let me in,"
I say in explanation.

"How is she?"

"Angry. She threw things...said things..." I shake my head.
"Doesn't matter. I just feel horrible. If there's any way I can
help you get her back..."

Liam shakes his head quickly. "I think you've done enough."

Right.

"The thing is, Hails. While this whole thing was a disaster, I think it made us both realize that we aren't quite ready
to get married."

Not a shocking revelation.

Liam runs a hand through his hair. "I want New York
and skyscrapers. Sonia wants the glitz and glamour of Hollywood."

"Right, but I thought your relationship was about compromise. You'd do this now—for her family and for her to
pursue a career in acting—then you'd re-evaluate and maybe
move back to New York in a few years. Balance in the relationship—you both emphasized how important that was. I
think maybe this...hiccup...has just made you two doubt the
strength of your commitment to that plan. To each other."
Doubts were natural, especially after such a setback, but they
couldn't throw it all away, could they?

My heart sinks at the thought. If they could after such a
strong connection, what hope do Warren and I have of finding a way back?

"We did say all that," Liam says with a nod, "but I think we
were just saying what the other person wanted to hear because
we were dedicated to making things work. But deep down,

we were both making compromises we really weren't ready to make. We love one another, but maybe not enough…"

"Wow."

"And a small part of me wanted to prove to my dad that I was confident in this decision…" He pauses and shakes his head. "Make some point or something. Apparently, the effects of childhood divorce include wanting to show my parents how relationships were *supposed* to work, but that's not something I should take on."

I nod and take a deep breath. It sounds like he's done some soul-searching about all of this and reached a conclusion that makes sense. "So, what now?"

"I'm hoping to try long distance…if she ever speaks to me again, and see how it goes."

"I hope she wants that too." Though the reality of the situation is that they've decided to pursue career over love and eventually the connection they have now will either strengthen or weaken. But their future is their business and I absolutely will not touch Liam's lifeline to warn him of what's to come.

Life is meant to be a surprise.

Liam smiles at me gently, then checks his watch as he gets to his feet. "Hate to cut this short, but I have a plane to catch for a job interview in New York."

I stand and we hug quickly from across the booth. A table between us, which feels like an appropriate metaphor for the distance between us now. There's no going back to what we were before. This has changed things. Too much history now to ever be friends.

"It was great seeing you again," he says.

I laugh.

"Okay, not really, but it was an…adventure as always."

I nod, feeling the slight sting of it. "Have a safe flight."

He nods and gives a small wave as he walks away.

I watch as my ex leaves the café and feel the closure I'd always sought wrap around me. Liam will be fine. Sonia will be fine.

Will I be fine?

The departures drop-off point at LAX is busy with travelers and taxi cabs as I put my Jeep in Park and turn to Liam. "Here you go."

"Thanks for the ride," he says gratefully.

We climb out and I take Liam's suitcase out of the back and set it down on the curb. We fist-bump and share a manly hug.

"Don't be a stranger, okay?" I know he needs to do this, but I'll miss having my best friend around. Over the years we'd lost touch, but spending time reconnecting these past few weeks has made me realize how much I value his friendship.

Though, I wonder how he'd feel if he knew I'd fallen for his ex.

Doesn't matter since it's over now. No sense telling him that the girl I'd always thought of as the Antichrist is actually the only woman in the world who has me feeling some type of way and without her, I'm feeling really lost.

He said he was meeting with Hailey this morning at the café before heading to the airport. I assume they finally discussed the kiss and what that means for them. I haven't had the guts to ask if they are rekindling the old spark. I don't think I could handle hearing it. But he seemed lighter, happier when I picked him up, so I can only assume the conversation went well. Not sure how the two of them together will affect our friendship moving forward. I'd be lying if I said I could be around them.

Fuck, if they ever got married, there'd be no best man speech from me.

My chest is tight and it feels even tighter when he says, "I'll be back more often now."

My mouth is dry. "To see Hailey?"

Liam looks confused. "No. To try to make things work with Sonia."

Sonia? She's still in the picture? The last time I saw her, she was singing "Roar" by Katy Perry, burning photos of her and Liam in an illegal bonfire on the beach outside the resort. "I thought you two had called it quits."

"We talked this afternoon when I picked up my things at the resort and she reluctantly agreed to try a no-pressure, long-distance thing. But I'll be honest man, I miss her already."

The tightness in my chest eases significantly.

"So, you and Hailey aren't...?"

Still doesn't mean he'll be cool with *me* dating his ex.

Liam sends me a knowing look. "That Hailstorm really dented your heart, huh?"

I shake my head quickly and scoff. "Don't know what you're talking about." Denial was the only way to deal with this one.

"Bullshit someone else, man. I saw you two. And I've never seen you like that around a woman before."

Shit. He's right. Best friends since childhood can call your bullshit like no one else can. I shrug and desperately try to sound unfazed. "It was just a forced proximity thing. That was never going to work."

"I wouldn't be so sure about that. Go easy on her." Liam taps my shoulder. "This wasn't her fault."

"That's generous of you."

"She had good intentions. She's a good person, Warren."

Hailey was the first woman I ever let get close and it backfired. Besides, I still don't know what to do about her revelation. How do you enter into a relationship with someone who claims to be psychic without trusting and supporting them in their claim? I can't say I fully believe it, but at the same time, I believe in her enough to know that she believes she possesses this ability. I'm at a standstill and have no idea how to move forward.

As if shit wasn't complicated enough.

I check my watch and punch Liam softly in the shoulder. "You better go."

"See ya, man," Liam says. He picks up his suitcase and heads toward the door.

As he enters the airport, I run a hand through my hair and ponder next steps. I have his blessing to pursue something with Hailey, but can I take that risk? Put it all on the line again? Go all in with her and see if this connection neither of us expected is real?

Another disappointment—if she rejects me or if we give it a shot and things don't work out—could be absolutely devastating.

But I'm not sure anything could be worse than this lovesickness that doesn't seem to have a cure.

TWENTY

HAILEY'S DAILY RULE FOR SUCCESS:
In the face of adversity, we can choose to run or
we can choose to fight—the right choice depends on
the height of our heels.

ON MY LAPTOP SCREEN IS THE SCHEDULE FOR the life coaching conference tomorrow. Miraculously, they haven't canceled my appearance—just a strongly worded email from organizers saying they'll be *monitoring* the situation closely and advising that I provide my own security detail if I feel unsafe.

I can't go now. And not because I'm afraid of a few angry, judgmental former fans. No one wants to hear what I have to say and I'll only draw a crowd because of the controversy. All my pre-confirmed meetings have canceled so there's really no point in attending.

I sigh and start to write an email withdrawing—

The gate buzzer sounds and I frown. I'm not expecting anyone. For a brief moment, my hopes rise—Warren?

I quickly fix my hair as I hit the intercom button. "Hello?"

Only static on the other end. It's still broken and I haven't had time to get it fixed. I hesitate for a second—what if it's some dangerous follower? Then I'll at least have someone to hear my side of the story.

Instead, it's Sonia standing on the front step when I open the door. She looks refreshed and well in a pair of flowing white pants and matching tank top and her expression is far more relaxed than our last encounter.

Still, I scan her for any sign of weapons.

All clear.

"Hi... Come on in." I step back to let her enter.

Sonia shakes her head. "I can't stay...late-night movie shoot."

"Right. I read the piece in *Variety*—again, congrats." She's really doing it, and the indie thriller is getting a lot of buzz already. She may only be playing a secondary character but given her status as a Banks, the movie press is highly focused on her acting debut. It will do wonders for future roles.

"Thanks," she says. "I just wanted to stop by and say that while what you did was shitty, you weren't exactly entirely wrong."

"I appreciate your forgiveness, but—"

Sonia holds up a hand. "I didn't say I forgive you." But a hint of a smile plays on her lips. "But you did help Liam and I realize that we need to figure out what we want in our own lives before we move forward together."

It's what he said too. I wish I could take solace in the fact that they do genuinely seem happier now not having gone ahead with the wedding, but unfortunately, this whole thing has illuminated so many flaws in my own character, the error of my judgment, that it's hard to feel any kind of victory in how this has played out.

Sonia glances at her watch. "Anyway, I have to go but I

also wanted to say thank you, for your unorthodox way of putting me on the right path...for me."

I nod, unsure what to say as I watch Sonia head back to her car. I know the likelihood of us being friends is next to none, and deep disappointment fills my chest. I enjoyed getting to know her. Strong female friendships have always eluded me and for a while, it had felt nice. But my situation hasn't changed and if the disaster of confessing my secret to Warren is any indication, I can't be truly vulnerable with a friend, so it's best I continue on my solitary path. But I am happy that I was able to get Sonia one step closer to her dream. I'll be cheering her on as her number one fan from afar.

Back in my office a moment later, I sit at my computer. I stare at the email I'm about to send canceling my appearance. It's the right thing to do. What value can I offer attendees now? No one trusts me anymore. No one believes in my value as a coach. Everything I had planned to say was just empty industry lingo—a sales pitch to draw new clients...

My gaze lands on my client pride shelf.

Alice's bestsellers, Frost God's Top Bakery awards, photos of Darren and me at the Brooks's Bar opening...

All of those people put their faith in me. Had I made their lives perfect? No. But I had helped them get to a place they wanted to go. And I'd done it from a place of sincerity and genuine interest in helping others succeed. I had to build that trust and reputation. It might be harder now, but I've always preached the value of hard work and commitment...

With the same focus and principles guiding my own actions this time, maybe I can do it again.

I delete the email.

Standing, I pick up the framed posters that are still propped against the office wall—"Hailey Harris—Top 30 Under Thirty," "Life Coach to the Stars"—and start to hang them back up.

I may have hit a roadblock, but these images aren't a lie. They are who I am—for better or worse—and I need to strive harder to live up to this successful version of myself staring back at me.

I lie in bed and stare at the ceiling. Since dropping Liam off at the airport, memories of the last few weeks have been flooding my mind. With his blessing and the knowledge that he and Hailey aren't planning to reconnect their relationship, I'm even more conflicted as to what to do.

It's been over a week since I pushed her away. I'm not even sure where her heart is right now. Putting myself out there and having her reject me would be even harder to come back from, but I'm not sure I have a choice.

I miss her. Everything about her. Even the bickering.

My pillow still holds the lingering scent of her, but it will be gone soon and there will be nothing left...

Reaching for my cell phone on the bedside table, I open her social media and see the hashtag #CancelHaileyHarris is still trending. The life coaching event is tomorrow.

Will she still attend?

Realization dawns and I quickly get out of bed. As I pull on my jeans and hoodie, I dial Marcus's cell.

Two rings then, "Hey, Coach, what's up?"

"I need you to meet me somewhere."

"Text me the location ping."

Twenty minutes later, Marcus and I stand at the base of the highway billboard with my ladder and cleaning supplies.

He eyes the height and shakes his head. "Thought you hated this chick."

"She's grown on me." Understatement.

"Enough to climb up there and risk breaking your neck?" Marcus scans the dark, empty street nervously, looking for signs of authority.

Enough for that and so much more.

"Hold the ladder and then toss me the supplies."

"Can't believe you dragged my ass into this. What happened to 'head down, nose clean, guilty by association'?" he asks, throwing my own words back at me with a hint of sarcasm.

I see the irony now—calling Hailey out for meddling in people's lives when I'd constantly interfered in Marcus's, even though it was from a place of genuine caring.

"Just hold the ladder, smartass." I climb the rungs, then catch the supplies as Marcus chucks them up to me. Then I climb the scaffolding to the top of the billboard. It's a hell of a lot higher than it looks and the wind is fierce at this height. I glance toward the ground and feel slightly nauseated.

Don't look down.

Instead, I stare at Hailey's face, larger than life, and my heart races as I start to clean away the graffiti.

Whether or not she's telling the truth about her gift, her impact on the lives of so many people means she deserves more respect than the public is giving her right now. And whether or not this gift of hers saved my life...or helped me see a way through to giving Marcus a second chance, she ultimately did both and how can I not love her for that?

Love?

The thought literally throws me off balance and I slip over the wet edge of the platform. "Whoa." My body starts to freefall and I grip the metal of the scaffolding in the nick of time, then I'm left dangling a hundred feet off the ground.

"Coach! You good?" Marcus calls from below.

No I'm not good. I'm falling in love and it nearly cost me my life.

Flashing police lights and a siren cut through the night air and I close my eyes as the squad car puts its headlights on me.

Fantastic.

"Hey! What are you doing up there?" the officer calls up to me.

"We were just cleaning the graffiti from the billboard," I hear Marcus explain.

I pull myself up and over the platform and then work my way carefully down the scaffolding and the ladder to the officer. "What the kid said," I say holding up the cleaning supplies.

The stern-looking thirtysomething officer whose nametag reads: "Perkins" glances up at the partially clean billboard and nods. "Get back to work then."

I must look surprised because his face breaks into a grin as he leans on the hood of his squad car. "Hailey Harris helped my brother start his own IT consultancy firm a year ago when he was struggling to find work with a new wife and baby on the way."

Ah.

"Didn't charge him a dime."

Another one of her private success stories. I'm willing to bet there's many more.

"She doesn't deserve the bad press she's getting. Anyone who studies body language for a living could see it was the groom's fault on that viral video."

I frown, intrigued. "Yeah? How?"

"The way he leaned in and there's a hesitancy in her that indicates she was surprised and if you watch real closely, she never actually returns the kiss."

Maybe I need to take a closer look at that video.

"You know her?" Officer Perkins asks.

"Coach was hot for her back in the day, but then she destroyed his football career, but now he's hot for her again," Marcus says, filling the guy in.

I shoot him a look then sigh. "What the kid said."

Officer Perkins laughs as he climbs back into the squad

car. "I'll stay and leave the lights on. Make sure no one else busts you."

"Appreciate that," I say as I climb back up to the top of the billboard. I stare at her face as I work, the undeniable feelings of love in my chest only amplifying.

Hailey Fucking Harris has struck again.

The event room in the West Beverly Hotel is already packed with people attending the life coaching conference. Exhibitor booths are positioned along the edge of the room—coaches and influencers showcasing their successes and meeting one-on-one with potential clients. In the center of the room, chairs face a main stage where the presentations and panels are set to take place. There's an electric vibe in the air as upbeat, motivational music plays.

I see a lot of familiar faces. Life coaches I've followed throughout the years and social media influencers that I recognize from TikTok. There's a lot of energy in the room and despite the pitfalls that can accompany this career, I know a lot of lives will be impacted today. I truly believe that.

I check the time on the wall and take a deep breath as I cross the room, then head held high, I make my way to the stage.

Coming today was the right decision, but my heart is pounding and I feel the judgment and hear the whispers. I need to drown out the noise and focus on why I'm here. Four weeks ago, I was coming to impart knowledge, sell myself, and grow my follower and client list. Now I'm desperate and clinging to my last shreds of hope that I can rebuild my own business, my own future, in the face of adversity and public scrutiny.

I've never felt this struggle for self-confidence—at least not since I was a dorky teenage high school mascot, desperate to fit in. Desperate for people to see me and accept me and let me be me.

Strange being back in these feelings, but they were the last time I felt true drive and determination to discover who I am. I had to be accepting of myself, then others followed.

I hope it works the same way now.

My palms sweat as I sit on the panel with Spencer Stanley moments later. He's dressed in a slim-fit charcoal suit and electric-blue dress shirt—power colors. Confidence and charisma ooze from him and I can understand why so many clients choose to work with him. As much as he's had a part in dismantling my reputation, he does have an energy about him that draws people. He turns toward me. "Gotta say, Harris, I'm surprised you're here."

I've been in competition with Spencer. In the sports world he was always two steps ahead and that bothered me, but not anymore. "I'm looking forward to hearing how you approach your business," I say sincerely. "I think I have a lot to learn still."

He was obviously expecting a more arrogant Hailey. That Hailey is gone. Humbled, respectful, grateful Hailey is the only Hailey I've got going for me anymore. The only one I care to be.

His expression takes on an unexpected look of respect as he nods. "You've got balls, Harris. You'll be okay."

The words cause unexpected tears to spring to my eyes and I swallow hard and blink them away quickly as the panel organizer joins us onstage and starts the session.

I stare out into the crowd of faces as people take their seats. Most seem untrusting and critical, the way I expected, but I take several deep breaths in and out and prepare for anything that comes my way.

Questions from the audience come in—all for Spencer. With each one, I realize that I'd been prepared for an attack—

for personal questions and for the crowd to want to drive the wound deeper with the same insults I've been receiving online. I hadn't been prepared for this—being completely irrelevant and ignored.

This is definitely worse.

No one wants to hear anything I have to say. Not my life coaching advice or my excuses.

I sit back in the chair and focus on the knowledge Spencer is imparting on the crowd. He's smart and successful for a reason. My jealousy and competition with him had always clouded how I saw him and his message. But he's doing good things for a lot of people and I'm suddenly appreciating the value of what that means.

A reporter from *Media Mag* stands and addresses me. "This one is for Hailey."

I sit straighter and force a smile. Here we go.

"Is it true that you learn personal information about your clients to use it to your own advantage?"

I was expecting to be called out, but it's still hard to calm my racing pulse and think through my response rationally. Honesty. Complete, transparent honesty is the only way to get through this.

"No. Not at all," I say.

"You didn't get close to Sonia Banks to steal her fiancé?"

"That was a big misunderstanding." Simple, honest answers.

"The kiss looked pretty straightforward," the reporter says.

Murmurs throughout the crowd as judgmental eyes stare at me.

I take a deep breath. "The kiss that went viral was the result of bad decisions and..." I stammer when I see the doors open and Warren enters. I blink, not expecting to see him here. My heart races even more. This public embarrassment was bad enough. Explaining myself to a room full of strangers in an attempt to rebuild my career was one thing. Having the man I'm in love with witness this moment is just torture.

We haven't seen or spoken to one another in over a week and I'd given up hope that there's any chance for us.

Yet here he is...

"Hailey, you were saying..." the panel organizer prompts.

Right. I swallow hard and try to remember where my train of thought was going. "I...uh..."

"You were about to make excuses for your actions," the *Media Mag* reporter says smugly.

No, I wasn't. My spine stiffens as I sit straighter, a little of my edge returning as I start to regain my confidence. Being questioned I can handle. Being bullied—fuck that.

But before I can respond, Warren approaches the reporter and takes the microphone. The reporter looks annoyed. "Hey!"

Warren ignores her as he turns toward the stage.

Shit. What is he going to say?

I don't even care really. Just the sight of him has my heart pounding for completely different reasons. He looks amazing in jeans and a dress shirt, sleeves rolled to reveal those addictive forearms that I've been craving since the last time they held me. His hair is trimmed short but still a perfect mess that I long to run my fingers through and he's clean-shaven today, meaning he's made an effort...for what though?

Is he here to call me out even further? Reveal my secret to this room full of people? Tell everyone how I've cheated my way to success? To do that, he'd need to believe me.

And that's too much to hope for.

"I have a question...actually it's more like a comment," Warren says into the mic.

Eye rolls in the crowd. There's always that one guy.

I fold my hands in my lap tightly and sit even straighter.

"Hailey Harris saved my life. I mean, she totally destroyed my football career, but she saved my life."

I send him an exasperated look, but my eyes fill with tears. Does he believe me now? Is that what this is about?

The crowd recognizes him now and a murmur rumbles through.

Warren runs a hand through his hair and continues. "What I want to say is, we all expect celebrities and athletes to be on display. We want full-time access to their lives without allowing any room for a mistake. Well, news flash, we all make mistakes. We are all flawed. Hailey is human…just like the rest of us. She made a mistake, but would you want a coach who was unrelatable? Who hadn't struggled or learned to overcome obstacles?" He pauses and his gaze locks with mine onstage.

As I listen, I'm touched by his grand gesture. He's standing in this room full of people defending me?

I appreciate the effort though I'm not sure I deserve it, but more than anything, it fills me with a sense of hope that maybe there might be a chance for us.

"I want advice from someone who has been there, who has bounced back from adversity, someone with experience in rebuilding courage…and I think Hailey being here on stage today proves that she's brave enough to accept her flaws and mistakes and keep pushing forward." Warren pauses, his gaze burning into mine.

I can barely breathe.

"For what it's worth, that's the coach I'd want." Warren reluctantly turns his gaze away and hands the microphone back to the reporter. He walks away and stands in the back of the room.

I'm more than a little overwhelmed with emotion as I stare at him and the panel resumes.

"Okay…well, any other questions?" the panel moderator addresses the crowd.

A reporter from *Influencer Central* stands. "I have one for Hailey."

I nod and force a smile as I tear my gaze from Warren.

"What one element—more than any other—makes a person or entity successful? The 'IT factor' that ensures success above all else."

Good question. I take a deep breath before my true feelings pour out. "The truth is, my business is based on the concept that there are magical rules to success and that I somehow know what they are and you don't, but if you want something, *truly* want it, it will happen, because you'll do the work to get there, to reach those goals at all costs."

The crowd is much more engaged now.

"I can help—" I gesture toward Spencer "—Spencer can help, but we can only offer advice and at the end of the day, the decisions, the choices are up to you. Putting in the work consistently is up to you. Believing and having faith even through setbacks and failures is up to you. Knowing in your core that you want this dream to become a reality and drowning out the noise of haters and naysayers is up to you. It takes commitment, dedication, focus but that's something we all know—it's no secret," I say and take a deep breath. "But sometimes what can make the difference is someone truly believing in you to help you reach those goals." I'd always felt like a fraud because I used my gift to see the future, discounting the value I added by having that full confidence in my clients that they lacked until they got there themselves. My unwavering belief in them was a solid foundation they could cling to when things were challenging.

Just like the belief my mother always had in me…

I force a wave of emotion away as I conclude, "But one thing I will say—a universal truth that took me a while to learn—the ultimate secret to success, the best path forward, is always the one that makes you happy now...not someday."

The reporter nods and smiles. "Thank you. Great answer."

They take their seat and the questions continue to fly in. I relax more and more now that the elephant in the room has been addressed and the crowd has predictably moved on.

I'm already yesterday's news.

Moments later, the panel disperses and I climb down from the stage. Several reporters approach with their business cards and a young woman asks about a client meeting. Better than I expected this day to go and I have Warren to thank. He's still standing at the back of the room and all I want is to go to him. But I'm at a loss of what to say. He defended me today, but what does it mean?

Can I get my hopes up that maybe he's here because he still has feelings for me too?

I make my way through the crowd and meet Warren in the back of the room and an awkwardness simmers between us.

"That was quite a speech," I say. "Not as good as the best man speech you didn't get a chance to deliver, but not bad."

"I decided to wing this one." He pauses and looks at me with sincerity reflecting in those deep blue eyes. "You didn't deserve the way that reporter was witch-hunting you."

"Oh, I think I deserved it a little."

"Maybe a little," he says with a grin. He pauses, then... "And I wanted to tell you that Marcus impressed the scout. Looks like he'll be getting that scholarship to UCLA in the fall."

Oh, thank God. I sigh in genuine relief. "That's wonderful."

Warren nods and hesitates. "Thank you for convincing me to give him another shot."

"You just said it yourself, sometimes people need a second chance," I say gently.

Warren steps toward me. "Like us?"

Air traps in my lungs and my heart pounds. I don't trust my voice to speak and all words are eluding me anyway.

"You know why I've always called you Hailstorm?" he asks in my silence.

I swallow the emotion welling in the back of my throat. "Because they're loud, painful, and damaging?"

He stares into my eyes. "Because hail is caused by strong updrafts in a storm. You've always embodied that relentless, against the grain strength that sometimes results in a natural disaster."

I cock my head to the side and raise an eyebrow. "That's supposed to be flattering?"

"No, it's supposed to be the truth. And so is this—all I know is that nothing feels better than when I'm with you."

"We argue all the time..."

"Not all the time," he says huskily as he moves even closer.

I swallow hard as I stare up at him. I want this with him, but I've been completely vulnerable and I'm not sure he can accept me—all of me. "I know what I told you seems hard to believe..."

The floor beneath my feet rumbles as a crumbling noise drowns out the motivational music in the event room. Items fall from exhibit booths and attendees hurry to seek security as an earthquake shakes the room.

It knocks me off balance, but Warren's quick to catch me before I tumble. One arm around my waist, his other hand touches mine. Palm to palm. Our lifelines connecting. Gazes locked on one another.

The floor beneath us sways and it's as though the universe is bookending this topsy-turvy ride I've been on.

A second later, the tremor stops, but Warren holds tight. He glances toward our hands pressed together and then his questioning gaze searches mine. "Well?"

I wait but see nothing. No visionary powers activated. No glimpse.

It confirms what I already know. "I can't see your future anymore because… I'm in love with you."

Warren takes me into his arms and stares into my eyes. "I know exactly what I want my future to be and who I want in it."

My heart pounds and my pulse races as we feel the aftershocks of the earthquake. Maybe sometimes tremors open gateways to new possibilities…

"I love you, Hailey," he says as he brushes my hair away from my face and lowers his mouth toward mine.

I stand on tiptoes to wrap my arms around him and press my body closer. "I love you too."

His lips brush against mine with a heated passion before he kisses me—the real me, the complete package me, with all my flaws and secrets—with all the love and affection I've never thought I'd be lucky enough to find.

A happily ever after even *I* could never have predicted.

★ ★ ★ ★ ★

ACKNOWLEDGMENTS

This story was one of those ideas that stuck with me and demanded to be written even though I wasn't quite sure making the leap to speculative fiction was the right direction for the next chapter of my writing career. But I am so happy I followed my intuition and wrote this passion project as it is truly my favorite novel to have written. Thank you to my agent, Jill Marsal, for helping me find the perfect home for it and the biggest of thanks to my editor, Dana Grimaldi, and the team at Canary Street Press for loving it as much as I do. Dana, your notes and feedback have helped shape this book into the story I wanted it to be. Thank you to the marketing department at Harlequin and a very special thank-you to Crystal Patriarche and the amazing publicity team at Booksparks—this book would not have found its way into the hands of so many readers without you! So much appreciation for my family—my husband and son who are always my biggest cheerleaders—I couldn't do this without your support. I'm so grateful to be fortunate enough to do what I love as a "job," so a heartfelt thank-you to all my readers! XO Jen

QUESTIONS FOR DISCUSSION

1. What are the main themes of *All Signs Point to Malibu*? How are those themes brought to life by character, plot, setting, etc.?

2. Do you ever check your daily horoscope? Why or why not?

3. In the first scene, Hailey gets up early on a Monday morning to post about hustling hard, but then she goes back to bed. What did you think about the disconnect between her words and her actions? How do the unrealistic expectations of hustle culture affect your own life?

4. What scene resonated with you most? Why?

5. If you got the chance to catch a glimpse of the future, would you take it? For yourself or someone else?

6. What character or moment prompted the strongest emotional reaction for you? Why?

7. Would you ever talk to a life coach about your own plans for the future? Why or why not?

8. Why do you think Sonia trusts Hailey with her secret dream of becoming an actress?

9. Were there any quotes or passages that stood out to you? Why?

10. Liam and Sonia get engaged after dating for only six months. Do you think this is too fast, or do some couples know they've found "the one" even if they've just met?

11. Are there any books you'd compare this one to?

12. Were you rooting for Hailey and Warren to get together the whole time? What about Sonia and Liam? Compare/contrast the two relationships.

13. What did you think of the writing style and structure of the book? Do you prefer stories written in first person point of view or third person?

14. Have you read other books by Jennifer Snow? How does this one compare in your opinion?

To access bonus scenes, behind-the-scenes info and movie news, visit jennifersnowauthor.com and subscribe to her newsletter.